Dare to Surrender

Dare to Surrender

KAREN ROSSI

A Karen Rossi Romance

Wisteria Publications

Wisteria Publications
507-4 Briar Hill Heights
New Tecumseth, ON
L9R 1Z7

Dare to Surrender
ISBN: 978-1-988763-08-8
Copyright © 2018 by Kaarina Brooks

Published in Canada 2018

Layout and Cover Art by Taria van Weesenbeek

Please contact the author at brooks.kaarina@gmail.com for any questions or comments.

Dedication

This book is dedicated to my friend Marjatta Mustonen, whom I have known since grade three.

Other Books by Karen Rossi

"Portraits of Love" Series
    Dare to Dream
    Dare to Love
    Dare to Trust

Beyond Forgiveness
No Home for My Heart
Despite Everything

Acknowledgements

I want to thank my sister Raili for her great editing and Taria van Weesenbeek for her work on the layout and cover design.

Chapter One

Damn! Why couldn't *his* luggage ever be the first to roll down the chute? With all the traveling he did, surely he was owed that much by the god of travel—whoever that was.

With sleep-deprived eyes Mika Laine stared at the luggage circling around on the carousel at the Helsinki airport. The four-hour layover in Amsterdam had added to the travel time and didn't help to lower his irritation index. But what was worse, during the seven-hour trans-Atlantic flight from Toronto to Amsterdam there had been kids crying almost the whole time, either singly or in a chorus. Surely to God airlines could arrange for people with kids to sit in one section of the plane, preferably separated by a sound-proof wall, letting the other passengers try to catch a few hours of shut-eye during the flight. Was that too much to ask?

There was his suitcase, finally coming around. Mika grabbed the handle, set it up on its wheels and headed toward the Exit sign. He hoped the person from the university was already at the Arrivals, because if he had to sit there and wait for her . . . She was supposed to meet him and take him to his dorm room to sleep. At last.

Sleep. That was all he could think of as he bypassed the Customs. He had nothing to declare—no alcohol, no tobacco. Just paints, brushes, a stack of good quality watercolour paper and some books on the history of art in Canada to use for his lectures. Plus a few sundry items of clothing. It was summer, after all, and he knew Finland had perfectly respectable department stores where he could replenish his wardrobe as needed. And when winter came, he could buy suitable outerwear without lugging his boots and parka all the way from Canada.

Mika stepped through the doors that led to the Arrivals area where people were milling around, hugging and kissing, and handing bouquets of flowers to long-awaited friends or relatives. But which one was the woman from the university? He knew her name was Anna-Liisa Saari and Mika hoped she would be carrying some sign, like *"Helsingin Yliopisto"* or maybe even "The University of Helsinki" in plain English. Even though his grandparents had emigrated from this country, his Finnish was limited to a handful of polite—and some not-so-polite—words. But that didn't worry him because he'd been told everyone here spoke

English, especially in the university circles.

"Mika Laine?" A woman approached him. She pronounced his last name the Finnish way, *"Lie-neh"*, which—he'd known since he was a kid—meant "a wave".

"I am Anna-Liisa Saari," she said and extended her hand. "Welcome to Finland." Her wide smile exposed a row of white, even teeth surrounded by a pair of full, pink lips that immediately made Mika want to do what so many others around him were doing—kiss her.

"Th-thanks," Mika stammered. The woman was beautiful. Her blond hair—somehow he knew it had to be natural—reached her shoulders and was combed loosely around her face. Her skin was pure peaches and cream. There was simply no other way to describe it.

She looked so soft and feminine. To say she sparkled would have sounded too sharp, but "glowing" definitely described her. The blue eyes that looked directly at him were smiling too, but in a calm, friendly way that made him forget his fatigue and feel almost rejuvenated.

He'd never expected a Finnish beauty like her to come and meet him. Thinking about university professors he'd imagined some middle-aged, scholarly type with graying hair in a bun and no-nonsense lace-up shoes. This woman was wearing light strappy sandals and a short-sleeved dress with a bold, colorful floral print. Was this the *Marimekko* design he'd heard so much about? It probably wasn't appropriate to ask at this point, but whatever the design, the dress sure looked pretty on her slender frame.

He, on the other hand, probably looked like a damned scruffy slob after a night on the plane. He'd brushed his teeth with the miniscule toothbrush from the freshen-up kit, had rinsed his face and run a comb through his unruly hair in the WC, but he knew he definitely did *not* look like those spiffy business travelers who'd come on board in Amsterdam and were now striding briskly toward the Exit, pulling their shiny leather cases on wheels. He'd spilled some mustard on the front of his cotton sports shirt while eating a sandwich in Amsterdam and, trying to rub it off, had only made it spread even more.

"Hyvää päivää," he finally remembered to say in a well-rehearsed greeting. *"Hauska tutustua."* He hoped the words were at least somewhat recognizably pronounced.

"Good day. I am glad to meet you, too," the Finnish beauty said.

"How did you recognize me?" Mika asked.

"There was a photo in the dossier you sent."

"Right. But surely I don't look much like that now." Self-conscious, he ran his fingers through his longish hair, brushing it off his forehead. "Not after fourteen hours of travel." Like he needed an excuse.

"You look fine after fourteen hours of travel." She reached for his flight bag on the floor. "Let me help you with your luggage."

Mika quickly took it from her. "That's okay, thanks," he said. "I can handle it. I only have the suitcase and this carry-on. But *kiitos*, anyway."

They walked out, she leading the way to the parking garage where she opened the trunk of a dark blue Mercedes with her remote. He noted the vehicle had a University of Helsinki license plate. Mika stuffed his luggage in and they were on their way.

After clearing the pay booth at the exit, they joined the early afternoon traffic, and Anna-Liisa told him about his lodgings. "I hope you will be comfortable in the university dorm during your stay."

"I'm sure I will be." At this point even a park bench would have been welcome, so he could catch a few winks. If it hadn't been for this lovely woman beside him, he would already have dozed off. Now he just wanted to keep awake, so he could look at her and admire her competent moves at the wheel as she drove along the busy expressway. She even handled the manual transmission with skill and dexterity, like one born to drive. Mika felt surprisingly at ease, which wasn't usually the case when he was with a woman driver. Of course, that pretty well never happened, because he always made sure he was in control of the steering wheel.

He waited for her to ask him how the flight was, or something, but nothing seemed to be forthcoming. "So, I'll be returning to Canada when the fall semester is over," he finally volunteered, simply to have something to say.

"Yes. I read so in your dossier."

Her soft accent was fascinating. It reminded him of his grandmother's, except Grandma had never learned to speak English very well . . . so actually there *was* no comparison. It just sounded familiar, somehow, adding to the feeling of comfort this woman exuded.

"Yes, I'm planning to be home after Christmas," he went on. "But as soon as the exams are over I thought I'd play the tourist for a while, even though it'll be winter. I've never been in Finland, but I've sure heard a lot about it from my grandparents. They bragged it was the most beautiful country in the world."

Anna-Liisa smiled. "Yes, we think so, too. Especially in the summer. That is why many Finns travel out of the country in the winter."

Such a beautiful, full smile. Mika shook his head to clear his brain from the almost magical effect this woman was having on him. "I expect they want to get away from the cold."

"Yes, and the darkness. If there is no snow to brighten up the land, it can be very depressing."

"Maybe that's why so many Finns drink?" Mika wasn't sure if that was where he should go, but the words were out. To his dismay he observed a change in Anna-Liisa. She seemed to shrink into herself right before his eyes and all the glow drained out of her. He *definitely* shouldn't have gone there.

"Yes, perhaps that is why," she said quietly.

They were both silent for a few minutes. Mika didn't know what to say after his obvious gaffe, and was grateful when she turned to him again.

"I have been put in charge of entertaining you for a few days. I hope that is agreeable to you."

That certainly was agreeable to him. But her serious, business-like face banished any suspicion her words might contain a double meaning. Her "entertaining" obviously didn't mean what he would've wanted for it to mean. Mika was relieved he didn't blow it with some lascivious joke.

"You have something specific in mind?" he instead asked. But was that any better? He hoped desperately she didn't take the question the wrong way. Or would that be "the right way"?

He better stop thinking along these lines, before he messed up for real. But, hell, she was a very attractive woman and he wouldn't have been alive if he hadn't at least *thought* about such things. Especially having been without a girlfriend since before his African adventure, over a year ago.

"I thought after you have had a chance to rest, I would take you for your first dinner in Finland."

"That's great." He really, really liked the idea of dining with her.

"You probably ate something in Amsterdam, but if you are hungry now, the cafeteria is open. You can get a snack from there before you go for a rest."

"They served us breakfast on the plane before we landed in Amsterdam, and then I had a coffee and a sandwich at the airport before we took off," Mika told her. "I'm okay for now."

Anna-Liisa maneuvered a lane change and got off the expressway. "Tomorrow I will take you on a tour of the city, if you are interested. And in the evening the department will host a welcome barbeque for you."

"That sounds great. And you'll be there?" He hoped.

"I will be your chauffeur. Unless you have other plans."

"No, please, *you* make the plans," Mika said quickly. "I wouldn't know what to plan at this stage."

The idea of spending all day tomorrow with her sounded fabulous.

She pulled into the university grounds and parked in front of a five-storey building.

"I will take you up to your room. But if you would rather sleep and not go for dinner tonight—"

He didn't let her finish. "I'm sure I'll be ready to eat by six o'clock, so if you don't mind coming to pick me up—" He gave a short laugh to cover up for the fact that he sounded almost desperate. "Otherwise I'll be too hungry to fall asleep."

They went into an elevator and she pushed the button for the fourth floor.

"You will have a lovely view of the ocean from your window. I especially wanted you to have a room on this side of the building. Luckily one was available."

She sounded so efficient it wouldn't have surprised him if some unlucky bastard had been kicked out so he could have this room with a wonderful view.

They entered and, as she had promised, through the large picture window the ocean glimmered in the distance.

"This is great. I appreciate the effort you've put into looking after me."

"It is part of my assignment to look after your comfort," Anna-Liisa said simply.

Again Mika was taken aback by the serious way she said all these things, which some rake would have interpreted as lewd. Other than he, of course.

The room was small and the single bed, dresser, desk and the chair almost filled it. But since they were of light, modern design, the room still appeared spacious. A couple of colorful throw-rugs on the light wooden floor gave it a cozy, home-like ambiance. Mika was glad there was also a bathroom with a shower, so he wouldn't have to use some common facility down the hall.

After Anna-Liisa left, Mika stretched out on the bed

and sighed. He'd landed in Helsinki in a terrible mood, but here he was, feeling incredibly light-hearted, and looking forward to seeing Anna-Liisa again this evening.

What an amazing person she was. Wasn't he a lucky stiff to have been assigned to her. He couldn't imagine how down he'd be feeling now if that woman with gray hair and lace-up shoes had been at the air-port to meet him instead. Not that he had anything against gray-haired women, or lace-up shoes for that matter, but this Anna-Liisa was so much more prefer-able.

A persistent ringing of the phone forced itself into Mika's dreams and finally pierced through his sleep. He groped for his cell on the table beside the bed and, after fumbling with it for a few seconds, was finally able to press the talk button.

"Hello?" For a moment his groggy brain didn't com-pute. Where was he? But then the voice speaking to him made the clouds evaporate and his mind quickly cleared up.

"Hello, Mika? I am sorry if I woke you up, but it is now 18:30. I have to know if you want to go for din-ner."

That would be . . . 6:30 "normal" time, Mika quickly computed.

"If you want to go back to sleep, it is okay, but—"

"Oh no, not at all. I'm glad you woke me up," he said quickly. "I'm feeling pretty hungry, as a matter of fact." His stomach growled right on cue.

"Good. I will pick you up at nineteen—" Anna-Liisa stopped. "I am sorry. I should use the North American way of telling time until you get used to the twenty-four hour clock. I will pick you up at seven?"

"Perfect." He would have a chance to take a quick shower and change into some fresh clothes.

Mika whistled in the shower. The happy lightness he'd felt when he fell asleep thinking about Anna-Liisa, was back. After getting dressed, he strode down the hall with a bounce in his step, feeling like a kid, waiting for something fantastic to happen. Like going to watch a hockey game where his favorite team was playing, or going to a movie with some buddies, without adults tagging along.

Instead of using the elevator, he took the stairs down three at a time and emerged out onto the sidewalk. The sun was still riding high and Anna-Liisa was waiting for him, standing beside the Mercedes parked at the curb. She smiled at him and he didn't know which was brighter, she or the sun. She wore the same floral dress as in the afternoon and looked just as charming as before. Mika had been half-afraid it had only been his sleep-deprived brain that had made him imagine she was so fabulous, and was relieved to see it was all for real.

"*Hei,*" she said. "You look refreshed after your nap."

"Thanks. I do feel better." Mika sat beside her on the grey leather seat and again he marveled at her skill with the gearshift. "You drive very well," he said.

Her short laugh rang pleasantly in Mika's ears, and to him the sound was light, like everything else about her. He wondered if he could paint a picture of her laughter, which made him think of pure, perfect pearls dropping into a pool of crystal clear water.

"I think it is because of our very strict driver education program," she said, her pragmatic reply dispelling the image of the falling pearls. "I am not any better than other drivers in Finland."

"Well, you're the only driver I've seen so far, and I'm certainly impressed," Mika said. "You handle the gearshift like a man."

"Thank you." The reply was cool and crisp.

Right. His sexist comment fell flat, like it should have, and he was sorry the moment it came out. Now she knew what he thought about women drivers.

"I meant to say, you handle it like a *pro*," he amended his words but received no acknowledgement from her. Mika was beginning to suspect that under the soft exterior lurked a woman who wasn't to be trifled with.

Was she always this serious? Did she even posses a sense of humor? Mika wanted to find out, but a knock-knock joke probably wasn't the way to go.

"I understand Finns are a pretty serious bunch of people," he ventured to say. "A friend of mine was lecturing here a few years ago and warned me not to expect too much idle chatter from the students."

Anna-Liisa nodded. "Perhaps they are thinking, instead."

Touché! What could he say to that?

She found a parking spot in front of Jussin Baari and they entered the dimly lit establishment, where Finnish pop music was playing loudly.

Mika would rather have sat with her somewhere with a more tranquil ambiance, but it wouldn't have been proper to make his host think he was unappreciative.

"Hey, this is *fine*," he said, looking around and feigning enthusiasm.

"Too noisy?"

She *had* to be a mind reader, or how else could she have known that? He'd better learn to control his errant thoughts when he was around her. The idea made him smile. There was bound to be at least a few occasions when he'd be thinking about her in rather "errant" ways.

"Maybe a bit," he admitted. "How did you know?"

"I heard you think," she said, smiling playfully.

He laughed. "So you're a mind reader as well as a good driver?"

"Most women are mind readers, I think. Especially

mothers."

Mothers? Mika frowned. He'd forgotten to check her finger for a wedding ring. A woman like her would more than likely be married. Probably with kids.

As soon as they were seated at a table, he looked at her left hand—and sighed with relief. The ring finger was bare.

But just to make sure the ring wasn't lost or sitting somewhere at home, he decided to take the bull by the horns. Crossing his fingers under the table, he asked, "So does your husband also teach at the university?"

"I am divorced."

Mika could hear the huge period at the end of the clipped statement. Right. This matter was none of his business. He felt sheepish. "I'm sorry. I didn't mean to probe." Yes, he'd meant to probe. And he knew she was sharp enough to have figured that out.

"I think you did," Anna-Liisa said, raising her menu, but not before Mika had seen the smile. "What would you like to eat?" she asked. "The fish chowder is delicious. It comes with dark rye bread and butter. Or would you rather have a hamburger?"

"I'll have whatever you're having. I don't want to get *too* adventurous until I become familiar with the food in this country."

"I eat my main meal at noon at the university cafeteria, so I am only having a salad now."

He scowled. "A burger, then."

"A burger is good. And a beer?"

"Sure. What're you drinking?"

"Coffee. I am driving."

"Right." Was everyone in Finland this law-abiding? Or just she?

They sat in silence while they waited for their food. Mika was becoming fidgety, but Anna-Liisa simply sat, calmly looking around her at the other diners. Students didn't talk much? Well, it looked like their teachers didn't indulge in small talk, either.

Why didn't she ask him about his flight? That was the typical North American way to fill a void in a conversation. Besides, people *always* asked that whenever someone had just disembarked.

He waited. And waited. "My flight was pretty good," he finally blurted out.

"Was it? That is good," Anna-Liisa smiled at the waitress who brought their food.

Mika nodded. "Yeah, except for a bunch of yowling kids," he went on. "They kept everyone awake."

"That sometimes happens, but families have to travel, too." Her tone was conciliatory. He noted that as she cut up a tomato wedge, she held the knife in her right hand and the fork in her left, like most Europeans.

"True. But I'd like to see them in a separate, soundproof compartment of some kind," he countered and bit into his burger. It tasted the same as hamburgers in Canada. "Kids and I don't even belong in the same room, never mind on the same airplane for seven hours."

Anna-Liisa kept on eating, but Mika had the feeling he'd overstepped his welcome with his judgmental opinions. But what the hell, that's how he felt. Why mince his words? He hoped she wasn't a Pollyanna who would rather say nothing if she didn't have anything nice to say. He'd always resented "goody-two-shoes" types.

After a while, as though starting on a brand new topic, Anna-Liisa looked up and asked with great interest, "And do you also offer art lessons to children?"

Touché. The question sounded innocent enough, but Mika knew better. She was definitely *not* a Pollyanna. Her question contained a veiled rebuke at him for his harsh comments about kids.

"Um . . . I guess I deserve that," he said. "But in my defense I have to tell you that—"

Anna-Liisa raised her fork. "Please. You do not need to explain. You are allowed to have your own opinions."

"But I *want* to explain. I was the oldest of four kids and had to take care of them while my mother worked. My father was—"

He stopped abruptly. If he went on he'd end up telling her his whole life story and this wasn't the time for those kinds of intimate, unpleasant revelations.

Maybe there never would be a time for them. Their relationship might never progress beyond the few days she showed him around the city. After that he might never see her again, except for an occasional glimpse around the university.

The thought caused an unexpected dip in his mood. Time for that joke.

"Knock, knock."

"Who is there?"

Good. She was familiar with knock-knock jokes. "Plato."

"You mean a plate o spaghetti?"

Mika burst out laughing. "Hey, that's *my* line."

Anna-Liisa laughed, too. Mika was fascinated. The beautiful pearls dropped into the pool of crystal clear water again. He definitely would have to see about painting that.

"Sorry," she said. "I didn't mean to spoil it for you."

"You couldn't have heard it before because I just made it up," he grumbled.

"Yes, you *are* very talented."

Mika grimaced. "Why does that sound more like a put-down than praise? As if knock-knock jokes are the best things I can produce."

"No, it *was* a good joke," Anna-Liisa insisted and Mika could see she was trying not to smile. "Predictable, but not bad."

"And should I say thank you?"

"You are welcome."

During the rest of the meal she told him about the plans she had for the next few days.

"I will not call on you too early tomorrow," Anna-Liisa said. "You will get used to the time difference soon. The cafeteria opens at six-thirty so you can get your breakfast when you wake up."

When they left the bar an hour later, the late July sun wasn't even close to setting. The evening was still soft and warm.

"I'd like to walk for a while," Mika said. "Would you walk with me?"

"I am sorry, but I have to get home." Anna-Liisa already had the car keys in her hand.

Disappointment hit him unbelievably hard. Damn, what kind of magic spell was this woman weaving on him? It was totally unreasonable to feel this bad simply because she wasn't going to walk with him. Like it was an effing big deal.

"That's okay," he said casually. "I'll walk back to the university by myself. I need the exercise. If I just keep going down along this street I'll get there. Correct?"

"That is correct. You cannot go wrong." Anna-Liisa opened the car door and got in. "Good night."

"*Hyvää yötä*," Mika said in turn and was gratified to see this bring a wide smile to her face. She seemed to like it when he spoke Finnish. Or tried to. He'd have to make a point of doing so more often, and make better use of his few words.

Maybe then he'd hear more pearls dropping into water.

Chapter Two

Anna-Liisa locked the door behind her and hurried to the Koivus' townhouse across the courtyard, holding four-year-old Aleksi by the hand. Leila Koivu was her best friend and had been her babysitter since she'd moved to this townhouse complex after her divorce. Too bad she hadn't been able to simply disappear somewhere, and never let Aaro know where she was, and never again have to hear his drunken voice on the phone threatening her. Unfortunately the child welfare office felt it necessary for Aaro to know her phone number. "It is better if the children have a relationship with their father," they'd said. Like heck it was better. He didn't care about the children, all he wanted to do was drink. And harass her.

For three years now, ever since the police had arrested him for trying to barge his way into the house, Aaro had left her alone, except for the phone calls that came at regular intervals to warn her not to "start screwing around with anyone".

She'd left Johannes and Elina at home, where they were having a leisurely breakfast. They would stay around home, playing with the neighborhood kids in the nearby park. They could always go to Leila if they needed something, but otherwise they were on their own for the day. Elina, at nine, was very capable of making herself something to eat, and seven-year-old Johannes was able to assemble a cheese sandwich on rye and pour himself a glass of milk without spilling.

"No fair that Johannes doesn't have to come to the babysitter," Aleksi now whined, slowing down his steps. "He's lucky."

"Johannes is a big boy. He can stay home with Elina. You always said you like having Leila as your babysitter," Anna-Liisa said. "Why are you complaining?"

"I want to stay home like Johannes," Aleksi muttered. "How come he doesn't have to come?"

She smiled and tousled his blond hair. "You tell me." They'd gone over this on a regular basis since school closed at the end of May.

"Because he's almost eight, that's how come."

"Right. And in a few more years you will also be staying home with Elina and Johannes, while I go to work."

At the Koivus' door she kissed Aleksi on the cheek and waved to him as she dashed across the courtyard back to her townhouse. The big, blue Mercedes was sitting in her carport, looking slightly out of place in this modest neighborhood. Soon she was sitting in it, heading toward the city and the university. It was nice to have the use of this car while she was in charge of showing Mika Laine around Helsinki. Quite a change from her own modest vehicle.

Mika Laine. An interesting man. But obviously not a child-friendly fellow. So inviting him for a home-cooked meal at her house—which was supposed to be one of the welcoming activities—didn't seem like such a great idea any more. No problem. One of her child-less colleagues could invite him instead.

From having read his dossier, Anna-Liisa knew he was around her age, but unmarried, while she had three children and an alcoholic ex to her credit. She knew a great deal about Mika, like the fact that he had a business in Toronto—Triple M Graphic Design and Production, that he ran with two other artists, Miguel Cordova and Michael Merrick. They taught watercolor painting on the side, while pursuing their own artistic careers. She also knew the men took turns going off for a year to—how had he phrased it in his dossier?—to "rejuvenate themselves artistically" or something like that, while the other two stayed behind to take care of the business.

In his dossier Mika Laine said he'd been to South Africa on his last trip, and he had included interesting prints of the art he'd produced on his return to Toronto. He was a very accomplished artist, indeed.

And what were *her* accomplishments, besides her three wonderful children? A career as a lecturer of Swedish literature at the university. And a failed marriage.

Anna-Liisa pulled into the university parking lot and glanced at her watch. She could grab a cup of coffee before going up to see if her charge was awake. In the cafeteria she joined the line-up and then carried her cup to a table, where her friend and colleague, Stefan Willner, was sitting. He was the French lecturer and for some time now had thrown strong hints that he wanted her to be more than a friend. Anna-Liisa had refused to take the bait.

She had just seated herself across from Stefan, when Mika Laine appeared out of nowhere and stood beside her chair, holding a cup of coffee.

"*Hyvää huomenta*, Anna-Liisa," he said and glanced questioningly at Stefan.

"Good morning, Mika. You are up early," Anna-Liisa pulled out the modern-design, light wooden chair beside her. "Please join us. Have you eaten yet?"

Mika sat down. "Yes. I woke up early and came to see what was for breakfast." His eyes went back to Stefan.

Anna-Liisa made the introductions. "Mika, this is Stefan Willner. He is a Swede, but is pretending to be a French lecturer. I have told him about you."

She saw the men eye each other for a split second before they reached across the table to shake hands.

"Glad to meet you, Mika," Stefan said. "I hope you enjoy your stay in Finland."

"I'm sure I will," Mika replied. He wanted to add that so far his stay had been very delightful with such a lovely guide, but he didn't think his lovely guide would appreciate such a comment. Funny, but after having been with Anna-Liisa for only a few hours, he felt he already knew quite a lot about her, like her subtle, dry sense of humor, and what she would or would not approve of.

"When you are ready to go, we will leave for a city tour," Anna-Liisa said. "There is no hurry."

"I'm almost done with this coffee," Mika told her. "I think it's my fourth."

"You sound like a real Finn already," Stefan put in. He turned to Anna-Liisa. "How does Johannes like the idea of going to grade one in September?"

Anna-Liisa laughed. "Oh, he thinks he is so big."

Mika was annoyed. *He* wanted to be the one to make her laugh. Not this big Swede with curly blond hair and wide blue eyes.

In fact it seemed that everyone was blond and blue-eyed here. He looked around him at the people in the cafeteria. Yeah, everyone except him. His eyes were brown, like his mousy-brown hair. Okay, so there were a few dark-haired people, and even a couple with dark skin—would they be called African Finns? But the over-reaching impression was one of general blondness.

This Stefan fellow seemed to know Anna-Liisa's family intimately. How good a friend *was* he? So she had a son? Damn. Kids always spelled trouble. And responsibility.

"I'm free till lunch. Mind if I tag along this morning?" Stefan asked.

"Of course we would not mind. Please come," Anna-Liisa said.

Mika tried to gauge the level of enthusiasm in her voice and found it too high to suit him. He tried not to frown. How come she made him part of the "we" without asking his opinion? Although, if she had, what could he have said? Sorry big buddy, but I want this lovely woman all to myself today.

Right.

"So, where are you taking me today?" he asked instead.

"I was thinking an overview of Helsinki would be good." Anna-Liisa addressed the reply to Stefan as though seeking his opinion.

"A good idea," the Swede agreed. "Then he can pick out the places that interested him for more intimate, detailed visits. Like the art museums."

Nice way they had of leaving him out of the

conversation as though he wasn't even present.

Half an hour later the three were in the Mercedes, heading toward the centre of the city. As the guest, Mika sat beside Anna-Liisa, which was the first good thing that had happened today.

"Did you sleep well?" Anna-Liisa asked, negotiating a sharp turn.

How about that. Small talk coming from Anna-Liisa. What brought this on?

"*Kyllä, kiitos.* I slept like a log until six," Mika replied. "That's around midnight in Toronto, which is when I usually hit the sack back home. So I thought I might as well wake up and get used to reversing my daily schedule."

He expected that would get a laugh. It did.

But his mood wasn't the best. His head felt like it was wrapped in a thick wool blanket, and it didn't help matters that Stefan, in the back seat, kept leaning over constantly between them to point things out. Once, in his eagerness, he hit Mika on the nose with his finger.

"Sorry," he said, while Mika counted to ten, trying to remain civil.

Again the man leaned forward over Anna-Liisa's shoulder. "I'm sure Mika would enjoy stopping at the Senate Square and seeing the cathedral and the old university buildings."

Would it have been too much for the guy to ask him directly? But at least he was speaking English. It would *really* have put the frosting on the cake if Stefan had spoken to Anna-Liisa in Finnish because at that point Mika would have exploded for sure. Stefan seemed to speak English with less of an accent than Anna-Liisa. Probably, Mika decided, because Swedish was so close to English, whereas Finnish was a totally different ball game.

"So how come you're teaching French, instead of Swedish?" Mika asked.

"Since Finland is a bi-lingual country, everyone speaks Swedish," Stefan said. "So teaching French gave me a better opportunity to get a job."

Mika nodded. "Smart move."

At the Senate Square Anna-Liisa parked the car and they got out to walk around. A tall statue of Tsar Alexander II of Russia on horseback was in the centre of the square, which was surrounded by the white, majestic Helsinki Cathedral, the old government building, and the main buildings of the University of Helsinki. They entered the Cathedral and Mika admired the clean, white lines of the interior that was almost totally bereft of the excessive gilded decorations he'd seen in most churches in Europe.

As they descended the seemingly hundreds wide steps from the church, Mika squinted in the bright morning sun. "That was really impressive in its beautiful simplicity," he commented.

"Finns are like that. Simple," Stefan replied, and

then chuckled at his back-stabbing joke.

"Swedes think they are so superior," Anna-Liisa said to Mika, but there was no rancor in her voice. It seemed this was an old battle between the two nationalities inhabiting Finland.

"The Kauppatori market square would be interesting to see on a Saturday," Stefan said as they got back in the car. "You'd see the docks with the fishermen in open fishing boats selling their fish, many still flopping around. The fish I mean." He chuckled again at his own joke.

Mika suppressed a snort. Quite the jokester, this Stefan fellow.

"And from there you could take a ferry to the historic Suomenlinna Fortification," Stefan continued, "They're on a bunch of islands just off the mainland."

"Might be interesting to go stroll around there some time," Mika suggested, looking directly at Anna-Liisa to make sure she knew he was addressing her and not Stefan.

"Yes, you would probably like the military history," Anna Liisa said but didn't indicate whether she would. Mika had absolutely no intention of venturing there unless Anna-Liisa suggested they go together. Without the big Swede.

The morning drive around the city would have been infinitely more pleasant without Stefan acting as an over-eager tour guide. By the time they returned to the university for lunch, Mika was gratified to see the back-end of the fellow.

"We will see you at the barbeque at Pekka's house tonight," Anna-Liisa called to Stefan as he turned to walk to his sports car on the parking lot.

Mika and Anna-Liisa lined up with their trays in the cafeteria.

"Pekka?" he asked. A new name to add to the growing list. That, on top of jet lag, and his head was starting to spin.

Anna Liisa smiled. "Pekka Miettinen. His wife's name is Sanni, by the way."

"Thanks. I'll try to remember." As if.

It was nice to have her back all to himself. He could feel the tension leave him as they chatted while eating. He didn't even mind the crowded cafeteria, because when she talked, it was easy to tune out everyone and everything around him and concentrate on her calm, low voice.

What was it about her that he found so pleasant? It was as if he were drinking some soothing tonic instead of the caffeine-infused, strong Finnish brew. Could it be her voice? If she were a singer, she would definitely be a second alto. He could almost hear her sing a peaceful lullaby to this Johannes-kid of hers. The lucky boy would be asleep in no time at all.

Or maybe it was her sedate composure? There was nothing hurried about her—not when she spoke, not when she moved. She wasn't slow, but rather almost deliberate and studied in her movements. He couldn't see her knocking over a cup of coffee or dropping her fork. That was *his* specialty. And how often did he blurt out something he should have had the sense to keep to himself? Or wave his hand, upsetting a glass of wine on some pure white linen tablecloth? Too often.

Of course when he was painting, things were different. Then he had the patience of Job to work for just the right effect, no matter how long it took, no matter how many times he had to correct some detail. He didn't speak for hours and often didn't even remember to eat for the entire day.

Mika studied her. Her laughter he'd already pictured in his mind. But what else was there that he found alluring and irresistible? She was light. That was it. There was an almost ephemeral, airy lightness about her. And yet she was all woman in the places where it counted—beautiful, desirable and— Mika swallowed. He wanted to feel her lithe body in his arms, and even just imagining it made his pulse kick up a notch.

"Is something wrong?" Anna-Liisa was looking at him, lines of concern on her usually smooth forehead.

Mika quickly stabbed a cucumber with his fork. "No. Not at all. I'm probably starting to fade." He glanced at his watch. "Maybe I should have a snooze before the barbeque."

"That is a good idea," Anna-Liisa said and rose. "I am done eating. You finish up and go up for a rest. I will come and get you about five-thirty and we will drive to Pekka and Sanni's home."

When evening fell—although it didn't really fall at all but lingered for hours--they arrived at the Miettinen home. It was situated in what looked to Mika like a fairly new subdivision, where many of the houses were two-storied, with stained board and batten exteriors and red tile roofs. But despite these similarities, there was no cookie-cutter look to the neighborhood.

As Mika and Anna-Liisa rounded the corner of the house, he saw that people were already gathered in the back yard, standing around a long table with snacks and drinks. The barbeque was fired up and music was playing. One or two couples were even dancing on the spacious deck. Mika had heard that Finns liked to dance at parties, or wherever music was playing and beer was flowing. This was obviously such an occasion.

Before they'd advanced too far, out of a group of kids at the rear of the yard, a little blond boy ran up and hugged Anna-Liisa around the hips. She hoisted him up in her arms and kissed his cheek.

Johannes? He looked too young to be going to grade one.

"This is my son, Aleksi" Anna-Liisa told Mika.

"Aleksi, this is my friend, Mika. Remember I told you about him? He comes from Canada."

"*Hei*," the boy said with a shy smile and hid his face against his mother's neck.

Okay. So she had two kids, not one. Mika wanted to make sure he started out on the right foot with the child, so he pasted an over-friendly smile on his face. "*Hei*, Aleksi," he said. "Nice to meet you."

"Aleksi speaks English quite well," Anna-Liisa said with a touch of pride in her voice. "And he understands even more. We spent a year in England when Aleksi was one. Elina and Johannes went to school there. I have been speaking English to my children since they were born and they go to an English school." The information failed to impress Mika. Elina? How many kids did she actually have?

"How come you never told me you had all these kids?" he blurted out frowning. He didn't quite manage to hide his annoyance at this new revelation.

Anna-Liisa looked at Mika calmly. "It is not part of my assignment to share my personal life with you." She put Aleksi down and he ran off to join the other kids on the lawn.

Assignment. Mika didn't know how to respond to such a blunt statement. "And you certainly haven't," he muttered.

"Yes. I know that is not fair since I know so much about you from your dossier," she replied, not sounding at all put off by his words.

So she considered him simply as part of her assignment and had no intention of creating a close personal relationship with him. It was going to be strictly business, and not even a friendship as far as she was concerned.

He, on the other hand, had been seriously thinking about asking her to go out with him after this introductory period was over and they wouldn't be meeting daily any more. The thought of only seeing her in passing in the halls of Helsinki U didn't sit too well with him for some reason. But it was quite obvious that she had no similar thoughts about *him*. To her he was only an assignment, forced on her by some committee or other. She was probably waiting anxiously to be done escorting him around and to be rid of him.

"Maybe I should have asked for *your* dossier," he said, trying to add a touch of humor to the conversation. His mood had plummeted and his interest in meeting all these laughing people was quickly evaporating. He would just as soon have turned around and left, but naturally that was out of the question. He couldn't use jet lag as an excuse any more, not after having told Anna-Liisa he'd had a very refreshing nap. Besides, people were becoming aware of their arrival and were starting to edge toward them, some saluting with their beer bottles, welcoming him.

Anna-Liisa started to make the introductions, but

at that point another boy ran up to her and stood there, looking up at Mika with narrowed, suspicious eyes. It was as though the kid considered him a public enemy number one. But why?

"This is my son, Johannes," Anna-Liisa said and tousled the boy's blond hair. "Johannes, this is Mika, my friend from the university."

Mika did his best to at least *appear* child-friendly. "*Hei*, Johannes, you having fun?"

"Yes." The nippy reply didn't invite further questions. Like his mother's answers, when she didn't want him to know more. And frankly, as far as this kid was concerned, that was okay, because Mika wasn't interested in finding out anything more about him, thank you very much.

A young girl now appeared out of the shadows and slipped her hand into Anna-Liisa's.

"Mika, this is Elina," Anna-Liisa said and stroked the girl's long, flaxen hair. Blond. Of course. "This is Mika whom I told you about."

"How are you?" Elina said shyly.

"Just great, thanks," Mika replied. The girl looked like a smaller, sweet version of her mother.

"So Uncle Stefan picked you up on time?" Anna-Liisa asked her.

"Yes," Elina replied. "We got here about half an hour ago."

Mika was dismayed. *Uncle* Stefan? Now didn't that

sound cozy.

"Stefan is your uncle?" he asked. Strange that Anna-Liisa had failed to mention that this morning.

Anna-Liisa laughed. "No, he is not related. But in Finland children call adult men uncles." She stopped to think. "It is a sign of respect, because they cannot call them by their first names."

Mika chuckled. "Okay. So when do I get that title?"

"Never, I should think," Anna-Liisa said, dashing ice water on his question. "It is for close friends."

Mika made a rueful face. "So I won't ever be a close friend?"

Anna-Liisa shrugged. "I do not know, because you are leaving at the end of the fall term."

Mika snapped his fingers. "Right. Glad you reminded me." He turned to Elina, who stood listening to this exchange with obvious interest, and decided he should make some effort to at least *pretend* he was a friend—even if he would never graduate into an uncle. "So, what grade are you in?" he asked, though he couldn't have cared less if she went to school at all. That was what one always asked kids. Right?

"I'm going to grade four when school starts," she answered.

"What do you like best in school?" He gave himself a mental pat on the back. Excellent question, Mika.

"I like art," came the unexpected reply.

Mika was taken aback. For some reason he'd

expected Social Studies or English, or anything but art. "You're good in art?"

"I got ten in my final grade three report card," Elina replied, looking down at her shoes.

"Ten out of . . .?"

"Out of ten," Anna-Liisa filled in, the pride in her daughter coming through in her voice.

Wow! "And you like drawing?" Mika asked the girl.

"Yes. And painting. I don't think I'm *that* good, but I like it."

"Elina is *very* good," Anna-Liisa interjected. "She is just too critical of herself."

"That's not such a bad thing, either," Mika said, thinking of his old man who fancied himself Picasso re-incarnated. "Maybe one day you'll show me your work?" The artist in him was interested, but more than that, the man in him had already figured out that his interest in Elina's art could be a ticket into Anna-Liisa's good graces. For some reason it was important to him that she should consider him to be more than an assignment.

Elina didn't reply, but instead kept looking down at her shoes.

"*Hei*, Mika!" Stefan called. "Come on over to the bar. Let's get you a drink."

Reluctantly Mika left Anna-Liisa and crossed over to a long table set up with alcohol bottles and glasses. Stefan dug into a cooler at one end of the table and handed Mika a bottle.

"Lapin Kulta, premium lager from Lapland," Stefan said and saluted Mika with his own bottle. "Lappish gold, in other words."

Mika took a swig. "Not bad."

Stefan introduced him to a few more people. There were too many new faces for Mika to remember half of them, but he enjoyed chatting with them, trying to get to know who was a colleague and who was a spouse, and what they did at the university. It was difficult to figure out who was single and who was part of a couple, but there were several kids milling about, so at least a few had to be married. Or living together. It surprised Mika that although there was some drinking and dancing, the evening seemed to be a family affair. Kind of like at a wedding, where kids mingled naturally into the scene.

"Here, Mika, come get a sausage," a man called Harri shouted from the grill he was tending.

Mika picked up a paper plate and Harri plopped a fat, sizzling, slightly cracked sausage on it. "Mustard's over there."

As Mika helped himself to the condiments, Harri explained some of the "laws of the land".

"You know it's the law in Finland that you have to have some sausage when you're at a party," Harri said with a grin. "There's chicken and salmon steaks on that other barbeque, but sausage beats them all."

Mika grinned. "I'll be the judge of that."

As he stood against the railing, eating, a couple of women came up to join him. They were about his age and very pretty in that blond, long-haired Finnish way. He couldn't recall whether he'd been introduced to their husbands or partners, but Johanna and Marita chatted easily, and even flirted with him. Mika laughed and welcomed these attentions which made him feel like they were interested in him as a person, and not only as an assignment.

But although he tried to get into the spirit of the moment, Anna-Liisa's words still stung. He snorted. An assignment, was he? He made a valiant attempt to throw back some flirtatious remarks at the women, but somehow he couldn't keep his eyes from following Anna-Liisa's movements. As far as he could tell she didn't hang around with any particular man, which pleased him, until it occurred to him that maybe she was seeing someone outside the university.

Well, was she or wasn't she? He wanted to know, for no other reason than simple, natural curiosity, of course.

"So, Anna-Liisa's special squeeze isn't here tonight?" Mika asked, bringing an unexpected burst of laughter from both women.

"Anna-Liisa's special squeeze?" Marita said, sounding incredulous.

"Yes, well . . . She didn't introduce me to anyone

with that specific title." Mika hoped they wouldn't think *he* was interested in her.

"Since her divorce I haven't seen Anna-Liisa showing interest in *any* man," Johanna explained. "We call her the Snow Queen, because she's cold to all advances."

"No kidding? I wonder why?" Mika tried to make the question sound as casual as possible.

"Maybe she misses her husband," Marita said with a giggle that didn't sit well with him at all. "He's a good-looking man, you know. Or used to be. He was a lecturer of German literature here."

"So where's he now?" Mika didn't want to know, yet couldn't help asking. He felt like a masochist, pumping the women for information that was irritating the hell out of him.

Johanna gave a dismissing wave. "Oh, somewhere around Helsinki, no doubt."

Later, when he was getting another sausage, Mika posed the question to Harri. "So, does Anna-Liisa have a boyfriend?"

"Not anyone I know of," Harri told him. "She looks so soft and desirable that plenty of fellows wouldn't mind changing that status quo, but she's not buying."

Soft and desirable. It was annoying to think that other guys also thought of her that way.

"And Stefan?" he asked, and he felt his fingers curl into a fist. Damn. Why did he keep asking, when he didn't want to know?

"You've noticed, too?" Harri said. "Yes, poor Stefan's the only one who still has his hat in the ring. Others have given up."

"So how long since her divorce?" If he asked any more questions his interest in Anna-Liisa would become way too obvious.

"Four years, I think. Something like that." Harri slapped him on the shoulder and laughed. "And good luck to you. You'll need it."

"Hey, I wasn't thinking about—" Mika protested but it didn't come out strong enough.

Harri guffawed. "Yeah, right."

The sound irritated him. "I'm only here for the semester. I can't start anything." He took a swig of his beer. Sadly, that was true, but he preferred not to think about it.

"Listen, friend, those short-term relationships are the best," Harri said with a wink. "No consequences. Love 'em and leave 'em. Of course that's not for me, anymore," he signaled with his spatula towards a woman who was putting out more paper plates on the table. "There's Pirkko, my beloved wife. But you're a free agent."

Mika chuckled and joined in the bantering to throw Harri off his trail. "Yeah, you're right. That's the only way to go." He looked around. "So which one of those beauteous ladies do you recommend I put my feelers out for?" One-night stands weren't generally his modus operandi. His affairs were temporary, but not quite that short. And he always made sure all facts were clearly understood. If the woman preferred something more permanent, he simply refrained from starting anything.

With his beer bottle Harri pointed to a particularly pretty brunette to whom Mika had been introduced earlier. She was chatting with Stefan by the bar. "Arja has no one at the moment," Harri said, "so if she's willing, you wouldn't be stepping on anyone's toes. And you might be in for a really fun ride, too. A great gal, Arja."

"Thanks for the tip, Harri. I just might take your advice and give her a whirl."

Not likely.

Pirkko came up and began to sway in front of Harri, who grinned widely as she tugged him onto the dance floor by his arm. "My lovely, sexy wife is trying her best to seduce me. I better pretend to go along."

"Find a lovely sexy lady of your own to dance with, Mika," Pirkko called over her shoulder. "Lots of them here."

"Right. Will do!" Mika leaned his back against the deck railing. Some of the kids had joined the dancers, goofing around and laughing. He took in the scene—the sky with its soft light, slowly getting ready for the sunset in an hour or so, the tall birch trees at the far end of the yard—and the awareness of Anna-Liisa standing not too far from him, talking with a colleague.

Was it possible he was starting to be *too* much aware of her? Mika shrugged off the thought. It was because she was basically the only woman he was acquainted with at the moment. He definitely needed to widen his search.

As if on cue, Arja sashayed up and put a hand on his shoulder. "Hey, you handsome Canadian," she crooned. "Would you like to dance?" She hooked his arm. "We haven't had a chance to get to know each other yet. What better way to do that than to the rhythm of the music."

Mika wondered if Harri had talked to her, or was this her own initiative.

"Sure, I'd like that," he replied and took her in his arms. It was a fast-paced two-step and Arja was a very capable dancer. And she was also very sexy in the way that all red-blooded males appreciated. Full, firm breasts, the fetching cleavage in full view, a nice narrow waist, and rounded hips that undulated to the beat of the music. Now and then they brushed against his thighs, causing the expected reaction to pulse through him.

"So what do you teach at the university?" Mika asked to get his mind off the possibilities this woman's body offered.

"Finnish literature," she answered. "Are you familiar

with any of the works of the Finnish authors and poets?" She twirled under his arm, as he held her hand.

"I'm afraid I only know of the most well-known work, *The Kalevala* epic."

"Well, if you know about *The Kalevala*, you're doing well. But there are many others." She cast a look from under her thick, dark lashes. "If you like I could familiarize you with some." She did a smart pirouette in front of him.

He would've had to be a total jerk not to hear the invitation in her voice, asking him to partake in something more than Finnish literature. At this point his next line should have been, "Maybe you'll give me a few private lessons?" But somehow he couldn't make himself say it. Not with Anna-Liisa standing almost beside them.

"Yeah, I'm sure there are some good ones," he said instead. "I probably should read a few of them while I'm here."

When the dance was over, he excused himself and strode over to the bar table for another beer. Tonight, on the dance floor, would be a prefect opportunity to hold Anna-Liisa in his arms, because that's what he'd wanted to do since they met at the airport. As far as he had seen, she hadn't danced with anyone. So would she dance with him if he asked her?

This was crazy. He hadn't felt this unsure of himself

since his grade eight graduation dance, when he'd been too scared to ask lovely Jessica Miller to dance, even though his whole thirteen-year-old body had ached to hold her. And now he was feeling the same angst. It was ridiculous to think he hadn't learned anything in more than two decades.

Mika straightened his shoulders and, with a determined step, approached Anna-Liisa. "Would you like to dance?" He mentally crossed his fingers.

Chapter Three

Anna-Liisa looked up at him and surprise flashed in her eyes. "I—um—yes, thank you," she finally said.

Did he detect a slight blush on her cheeks, or was that only the way the sunlight, low in the sky, shone across her face?

Mika put his beer bottle on the flat railing and took her in his arms. It felt even more wonderful than he'd imagined. She was slender, yet soft, almost vulnerable. The piece was slow and rather sultry, and even though Mika didn't understand the words, the female singer sounded very sexy. One could almost say desperate. For a while they danced discreetly apart, but then, as a test, he pulled her imperceptibly closer. He was pleasantly surprised to feel her body yield. This gave him courage to tighten his hold even more. She didn't resist or stiffen, but somehow he sensed that this was as far as he could hope to go at this point. And something told him that putting his cheek against her hair would be an absolute no-no.

They continued to sway in rhythm, and whenever her hip lightly touched his thigh, it sent a shot of pleasure through him. Because the slow piece had drawn almost everyone onto the deck, they didn't make much headway, and had to undulate on the spot. It felt so good that Mika wished they could continue this for the rest of the evening. How about till the end of the semester when he had to leave?

All at once he became aware of little Aleksi standing beside them, looking up, hands behind his back. They stopped dancing and the boy said something in Finnish to his mother.

Mika could hear his name mentioned. "What did he say?" he asked, and was surprised to see a blush rise on Anna-Liisa's face. This time he knew for sure the color wasn't caused by the setting sun.

She shook her head. "Oh, nothing."

Harri was dancing by with Marita, and Mika put out a hand to stop him. "Hey, Harri, ask this kid what he just said to his mother. Something about me."

Aleksi repeated his words to Harri, who broke into roaring laughter. "He said you and his mother look very nice dancing together. Way to go, Laine!"

Mika grinned at Aleksi and gave him the thumbs-up sign. The boy signaled back.

"Yes, nice," Aleksi said with a firm nod, and they bumped fists to further seal their agreement on the issue.

Anna-Liisa broke away from Mika's arms and headed for the railing. "Stop that, now," she scoffed, shaking her head.

Mika followed. He placed a hand on her shoulder— a move he thought would be admissible after the dance, but he was dead wrong.

She shifted away from him and ran a hand across her face, as though to remove any lingering blush. "Aleksi is silly."

"But he's right," Mika countered. "I thought we danced smoothly together."

Anna-Liisa didn't reply and he tried desperately to think of something to say that would lighten up the situation.

"The kid should think about a career as a judge on 'So You Think You Can Dance'," he at last quipped. "Do you get that program on TV?"

That worked, and Mika was rewarded with the sound of her laughter. "Now *you* are silly."

Before Mika could ask her to dance again, Pekka came up behind them.

"So, Anna-Liisa, have you thought about when you're going to have Mika over to your house for that home-cooked meal?" He turned to Mika to explain. "We decided at the last meeting that Anna-Liisa should be the one to offer it, since she's your hostess."

Mika was pleased to hear that such a thing was in

the works, but for some reason Anna-Liisa shook her head.

"I think Harri and Pirkko should do it," she said. "They don't have kids and—"

"Anna-Liisa, your kids are no problem!" Marita exclaimed. She was standing within earshot. "They're beautiful children." She turned to Mika. "Aren't they? I saw how you bumped fists with Aleksi. He's a real cutie, isn't he?"

"He sure is," Mika said. And, oddly enough, he meant it. Cutie? He would never have thought he'd find himself saying that about *any* kid.

Anna-Liisa's smile was tight. "We will see—"

"Hey, I'm free any time," Mika put in. "Until classes start I have nothing on the books other than what you've cooked up for me. If you'll pardon the pun."

"We will discuss it later," she said in a tone that told him the matter was closed.

Pekka danced off with Marita, and Mika and Anna-Liisa remained standing, listening to the music.

Mika was gathering up his courage to ask her to dance again, when she turned to him. "You must be getting tired. I think I should drive you back to the university."

Hell, no! Mika wanted to shout. He was just coming alive. He wanted to dance with her again. All evening, if possible.

"And my children should get to bed," she said. "But

if you want to stay, Stefan can drive you back," she added. "I am sure he will not mind."

That sealed the deal. Without question Mika would much rather go with her than with the Swede. "Okay," he said. "I'll say thanks to Pekka and Sanni."

Anna-Liisa collected her children and they all got into the Mercedes.

"Tomorrow I will take you to the Ateneum," she told Mika as they drove through the city, buzzing with nightlife. "You may be familiar with it and have seen pictures of the paintings, but they are much more impressive in real life."

Mika wanted to warn her that he definitely didn't want Stefan tagging along, but refrained. Still, he didn't feel nearly as antagonistic toward the fellow now that Anna-Liisa hadn't even danced with him. Nor with any other guy, for that matter. Except *him*. Even if she did it only because he was her "assignment" and she felt it was her responsibility to indulge him, it still made him feel smug and satisfied with the evening.

Anna-Liisa dropped Mika off in front of the dorm building and headed for home. The two boys were asleep in the back seat, but Elina, who had come to sit up front after Mika left, was still wide awake.

"Mika is a good artist, isn't he?" Elina said.

"Yes, I think he is," Anna-Liisa replied. "I am no expert on art, but from what I have seen of his work, he is very good."

"Do you like him?"

Anna-Liisa started. Had the girl seen something to make her think that, or was this a simple case of childish curiosity? Because, yes, she was starting to like him. And dancing with him tonight had been . . .

"Yes, I like him," she admitted to Elina. It would have been useless to try to lie to her daughter. The child was much too perceptive.

Yes, dancing with him— A shiver surged through her and made her sigh. She hadn't danced for years, except sometimes by herself. She, to whom dancing and singing had been as natural as breathing when she was young. But Aaro had cured her of such frivolities during their brief marriage. And now, who could dance and sing with the threats always lurking in the background, if she even looked at a man?

But dancing with Mika tonight, with his arm so firmly around her, had made her feel light and young and carefree. She'd enjoyed it way too much. And hadn't thought once about Aaro and his threats.

Elina interrupted her dreams. "So, he's lecturing at the university only for the fall semester?"

"Yes."

Elina leaned back against the seat. "He asked to see some of my pictures. Maybe when he comes for dinner I'll show him. I want to hear what he thinks of them."

Anna-Liisa was surprised by the girl's bravery. Elina

usually didn't show her art to anyone but her family. And knowing how Mika felt about children, she was dismayed to hear what Elina was planning. She didn't trust him to pay her any attention and didn't want Elina to get her hopes high.

"I'm afraid Mika will be very busy at the university," she said. "I do not know when, or if, I can have him over for dinner."

It was unfortunate that Pekka had brought up the dinner in front of Mika before she'd had a chance to let the committee know she would not be able to act as the hostess. Now it was out of her control.

All she could hope for was that Mika would be too busy to come.

"I hope you like walking," Anna-Liisa said and sat down to wait for Mika to finish his oatmeal porridge in the cafeteria. She took a sip of her coffee. "It is only about fifteen or twenty minutes to the Ateneum and I thought we could walk there."

She looked so fresh and beautiful again this morning, Mika had felt uplifted just to see her enter the cafeteria. "Absolutely," he said. "It's a gorgeous day."

When he had finished his breakfast they left, and she led the way down one of the main streets of Helsinki, with a very long name. Mika tried to say it, but got totally tangled up in all the letters.

"Kai-sa-nie-men-ka-tu," Anna-Liisa said slowly,

splitting up the word into syllables for him, and then burst into gales of laugher when Mika bungled up the pronunciation even worse.

"Way too many letters," he grumbled, but actually he was happy that his funny pronunciation had produced the happy laughter from her.

She was too serious and needed to laugh more often. Thinking about her last night as he lay in bed, he'd decided that making her laugh would be his own "assignment" while in Finland. Laughter would not only be good for her, but it would also bring him the incredible pleasure, whenever they were together, of hearing the sound he had grown to love.

Hey, what exactly was going on? Was he looking forward to being with her so he could hear her laugh? He shook his head. Things were definitely heading down some new, unbeaten path. Never before had he been charmed by a woman's laughter, nor looked forward so much to being with anyone.

But, as he'd reasoned to himself before, this strange fascination with Anna-Liisa was probably because she was the only woman he'd been with here in Finland. Except for dancing with voluptuous Arja last night at the barbeque, and the brief exposure to flirtatious Johanna and Marita. Yes, he definitely needed some other female company in his life. But what really bothered him was the strange way his gut clenched whenever he thought about leaving at the end of the semester and never seeing Anna-Liisa again. Never, for the rest of his life!

God, what was the matter with him? It wasn't like she was the most gorgeous woman he'd ever had dealings with. Not by a long shot. If he was truthful with himself, he would have to admit that Anna-Liisa wasn't even sexy. Not in the way he'd always defined the word, in a physical sense. Like Arja, for instance. Now, there was one sexy lady. Yeah, that's what he needed—someone like Arja to go out with.

But Anna-Liisa was definitely feminine. And absolutely desirable. She had felt so soft and yielding in his arms when he danced with her last evening that the feeling had stayed with him all night. It had produced some pretty erotic dreams that he now tried hard to dispel as she strolled beside him in her floral summer dress. It wasn't the same one she'd worn on the first day, but some gauzier, lighter fabric, with small multi-colored flowers. He enjoyed the way it flowed around her legs as she walked, especially when a wayward breeze caught the hem and it fluttered up enticingly. *Very* feminine. And the wedge-heeled sandals emphasized her trim ankles. Yes, in a totally different way from Arja, she actually *was* sexy.

Inside the Ateneum Mika was soon absorbed in the works of the major Finnish masters. For a long time he stood in front of a large painting by Helene Schjerfbeck. It was a moving portrait of a little girl who was convalescing from an illness, holding a small budding branch—a symbol of hope and healing.

Anna-Liisa watched Mika. Here was a man who professed to dislike children, now completely absorbed in a painting of a child with tousled hair, who had obviously lain in bed for a long time and was finally allowed to sit up. Anna-Liisa had always loved that painting, perhaps because it reminded her of the few times her own children had been ill and were getting better.

"That's very touching," Mika said, his voice thick with emotion.

Slowly they meandered on. In front of a huge canvas by Albert Edelfelt Mika again stopped, and Anna-Liisa waited, watching him. He seemed taken by a little girl in a black dress, sitting in a rowboat bedside the small wooden coffin of a baby. Obviously her brother or sister. She was in the middle of the painting, clutching a little bouquet of field flowers, her solemn eyes gazing down at the passing waters. The rest of the family—father rowing with strong arms, mother and grandmother sitting with grim faces—all seemed resigned to the sad, inevitable fate of the baby.

But when they came to a painting by Juha Rissanen with the title, "Death of Father", Anna-Liisa felt her insides stiffen. It depicted a drunk man, lying on his back in the snow, clutching a bottle. How well she knew that painting. And each time she saw it, she felt guilty for thinking how wonderful it would be if the man lying dead in the snow could have been Aaro. It wasn't right to wish the father of her children dead, even if he was no father to them at all. And even though he'd beaten her up several times during their marriage, those actions weren't deserving of a death penalty. But she could, without a sliver of guilt, wish him all the way to the darkest corner of Lapland where he wouldn't keep intruding into her life with his threatening phone calls.

"Well, if that isn't a typical Finnish scene, I don't know what is," Mika snorted and continued on.

Obviously the painting hadn't produced a similar reaction in him, proving that his past didn't include an alcoholic father. Lucky for him to have had a happy childhood. Although hadn't he said something about having to look after his siblings while his mother worked? And he'd started to say something about his father, but had stopped. So, perhaps his was not a totally happy childhood after all.

By noon they had covered several galleries but still had much left to see.

"We could stop now and continue our tour after lunch," Anna-Liisa suggested. "Or we could walk home and finish looking at these another day."

"I hate to admit it, but I'm getting sleepy," Mika said, covering a huge yawn. "I think a nap would do me good."

"Yes. We will skip this afternoon's activities and instead you can rest. Tonight you might want to go and see Helsinki nightlife. If you like, I can give you Arja's phone number. I know she would be happy to take you."

Yes, Arja would be more than eager to accompany him. She'd given plenty of evidence of that at the party.

"You don't do night clubs?" he asked.

"No." She wasn't prepared for the feeling of regret that suddenly nibbled at her heart. She, also, would have loved to go dancing and enjoy herself.

Especially with Mika.

Arja and Mika arrived by taxi at an open-air rooftop nightclub where the music blared and bodies gyrated under strobe lights. They headed for the bar where Mika bought them drinks, and for a while they stood, leaning against the counter, taking in the overwhelmingly loud atmosphere.

After two more vodkas, consumed rather too quickly, Mika placed his empty glass on the bar and slipped an arm around Arja's waist. "Dance?" He led her onto the crowded dance floor.

As he'd noted before, Arja was a fabulous dancer and soon Mika was right into the whole scene, arms raised, hips undulating, responding to her suggestive moves. The alcohol dispelled any inhibitions he might have harbored, and by the time they stopped for a breather his hands had made their way down her back to her shapely bottom. Arja laughed and made no move to discourage his advances.

Mika wiped his brow. "Whew, I think I need some more liquid."

At the bar he ordered two beers and as they stood there, Arja leaned against his chest and snuggled into the crook of his arm. Mika blinked to clear a fuzziness inside his head caused both by alcohol and having danced with sexy Arja. What a heady combination. Enough to make any man fall victim to erotic sensations. He wrapped his arm around her shoulders and surreptitiously let his hand wander down to one full breast.

Arja laughed.

Not exactly falling pearls.

Damn! Anna-Liisa kept invading his brain at the most inopportune moments. What would she have thought of all this? Probably she never came to these kinds of places. Yes, she was a Good Mother with caps, like Virgin Mary. He snorted at the thought and pressed Arja closer to dispel the sound of Anna-Liisa's laughter.

"Here's to a great night in Finland," he said and saluted with his beer glass. Was it hello to Arja or good-bye to Anna-Liisa? Or vice versa? He didn't know, nor did he want to dissect the thought any further. "And to a lovely lady." He realized his words sounded somewhat thick. Which lady was he thinking of?

"Hey, any time, mister!" Arja said demurely. "I'll be happy to ensure your stay in Helsinki is good in every way."

He knew this was his cue, and he knew exactly what his response should have been.

But he couldn't say it. Damn it all! He had all the right words at the tip of his tongue, but somehow they wouldn't come out. Anna-Liisa's face was there in front of him, looking at him with those serious blue eyes.

"Knock, knock," he said instead.

Arja gave him a quizzical smile, but then shrugged. "Who's there?"

"Plato."

"Plato who?"

"Plato spaghetti."

Arja laughed. "That's a good one."

"Thanks."

But the joke sounded lame. "Hey, let's dance some more," he said and clunked his glass down on the bar a bit too hard. "I don't know how long I can keep awake, so let's make the most of the night before I snuff out."

With an inviting smile, Arja linked arms with him. "Let's!"

She moved her body fetchingly in front of him, and when he took her in his arms, he could feel every curve of her body rubbing against him. Any man with half the sex drive he had, would have had an instant erection. His barely made the grade. He remembered how, dancing with Anna-Liisa, his body had reacted much more strongly when her hip had barely brushed against his thigh. Maybe it was because that dance had been a sultry one, whereas this one was a rocking fast number. He and Anna-Liisa had barely undulated on the spot, and yet he had wanted to hold her, and keep on holding her. Now, although here was Arja gyrating in front of him, all he could do was try to keep his feet from stumbling. Obviously too much alcohol.

When a slow piece started, Mika made sure he held Arja as close as possible, in order to make full use of the ambiance. And to prove to himself he still had it.

But his body refused to co-operate, and he could only hope Arja didn't feel his embarrassing, half-cocked erection through his jeans.

After a few more dance numbers and several more shots of vodka, Mika gallantly escorted Arja to a waiting taxi. Although at this stage he wasn't sure who was escorting whom.

In the dark back seat he took her face in his hands and kissed her thoroughly. "Thank you for a lovely evening," he said, trying to sound cavalier, though the words came out thick and slurred.

He felt Arja's hand come down to stroke him, and did his best to conjure up the most masterful erection he could. But to his dismay, it was a far cry from his usual impressive size. They would have to do this another time without quite so much lubrication beforehand. By way of consolation, he partly unzipped her light fall jacket and slipped his hand inside her blouse. The way she thrust her firm, round breasts forward told him she was aching for him to caress her. He gently manipulated the puckered nipples and then zipped up her coat again like a fine gentleman.

"Fraid not tonight," he muttered and pretended to stifle a yawn. "Jet lag."

Arja giggled and gave the front of his jeans a consoling pat. "That's okay. Next time."

By twelve-thirty Mika was back in his dorm room. Alone. He couldn't believe he'd blown a chance to have sex with lovely Arja. How long could he keep using jet lag as an excuse? But the more relevant question was, why should he use *anything* as an excuse as far as Arja was concerned? Why didn't he just jump her bones when he had the chance?

He knew Arja wasn't the kind to give up easily. She seemed like a determined lady and normally he would have welcomed that type with open arms, but now . . .?

He knew damned well it wasn't jet lag.

It was Anna-Liisa.

Anna-Liisa parked the car in front of the dorm in order to dutifully pick Mika up for another tour of Helsinki. No, not dutifully at all, but with pleasure, although she found it difficult to admit this to herself. Why was it so nice to be with him? He was like any other man with two legs—long, and muscular ones, from what she'd seen of them under his jeans—and two arms. She knew they were strong and sinewy from the way he had held her while they were dancing. A man with two eyes—brown ones that had sparkled with delight or misted with emotion at the gallery. A man with light brown hair—somewhat on the long side, but it was nice the way the wind sometimes caught it and tousled it around his head. A man with a nicely-formed nose, and a chin that looked firm without being massive. And a man with hands that had long-fingers—artistic and sensitive, yet strong. She knew that because he'd held her hand after the dance. And it was nice to know he was impressed by—of all things!—her driving skills, and wasn't too macho to acknowledge it.

Anna-Liisa smiled. Was that why she liked being with him? A good-looking man who seemed to appreciate her. Fair enough. Nothing wrong with that, was there?

Mika was waiting for her on the sidewalk with his camera. "*Hyvää huomenta*!" he said with a broad grin as he opened the car door. "Did I say that right?"

"And good morning to you," Anna-Liisa replied. "You said it very well. Almost."

"So where's the laugh? My lousy pronunciation is

supposed to make you laugh." Mika buckled his seatbelt. "I like to hear you laugh."

Anna-Liisa pushed the stick shift into first and steered the Mercedes into the traffic. There was another reason she found the man so interesting. He was so candid when he spoke. Telling her he liked to hear her laugh, of all things.

"Why do you like to hear me laugh?" she asked. "Do I cackle?"

Mika turned his body sideways to look at her. "Absolutely not. Your laughter is delightful. I want to paint it."

Anna-Liisa shook her head in disbelief. "Paint my laughter?" The man was incredible. "Next you will say you want to paint my hiccups."

Mika's booming laughter filled the car in a very pleasant, masculine way and she suddenly realized this was another reason she was growing fond of him. She wanted to hear him laugh again.

"I haven't heard you hiccup yet," he said. "But when I do . . . yes, maybe I'll want to paint them, too."

"I *very* much doubt that."

"So where did you say you're taking me today? I understand it's a museum of some kind. Soor-saur or something? Sounds kind of like a dinosaur museum? Just guessing."

Anna-Liisa burst out laughing. "Seurasaari," she said. "It is an outdoor museum on one of the nearby islands and shows the way Finns lived as far back as the sixteen hundreds. The buildings are all original and have been transported here. Cottages, farmsteads, churches and manor houses. And saunas, of course."

"So my dinosaur guess wasn't that far off," Mika observed. "We'll just see fossils of a different kind."

"Very clever."

"Do we take a boat?"

"No, it is connected to the mainland by a bridge."

A short time later she parked the car in a parking lot next to the bay. After she had paid the admission, they crossed the long, white wooden bridge and started to wander along a meandering sandy path, taking in the displays.

As they strolled side by side, Mika was conscious of the fetching way Anna-Liisa's hips swayed beside him. Once, when their hands happened to touch, on a whim he caught hers and held it. He felt her start, but to his surprise and pleasure she didn't pull away. He hoped to make the situation less threatening by hooking fingers with her and swinging their arms as if they were a couple of kids out for a walk.

She looked up at him and smiled. "I have not walked like this for years."

"Yeah, I thought the day was perfect for a friendly sort of walk," Mika said and prayed she wouldn't pull away.

She didn't. And so he decided to push the envelope a bit by trying to find out more about her.

"So, how long have you been divorced?" he ventured to ask.

That was a mistake. She pulled her hand away and immediately he felt the loss and was sorry for the question.

"Four years." Anna-Liisa replied and by her clipped tone he knew no more information was forthcoming.

"See this rowboat?" she said instead. They were passing an open shelter that housed a tarred rowboat, several meters long. Mika snapped a few pictures of it, with Anna-Liisa standing beside it. Maybe he would do a painting of this one day, back in Canada.

She ran a hand along the rough and worn side of the boat. "It was used by villagers to get to church across a lake. That is why it is called—"

Mika put out his hand. "No, wait, let me guess. A church boat?"

"Nope. *Kirkkovene,*" Anna-Liisa said and laughed. "Okay, you are right. A church boat is correct."

"*Kirk* I understand. But '*koh-vey-neh*' doesn't sound like a boat to me in any known language."

"*Kirkko* is church and *vene* is boat."

To his surprise, Anna-Liisa began to sing softly, while she caressed the ancient tarred wood. The melody was so sad it almost brought tears to his eyes.

"*Vienan rannalla, koivun alla,*

kuulin laulun kaunihin,
aurinkoisen taivahalla
siirtyessä aaltoihin."

The song had several verses and seemed to tell some tragic tale. Mika didn't want her to stop.

When she finished, they stood in silence for a few moments.

"That was beautiful," he said quietly. "But it sounded so very sad."

"Yes, it is sad. My great-grandmother sang it to me when I was a little girl. She told me when the villagers rowed to church across the lake they always sang together, and this was her favorite song." Anna-Liisa's voice was melancholy, like the song.

"What's it about?"

For a while it looked like she wasn't going to answer. Then she swallowed. "It is sung by a girl whose lover has left her behind," she said at last. "He has gone to a far-away land. She sits by the river, under a birch tree, and plays her *kantele*—that is kind of like a zither—while the sun sets into the waters. She looks at the river with tears in her eyes and tells her lover that her youth is flowing by like the water, and she is fading like the lily flower. If he does not come back soon, he will find only her grave. And as she sings the nature settles down for the night, the lark stops singing, and soon the singer on the shore also falls silent."

"Being left behind by a lover—that's such a universal theme, isn't it?" Mika remarked. "I guess that has inspired some of the most beautiful and sad music and poetry in the world. Your song reminds me of 'Danny Boy'."

Anna-Liisa was silent, and Mika wondered if she'd been left behind by her husband, and was now remembering that. He wished she would open up about herself. She was divorced, had three children, and lectured at the university. That's about all he knew of her, while she knew everything there was to know about him, probably down to his shirt collar size.

"What do you do when you're not working? Or dragging around guests like me?"

"Do?" Anna-Liisa's pearly laughter rang out. "Oh my goodness, I am a working mother with three children and a household to take care of. I do cleaning, shopping, cooking, baking, laundry and preparing lectures. What else is there time for?"

"No time for love life?"

Chapter Four

Okay, he was probably jeopardizing the rest of the day with the question, but he had to know if there was someone in her life.

Anna-Liisa stepped away from the boat shelter onto the path and walked ahead a short distance before turning back to look at him.

"I do not have time for love life," she said, but her tone was somewhat softer, melancholy, as though she wished she did. Hadn't she let him hold her hand for a few moments? And hadn't she agreed to dance with him? That all had to mean something.

Or maybe not. She was hard to figure out.

They strolled on and then stopped in front of an ancient wooden church, painted red. *Karunan kirkko*, read the sign, dating from 1680, and again Mika took several photos.

"*Car-oonan kirk-ko*," Anna-Liisa pronounced the name slowly for him. Mika dutifully repeated the words after her and she smiled at his attempt. It looked like he would have to mess up the pronunciation more in order to get her to laugh. Luckily messing up Finnish words wasn't that hard to do. Getting them right was the difficult part.

"So what does the name mean?" he asked. "I know *kirkko*, but . . ."

"It is the name of the place where the building came from. The village of Karuna."

On the outside, only the arched windows and the steep roof identified it as a church, but nearby stood a beautiful, tall bell tower that was a sure give-away. They entered the church and found a large crucifix as well as several religious paintings on the white-washed wooden walls. While Mika inspected the ancient art with interest, Anna-Liisa followed him around.

"The church is still used for religious services and also for concerts," she told him and added, almost as an afterthought, "And for weddings."

Mika turned away from the relief of the Virgin Mary to look at Anna-Liisa. He felt she was about to tell him something else.

His intuition proved correct because after a few moments Anna-Liisa continued, "I was married in this church."

Mika let out his breath which he'd been holding in suspense. She'd actually *offered* to tell him something about herself. Was the wall of silence beginning to crumble? Was the Snow Queen starting to melt?

Outside, Anna-Liisa pointed to a nearby grave. "That is where Axel Olai Heikel is buried. He is the person who started this Seurasaari museum."

But Mika was still chewing on the previous piece of information. Being married in such an historic church had to mean that Anna-Liisa and her husband had every intention of making history together. It wouldn't have been simply an ordinary wedding, but a well thought-out ceremony for a couple who wanted to remain married for the rest of their lives.

"So what happened to the marriage?" Mika hoped he wasn't going to crash against another barricade.

"Alcohol happened," Anna-Liisa said simply. Again, he could tell this was all she was going to say about it.

Okay. So more than likely it was Anna-Liisa who had ended the marriage. And the sad, pensive look on her face after the song obviously was not because her husband had left her behind.

That cheered him up considerably.

As they continued along the wide, gravel path, they passed several log cabins, gray with age. In front of one such building sat a man smoking a cigarette. He was unshaven and somewhat disheveled looking, and when Anna-Liisa saw him she gave a startled gasp. Speeding up her steps, she passed by him without speaking.

The man's malicious grin sent a shiver down Mika's

spine. When they had rounded a corner, he took Anna-Liisa by the arm and turned her to face him.

"Who was that?" he asked.

For a long moment Anna-Liisa was silent, and stared at the ocean that sparkled through the tall birches.

"Who was it?" Mika asked again and this time his voice was firm, demanding an answer.

"My ex-husband," Anna-Liisa said at last, her voice quiet, almost resigned. "He must have followed us here. He would have no other reason to be here."

"Why would he follow us?"

"I assume he has seen me with you, and has been keeping an eye on us. Someone must have told him we were coming here today."

"Someone at the university?"

"Probably. He still has friends there who could be passing on information about us to him."

Mika frowned. This sounded like some cloak and dagger situation and he wasn't exactly happy about it. "I find it repulsive to think he's been spying on us. Is he jealous or something?"

"Yes, he is," Anna-Liisa replied. "There is a restraining order on him and he is not supposed to be anywhere near my house. But we are not in my house now, so—"

"Should we call the police?"

"Why? He has not done anything. This is a public

place. Being here is not a crime."

"I don't like this kind of business at all," Mika stated, shaking his head.

"I agree. And that is why I think I should not be your guide any longer. The department would not mind if someone else took over the job. It is only for one more week, and—"

"No!" Mika almost shouted and then coughed to hide his emotional response. "I mean, I don't think it's necessary to go that far. After all, the guy isn't danger- ous or anything." Or was he? Mika hoped Anna-Liisa's reply would be reassuring, but it wasn't.

"He has a bad temper and when he has been drink- ing he might do . . . things."

Mika's eyes narrowed. "What kinds of things?"

"Physical things . . ." her voice faded.

"Has he hit you?" Mika asked, although he couldn't fathom any man hitting sweet, gentle Anna-Liisa.

"That was years go, before we were divorced."

Mika's stomach turned. What had she gone through? And the kids? "What about your kids?" he asked.

"Aaro does not care about them. He hardly knows they exist. It is only me he is concerned about." She looked down.

Aaro. Now his enemy had a name. Something in his chest expanded and he felt he wanted to protect Anna- Liisa from this bastard.

"I still think you should alert the police."

"They have told me there is nothing they can do unless he actually does something."

"That's great!" Mika cried in exasperation. "They'll come and clean up the blood after he has beaten you up."

Anna-Liisa gave a short mirthless laugh. "Do not exaggerate, Mika. This is not some crime movie. He will not do anything as long as I . . ."

She started to walk quickly down the path. Mika followed and when he reached her, he caught her by the arm, twirling her around to face him.

"As long as you what?" he asked, his voice unyielding. "What is he demanding from you?"

Anna-Liisa tugged her arm free. "Nothing," she snapped. "And in any case, it is not your business."

Mika clenched his jaw. That's right. What went on between her and her ex wasn't his business. But from now on he would be keeping an eye out for this Aaro character whenever he was with Anna-Liisa. Or maybe he should be on guard even when out on his own, if the fellow was such a jealous type.

They continued to walk, but Mika couldn't help the creepy feeling that behind every tall, red pine or old building there lurked the jealous ex-husband.

At last Mika pocketed his camera. "All right. Let's finish up here at Soorus-dinosaurus."

Anna-Liisa's laughter dispelled all the unpleasantness

of the last few minutes. "I will have to remember that name so I can tell my children."

"Which reminds me, weren't you going to offer me dinner at your house?" Mika asked. "Or is it too bold of me to remind you?"

In the blink of an eye Anna-Liisa's smiling face changed into a serious one. "I do not know if that is—"

"Because of this Aaro guy?"

"No." She paused. "Not because of him."

He waited for her to explain.

At last she opened up. "I know how you feel about children."

"Babies!" Mika yelped. "I was talking about *babies* crying on the plane!" Although his dislike of kids was by no means limited to infants. "Your kids are great." He crossed his fingers mentally, hoping his voice didn't betray him, because he wasn't being exactly truthful. There was no such a thing as a "great kid".

"You know nothing about my children," Anna-Liisa said in that no-nonsense way of hers that didn't let him get away with any social niceties, like white lies.

"Okay, so I don't know much about them," Mika conceded. "But didn't Marita say at the party they were great? I trust her judgment. Besides, I've met them and they seem like awesome kids." He hoped.

"You Americans always exaggerate," Anna-Liisa scoffed. "Everything is so *awesome*."

"Hey, wait just a damned minute, young lady!" Mika

cried. "First of all, you have never heard me use the word 'awesome' before today. And secondly, I'm a Canadian, *not* an American."

"Same difference. You are all North Americans."

"That's true, but do you refer to Mexicans as Americans, too?"

"No. We call them Mexicans."

"I rest my case. Nothing against our southern neighbors, but USA is a different country from Canada, and from Mexico. We're not the same, even if all three of us happen to inhabit the same North American continent."

"Hmm," Anna-Liisa pursed her lips. "You may be right."

Mika laughed. "I *may* be right? Of *course* I'm right!" He took her by the shoulders and gave her a playful shake. "Now admit it!"

Anna-Liisa laughed and this time she didn't slip out of his hands. "Okay, I admit I was wrong. Now please release me!"

Mika wanted to do exactly the opposite. He wanted to crush her against his chest and hold her there so he could keep her safe from this Aaro-guy. But he knew it was best to obey, so reluctantly he let her go.

Their footsteps echoed as they returned along the white, wooden bridge back to the parking lot.

Anna-Liisa kissed the top of Elina's head. "Good

night, Elina," she murmured and tucked the colorful, cotton duvet around the girl's shoulders. She pulled down the blind to darken the room, shutting out the sun that at this time of year didn't set till after ten. Closing the door behind her, she softly walked past the bedroom where Johannes and Aleksi were already sound asleep in their bunk beds. On bare feet, she descended the light pine staircase into the living room.

She drew down the blinds, put on a CD of Finnish classical music to play quietly, and picked up her knitting. The light from the floor lamp behind her was the only illumination in the room and she cherished the dusk around her. Evenings were her favorite time of day. After the children were in bed and the house was quiet, she had time to herself. The cardigan she was knitting for Elina was cheerful and multi-colored, with a challenging pattern that usually kept her mind off things that would otherwise have bothered her.

Tonight the thought of seeing Aaro at Seurasaari made her uneasy, and even following the difficult knitting pattern wasn't enough to prevent her mind from thinking about his prying eyes. At last, frustrated at the unraveling she had to keep doing, she laid the work down on her lap and, with a deep sigh, lay her head against the backrest.

Aaro. How could a good man sink so low? She thought about the old church they had visited today at Seurasaari. Walking around inside had brought back so many memories of how, like every couple, they'd started their married life with great expectations. But the happiness had been short-lived. Exacerbated by his excessive drinking, Aaro's bad temper and his jealous streak had appeared. As the hitting and sexual abuse became more frequent, she lost her respect for him, along with her love. But by then they had two children, and she tried to keep the family functioning as normally as possible, while gently suggesting he should go for help with his problems.

He didn't. And Anna-Liisa finally got the courage to stop kicking a dead horse.

She picked up the knitting and tried to push the man from her thoughts. But immediately he was replaced by another.

Mika.

Today he had shown how caring he could be, and how concerned he was for her safety. And when he'd held her, she had wanted to lay her head against his chest and feel safe and comforted. That was something she hadn't experienced for a long, long time.

She knew her colleagues called her Snow Queen because she never went out with anyone. It wasn't because she didn't want to have a love life, but with Aaro lurking in the background it wasn't worth taking any chances with her safety. Yes, she missed having a lover and often dreamt of sex. But it was gentle, sweet sex that she yearned for, something totally different from when Aaro had forced himself on her.

Until now she hadn't met anyone with whom she'd wanted to have a relationship, and the Snow Queen title had conveniently kept men at bay, keeping her safe from Aaro's threats.

Until now.

Since Mika had come into the picture things had changed. She didn't even try to deny that she had feelings for him. Why kid herself? If Aaro were out of the picture, she would have a relationship with him in a heartbeat.

Anna-Liisa picked up her knitting. She wasn't deaf to her body's demands.

"Leila, what do you think I should do?"

Anna-Liisa had asked her neighbor to come over for afternoon coffee. On a tray were delicious slices of freshly baked *pulla* which Leila had brought over. Their children were playing at the park and Anna-Liisa could see them through the window, climbing and swinging with several of the neighborhood kids.

"About what?" Leila asked and took a big bite of her *pulla* slice.

"You and I have shared a lot these past few years," Anna-Liisa began, speaking in Finnish.

"Uh-huh." Leila nodded, her mouth full.

Anna-Liisa smiled at her best friend, a plump mother of three. As usual, her blond, straight hair was combed back and held with an elastic band in a rather messy bun.

"Well, I find I'm in a real conundrum," Anna-Liisa continued. "And I don't know what I should do."

"Work problems?"

"No. Would you believe it's a man?"

Leila clapped. "Hallelujah! At last!" she whooped.

"Leila, cut that out. You know very well why I haven't had any relationships since the divorce."

"I know, you're afraid of Aaro," Leila stated. "But I think he's bluffing when he calls and threatens you. He wouldn't dare do anything. Besides, he's not called you for quite some time, has he?" She dismissed Aaro with a wave of her hand. "He's a cowardly drunk. Now, who is this man? Do I know him?"

"He's the visiting lecturer from Canada, whom I've been showing around Helsinki in that fancy Mercedes."

Leila's face fell. "Oh. *That* guy. Too bad."

"Why do you say that?"

"Well, he's not here for the long haul, is he?"

"No, he's not," Anna-Liisa admitted quietly. "If I got involved with him, I'd probably end up sitting on the shore under a birch tree, waving my tear-stained hanky, like the proverbial girls of folk songs." She thought of the song she'd sung to Mika at Seurasaari. She didn't ever want to be in the same position as that sad maiden.

"How bad is it?" Leila asked, her voice full of sympathy. "I mean, are you in love with him?"

"No, of course not. I've only known him for such a short while. But, Leila, I can't deny that I find him very attractive and would have nothing against dating him. Even for the short haul."

"Has he asked you?"

"Not yet, but I have a feeling he might. And if things were different, I wouldn't mind taking this to a. . . to another level. I'd love to shed my silly Snow Queen title and show that I'm a flesh and blood woman with passions and needs."

Anna-Liisa stopped. Was she exposing herself too much, even to her best friend? Leila had been her trusted neighbor during the terrible divorce proceedings and since then had been her only confidante.

"So in other words, you wouldn't mind having sex with him?" Leila mused, reaching for another slice of *pulla.* "If I keep this up I'm going to get fat," she said and took a hefty bite.

"Yes, I think I would like that," Anna-Liisa said.

"What? That I'll get fat?"

Anna-Liisa laughed, also reaching for a slice of *pulla.* "No, the sex. But I also realize that at the end of the semester he'll be returning to Canada, where his life is waiting."

Leila frowned. "Yes, his life. So this affair with you would just be sort of an intermezzo."

Anna-Liisa smiled at Liisa's metaphor. "Musically speaking, yes."

Just then her phone rang on the table beside her and she gave a start. Something told her it wasn't going to be good.

"Anna-Liisa Saari," she said.

The heavy breathing at the other end almost made her slam the phone shut but then she heard Aaro's deep, guttural voice.

"So you got yourself a boyfriend after all!" he said. "I guess you think I was kidding when I warned you that if you start screwing around, you'll have to answer for it."

"I'm not dating anyone. This is an assignment from the university," Anna-Liisa retorted, trying to sound defiant. "I'm only showing a guest around Helsinki as a courtesy of the department."

Aaro's raucous laugh ended up in a hacking cough. "Sure you are. Walking hand in hand at Seurasaari sure didn't look to me like it was university business."

Anna-Liisa shuddered.

"You just remember that you're *my* wife and I won't share you with *anybody*. And if you start screwing this guy you make sure you're ready to face the consequences. And he better watch his back, too."

"I'm not your—" Anna-Liisa started to say angrily, but the line was already dead. Quietly she hung up her phone.

Leila's eyes were big. "That was Aaro?"

Anna-Liisa nodded and tried to look casual even though the threat to Mika made her stomach lurch. Aaro had never specified what the consequences would be if she started to date. And he had never before had a reason to spew his vitriol at any specific person. Nor did he now.

"He was threatening you?"

"As usual." Anna-Liisa picked up the knitting that always occupied the chair beside her, but immediately laid it down again. What could she do? The police were useless because they didn't arrest people simply for making a threat on the phone. She'd already found that out five years ago after their separation when she'd reported his behavior to the authorities. For a while the police had patrolled the townhouse complex, passing by on foot now and then, but when there'd been no further incidents, they had stopped coming around.

"Well, if he doesn't actually bother you physically, it's probably just so much alcohol-laced hot air. Right?" Leila poured herself more coffee and picked up the thread of their conversation. "So, you say this Canadian artist has no wife?"

But Anna-Liisa didn't want to go there any more. Whether she should or should not date Mika was now a moot point. It was out of the question. She didn't want to put him in danger, with Aaro's threats hanging over his head.

After Leila left to call in her kids, Anna-Liisa picked up the novel she'd recently taken out from the university library, hoping it would keep her mind occupied until it was time to start dinner. But instead, her thoughts kept drifting to Mika. Since he was here for such a short time, she hated to embroil him in her problems with Aaro. After the Seurasaari incident he was already aware that something was going on and now, after Aaro's threat, she should warn him that he should watch his back, as Aaro had put it. But, on the other hand, with the chauffeuring assignment almost finished, maybe Aaro would see there was nothing going on and would stop this behavior. Why raise the issue and alarm Mika if things were settling down?

Unfortunately, he already knew about the home-cooked dinner invitation and she didn't know how she could avoid it. She didn't want to explain to her colleagues why Mika shouldn't be seen around with her, and they didn't know about Mika's dislike of children. There didn't seem to be any other option but to have him over.

But this would be it. No more meeting him outside the university corridors.

Mika rang the doorbell of Anna-Liisa's townhouse and soon heard running steps approach the door and come to a halt. One of the kids.

Johannes opened the door and stood there, straight as a soldier, looking up at him with narrowed eyes.

"Come in," the boy said politely, but to Mika it sounded like he would rather have said, "Stay out." The boy's voice was that far from friendly.

"Thank you," Mika replied and obediently followed Johannes into the living room.

"Sit here," Johannes said and pointed to a specific corner of the couch. "Äiti is coming." He quickly turned and scrambled up the stairs, as though relieved to have carried out his assignment.

Mika sat down, puzzled by the boy's animosity. He recalled that at the barbeque the boy had exhibited similar aversion.

While he waited for Anna-Liisa to show up, he looked around at the compact, cozy home. From the living room, where he sat, an open pine staircase curved upstairs—he assumed—to the bedrooms. The living room, dining room and the kitchen were one open space, so he figured this set-up was what was called a *tupa,* or great room. The furnishings were light in construction, and the windows let in the late afternoon sunshine. The ceiling and floor were of light pine, and the walls were covered with pale, flowered wallpaper. The table was set for dinner, with a bouquet of field flowers in a glass vase in the centre. Some of the flowers were also on the low coffee table in front of him. There was nothing flamboyant anywhere, and

Mika could easily imagine Anna-Liisa living in here. Simple, understated and peaceful.

He heard her light footsteps descend the staircase and rose to meet her. It was incredible how the mere sight of her—like the proverbial ray of sunshine after a cloudy day—made him happy. She wore the same light, flowered dress she'd worn when they went to the art gallery and she smiled as she extended her hand to welcome him. Mika would rather have hugged her to show how glad he was to see her but that, he knew, would have been a huge *faux-pas*.

"Thank you for inviting me," he said. "Something smells very good."

"Thank you. It is the stew. I told you that you were getting a very ordinary home-cooked meal. You can always go to a restaurant if you want to eat fancy."

"I'm not into fancy eating. The stew sounds perfect. And smells even better."

As they talked, Mika was aware of Johannes standing right beside them. He had come down after his mother and was now looking up at him with big, blue, suspicious eyes.

"Johannes, go and get Elina and Aleksi so they can come down and meet Mika," Anna-Liisa said to him.

"They already met him at the barbecue," Johannes said. There was an unmistakable note of belligerence in his voice.

Anna-Liisa frowned at him. "Go and get them," she

said firmly, but not angrily. The boy turned and galloped upstairs.

Anna-Liisa turned to Mika. "Please excuse Johannes." With her hand she indicated for him to sit down. "He may be somewhat suspicious of you. I do not usually have male friends over."

Her unintended revelation made Mika very happy. She didn't have men over? Good. That further confirmed there was no boyfriend in the picture.

Soon Aleksi came scampering headlong down the stairs and screeched to a halt in front of Mika. Giving a wide smile of recognition, he stood there with his hands behind his back. "*Hei,*" he said.

"*Hei,*" Mika replied. "How's it going?"

"Good."

The conversation wasn't exactly enlightening, but there was something about the way Aleksi's eyes sparkled that made Mika smile. "So what have you been doing since I last saw you?"

"Playing," Aleksi said.

"Playing what?"

"Playing in the sandbox with my trucks with my friend Janne. And swinging. I like swinging."

"I like swinging, too," Mika found himself telling the boy. Because he suddenly remembered he'd always been fond of swinging when he was a kid. Not that he'd done much swinging lately—at least not the kind they were talking about.

Aleksi nodded. "I sing when I swing. Do you?"

"I don't . . . you know, I don't remember," Mika confessed. "It's been a long time."

"We can go swing in my park," Aleksi said. "And we can sing."

Mika grinned and tousled the boy's hair. "That sounds like a plan. We'll do that. Soon."

Anna-Liisa looked uncomfortable. "Mika, you do not have to—"

"It's all right," Mika assured her. "It's about time I got back into the swing of things. If you'll pardon the pun."

Chapter Five

"Hello, Mr. Laine." Elina had quietly appeared beside him. His name sounded cute coming from her lips, pronounced the Finnish way—Lie-neh.

Mika turned to look at her. How like her mother she was with her blond hair and sincere blue eyes. The same heart-shaped face and wide mouth looked at him. And because she looked like her mother, he didn't feel the usual apathy he normally felt toward kids.

"Hello Elisa," Mika said.

"Elina," the girl corrected him. "But lots of people make that mistake," she added with a smile, to let him know it was okay.

Mika could have kicked himself. He absolutely did *not* want to be one of those people. Anna-Liisa could easily take that to mean he wasn't interested in her kids. Which he wasn't. But he wouldn't be among her favorite people if he didn't even remember their names.

"I'm sorry. Of course I meant Elisa. I mean Eli*na*."

Damn! Could he mess up any more? "I really *am* sorry." Embarrassed, he shook his head. Out of the corner of his eye he glanced at Anna-Liisa, but nothing on her face told him whether she disapproved of his screw-up.

Elina obviously sensed his discomfort. "That's okay. It's not a big deal."

"Yes, it is," Mika said firmly. "It's important for people to call you by your real name. Your name is your identity. It's how you'll be signing your art one of these days." He recalled that Elina had received good grades for art in her report card.

She blushed and looked down at her shoes. "Yes . . . well, maybe."

"Do you have any of your art here at home?" Mika asked. This would show Anna-Liisa that he really was interested in her kids.

Elina's eyes sparkled. "Yes, I do. In my room."

"Do you think you could you let me see some?"

"Yes. I'll bring them down." And with that Elina turned and ran upstairs.

Anna-Liisa had listened to the conversation without a word. She now put her hand on Mika's arm. "Mika, Elina is a very sensitive girl," she said quietly. "Please try not to—"

"Don't worry, little mommy. I won't rip them apart," he said with a reassuring grin. Mika covered her hand with his. The gesture felt very intimate. "You'll see I can be very diplomatic."

With a smile Anna-Liisa withdrew her hand and Mika wished she'd left it there for a while longer. Like maybe for a few years.

"Yes," she said. "I know you can. I am just overprotective, I guess."

Elina returned, carrying a portfolio that she shyly handed to Mika. He couldn't help but be touched by the look of hope in her eyes. She was obviously eager to hear his opinion.

Mika placed the portfolio on the coffee table in front of him and opened it up. The first picture was a pencil drawing of a typical Finnish scene—a lake, a birch tree and a rowboat. The birch with its peeling bark and branching foliage was beautifully drawn and the shading was good, but it was the shape of the rowboat that made him give a low whistle. Mika knew how difficult boats were to draw, especially from this angle, and he was impressed by her effort.

"Elina, this is very good," Mika said and held the picture at arm's length. "The rowboat is excellent."

"Thank you," Elina said simply. "The art teacher told me it was good. I didn't know if she was only being kind. She always says nice things to everyone."

"She knew what she was talking about," Mika assured her. "I think you can safely trust her opinion."

He looked through the rest of the drawings and his favorable comments were sincere and had nothing to do with trying to impress Anna-Liisa. The girl was talented.

Anna-Liisa interrupted them. "I am afraid you will have to continue after dinner." She turned to Elina. "Get Johannes and Aleksi. But before you come down, make sure the boys wash their hands well. And you too."

She turned to go into the kitchen. "Please excuse me, Mika, while I put some finishing touches on the dinner."

Mika wanted to stand and watch her rather than sit in the living room. "I don't think it needs any more touches," he said. "It already smells so good."

Anna-Liisa opened the oven door and, with potholders, pulled out a dish that bubbled deliciously. It made his thoughts flash back to long-ago visits to his grandparents' home.

She took out some lettuce from the fridge and began to prepare a salad.

"I couldn't help noticing you don't use the word 'please' when you ask the kids to do something," Mika said. "Is that the Finnish way or something?"

"Actually, in Finnish we do not use the word 'please' the same way you do in English. You say 'Please keep off the grass' but we just suggest maybe you should keep off the grass: *Ethän kävele nurmikolla.*' So I do not use 'please' when I am telling them to do something even if I am speaking in English."

"Why not?"

"They are not doing me a favor. They are doing what I expect them to do. If I ask them to bring my purse or my book to me, I say please. And I say thank you."

"I guess that makes sense," Mika conceded. "But it does sound a bit . . . different. In Canada parents are always saying 'Please, go wash your hands,' or 'Go wash your hands, please and thank you.' I guess you think that's excessive?"

"Yes. Especially the 'please and thank you'. That does not even make any sense."

"I guess you're right. It doesn't. But, listen, can I help you please and thank you? I chop a mean tomato," Mika grinned.

Smiling, Anna-Liisa handed him a knife and a cutting board. "Here is the toma—" The phone on the counter rang and immediately she picked it up. "I do not allow the children to answer the phone," she said hurriedly.

As she listened, the lingering smile on her face changed into a frown and became almost fearful. After a few moments, without replying, she hung up and went to draw the curtains, although the sun was still out.

She returned into the kitchen and continued to tear up the lettuce.

"Bad news?" Mika asked.

Anna-Liisa swallowed before answering. "Yes."

"Want to share? I know it's none of my business, but—"

She turned to look at him, her face serious. "Actually, it does concern you, in a way."

This was the last thing Mika had expected to hear, but he didn't say anything, waiting instead for her to offer more information.

Anna-Liisa glanced in the direction of the stairs before speaking. "That was Aaro," she said quietly. "He is lurking around somewhere. He has seen you here and he told me . . ." She turned back to rip the lettuce.

Mika put a hand on her shoulder. "He told you what?"

"Even though I have told him you are a guest lecturer whom I am chauffeuring around Helsinki, he insists you and I are . . ." Anna-Liisa ripped more lettuce.

Mika took her by the shoulders and turned her to face him. "Are what?"

"Lovers." Her eyes were downcast and he hardly heard the reply.

After the incident at Seurasaari, this didn't come as a surprise to him. He raised her chin, forcing her to look up at him. "And I guess the fact that I'm here in your house only confirms that in his mind."

"Yes."

"Are you going to call the police?" he asked.

"He has not done anything. Making a phone call is not against the law. He only reminded me of what he always says."

"Which is . . .?"

Anna-Liisa shook her head. "He always says I must remember I am his wife—although I am *not.* We have been divorced for four years and it has been five years since we separated. He always says I must be ready to face the consequences if I start dating anyone."

Mika was very conscious of the hand that gripped his arm, although she seemed totally unaware of it. Was that the reason she never went out with anyone? Maybe she wasn't really a Snow Queen, but simply too scared to start a relationship.

Mika put an arm around her shoulders and to his surprise and pleasure she leaned her head against his chest. He wanted to hold her tightly with both arms to comfort her and make her feel safe, but was unsure how the gesture would be received.

"What consequences does he threaten you with?"

"Just consequences. I guess it is the uncertainly that makes it sound scary."

A fierce need to keep her safe from Aaro filled him and, heedless of how she would react, Mika wrapped both arms around her. "Nothing is going to happen to you, Anna-Liisa," he murmured. "I promise."

But what right did he have to promise her anything? After the term was over, he wouldn't be here to protect her.

She slipped out of his embrace and turned away.

"He cannot be trusted," she whispered.

The three children came scrambling down the stairs and Anna-Liisa once more resumed her role as the mother—positive, cheerful and competent. He knew there would be no going back to their conversation tonight, but perhaps he could bring up the subject of her husband—her ex-husband—at some later point. Maybe the man was only trying to scare her with empty threats, or maybe there *was* something to be concerned about. The whole scenario smelled of trouble.

But the way she'd leaned her head against his chest when he held her, told him she was in need of support and comfort. However, he knew that she would pull up the drawbridge if he started to talk about this. Which was probably good, because he was definitely *not* into starting anything with vulnerable women. Women with complicated pasts, who could get him involved in their lives. Women with kids who could run off with his heart. He had to remain vigilant because nothing could come of their relationship.

Nothing *must* come of it.

At the dinner table the children eagerly related everything that had happened to them during the day. Mika was surprised how much he enjoyed hearing it all and, taking his cues from Anna-Liisa, he asked a few questions of his own. Anna-Liisa was an active listener, always asking for more details from each child, and she kept the chatter more or less organized by making sure one didn't usurp the others' conversation. They all spoke English, and Mika was impressed with how well the kids were able to express themselves.

"Blueberry pie for dessert," Anna-Liisa told him. "Finnish style, with a *pulla* crust. Elina and Johannes, clear the table and bring out the coffee cups and dessert plates. They are on the counter. Then Aleksi can put out the little coffee spoons."

"And forks too?" Aleksi asked.

"Yes. Good thinking, *kulta*," Anna-Liisa said. She led the way to the living room and indicated for Mika to sit down on the sofa. "Would you like a cognac with your coffee?"

"Yes. Good thinking, *kool-tah*," Mika mimicked her, and that made her laugh. "What does *kulta* mean? Isn't that what you call your beer? Lappish gold or something?" He was surprised to see a slight blush rise to her face. He had no idea what he had just said to bring it on.

"Yes. *Kulta* means gold, or dear, or sweetheart, or love, or darling, all rolled up in one very important word. It is not just beer."

He wanted to tell her the word described her perfectly. "That's a very handy word to know," he said instead. "*Kulta.* I'll have to remember that."

Anna-Liisa went into the kitchen to put the coffee on and returned with a brandy snifter and handed it to him.

"Thank you, *kulta*," he said, emphasizing the endearment.

Elina giggled on her way to the kitchen with a load of plates.

"Do not overdo it," Anna-Liisa said sternly but Mika could tell she was hiding her smile.

"You won't have a brandy with your coffee?" he asked, wishing he could make her laugh again.

"No, I am driving you back to the university," she reminded him. She sat down in the armchair opposite him, although Mika had hoped—without expecting it—that she would sit beside him.

"And how is Finnish-style blueberry pie different from normal blueberry pie?" he asked to keep up the chatter. He wasn't comfortable with the silences which, he had noted, didn't seem to bother the Finns at all.

"This *is* normal blueberry pie," Anna-Liisa said. "Normal in Finland. We spread the blueberries on top of the *pulla* dough, which has been rolled out thin. You must be familiar with *pulla*, having a Finnish grandmother."

"Oh yes, and I love it. She used to make that delicious coffee bread every week and even taught me how to braid it."

When the dinner dishes were in the dishwasher, and the boys had washed the blueberry stains off their faces, everyone gathered in the living room to watch a comedy show on TV. Mika and Anna-Liisa sat on the sofa, this time side by side because Elina had commandeered the armchair. For which Mika was very grateful to her. The boys were sprawled on the shag mat in front of the TV and now and then burst into howls of laughter at something the actors said. And although Mika didn't understand a word of it, he had to grin as he watched their actions. At one point Aleksi, absorbed in the show and seemingly unaware, sat up against Mika's knees. The skinny back and shoulder blades pressing against his legs filled Mika with a strange feeling he couldn't identify. All he knew was, it wasn't unpleasant.

Something felt so right about all this, and yet Mika knew it was all wrong. This looked and felt too much like some cozy little family—a husband, a wife, kids—exactly what he never wanted to have around him.

"Well, time for me to hit the road," he said, and then gave a short, surprised laugh. "Oops, I don't have a car, do I?"

"Do you mind waiting until this show is over?" Anna-Liisa asked. "I will drive you back when the children go to bed."

When the kids were settled down, Anna-Liisa drove Mika to the dorm. Mika was tempted to bring up the subject of her ex-husband, but didn't want to spoil the moment. It was too pleasant sitting beside her, planning the following day.

Until she dropped the bombshell.

"So tomorrow will be the last day of our guided tours. I will give back the Mercedes tomorrow night."

Mika was stunned. He'd known their time together had been scheduled for only a couple of weeks, but somehow he'd neglected to count the days that accurately. Maybe he hadn't *wanted* to know.

"Naturally we have not been able to visit all the interesting places in the city, but there is no reason why you cannot go by yourself to the ones we have missed," Anna-Liisa said as she steered the car into the university grounds. "You have all fall and part of the winter to continue the sightseeing."

"But Helsinki won't be the same without you," Mika griped.

Anna-Liisa's laughter bubbled. "Now you sound like Johannes," she reprimanded him. "You will get even more out of the visits because there are *real* guides who can explain things in English much better than I."

"Nobody does it better," Mika said, feeling like a grumpy kid. Yes, like Johannes.

"Oh, I am sure Arja would do it better," Anna-Liisa threw out. "You could ask her to take you. She told me you two went to a nightclub, and she had a great time. I hope you did, too."

So she knew, and had said nothing. And judging

from her casual tone she didn't even care. "It was okay," he said. "Too bad I was bushed and didn't really get into the scene. Maybe now that I'm over the jet lag I would be able to enjoy it more." But he knew he didn't want to go out with Arja. And the thought of going to another noisy nightclub didn't appeal to him.

Was he getting old?

"What I'd like to do is go somewhere where we could enjoy nature. Somewhere peaceful and quiet." Where Anna-Liisa would fit in perfectly. He'd been thinking he'd like to paint her in some natural setting.

"Such as . . .?"

"How about an island?" he asked. "Could we go and visit one of those thousand and one islands that surround Helsinki? Would that be possible?"

Anna-Liisa thought for a moment. "Yes, I think so. I will make a few phone calls and let you know tonight if I can come up with something."

Perfect. A day out on an island together with Anna-Liisa. Walking with her. Talking with her. Sketching her. Taking photos of her.

Stefan sat at the helm, masterfully steering his long, low sloop out toward the open sea. Mika observed him—so carefree, laughing, his tanned hand gripping the helm, his blond curls covered by a smart sailor cap—looking every bit like the guy in a TV ad who'd won a huge lottery. The sleek Folk boat bounced on the sparkling waves as they sailed toward one of the islands off the coast.

The day hadn't turned out the way Mika had envisioned because it had been absolutely necessary for Stefan to come along, seeing as how the sailboat was his. Rather than renting one of the public motorboats that ran to the various islands, Anna-Liisa instead had asked Stefan. Which was a wise move, since Mika didn't know the waters around Helsinki at all, nor was he much of a sailor to begin with.

Mika frowned as the Swede kept up a constant, detailed lecture about the many picturesque islands on the archipelago. "Hey, you should take up a job as a tour guide," he couldn't help quipping at one point. "You sure know the area. *Very* thoroughly."

The sarcasm in Mika's words failed to reach its mark, and only caused Stefan to grin in appreciation and for his commentary to ramp up. But Anna-Liisa had obviously picked it up, because she frowned at Mika and shook her head disapprovingly, all the while trying not to laugh.

"It was so nice of you to help us out," she said to Stefan. "I thought Mika would enjoy sailing to an island instead of taking a rented motor boat. I hope you are enjoying this as much as Mika and I are."

"I certainly am!" Stefan gave a jovial wave to a fellow captain in a passing boat. "That's also a Folk boat," he informed them.

Anna-Liisa turned to Mika. "You *are* enjoying the day, are you not, Mika?"

Mika could tell she was being impudent. "I certainly am!" he enthused. With her uncanny mind-reading ability he knew she'd picked up on his rather negative feelings about Stefan. But did she know *why* he felt that way? Did she know it was because he considered the big Swede his rival? Or he would have *been* a rival if Mika had any inclination to throw his hat in the ring. Which he wasn't going to do. He only enjoyed being with her.

"Wouldn't your kids have enjoyed coming along for the sail?" Mika asked, surprising himself for even thinking about them. He knew Anna-Liisa had left them with the Koivus.

"I am afraid Elina and Johannes tend to get seasick," Anna-Liisa replied. "And, besides, there is not enough room on this boat for six people."

After an hour they pulled up beside a public dock on the island of Kaunissaari, where several sailboats and motorboats were already docked. Stefan hopped nimbly ashore, while Mika clambered out with as much dignity as he could muster. Which wasn't much. He was happy not to drop his phone, camera and sketchbook into the brine. Helping Anna-Liisa was unnecessary, as she seemed quite able to nimbly disembark on her own. That made him wonder, with a stab of jealousy, whether she often went sailing with

Stefan.

"Now, how about we hike over to the restaurant for a cup of coffee," Stefan proposed after securing the boat. "The exercise will do us good after all that sitting."

Great. Just after he'd brought his art stuff out. "That sounds fine," Mika said. "But Anna-Liisa, sometime today I'd like to sketch you by the rocky shore, if you'll consent to be my model?"

Anna-Liisa brushed aside his request with the wave of her hand and hurried after Stefan down the wide, sandy path, while Mika struggled back on board to tuck his art materials into the boat.

He jogged to catch up with Stefan and Anna-Liisa. "I meant what I said about wanting to draw you," he persisted, settling down to walk beside her. "You don't have to pose or anything. Sit wherever you wish and look out at the sea and let me sketch. Would that be okay?"

Anna-Liisa didn't reply until they were sitting at a wooden table in the rustic, red-stained restaurant, overlooking the quiet ocean and the rocky shoreline.

"If it means so much to you, I guess it will be all right if you sketch me," she said and took a sip of her coffee.

Mika reached over and gave her hand a gentle squeeze. "Thanks."

And just as he'd expected, Anna-Liisa pulled her

hand away.

Stefan had observed the gesture but only raised one eyebrow to indicate his thoughts. "If you want to sketch my boat, too, that's fine," he offered.

"Thanks. I think I'll just snap a photo of it to possibly use in a future painting," Mika said.

After coffee, they took a tour around the small island, which was only about two kilometres long and barely a kilometre wide, searching for a place to settle down for the day. Several campsites had been set up and people were sitting around their tents, enjoying whatever libations they'd brought along. Along the way Mika snapped many photos of the scenery.

Finally they found a quiet spot by the shore and sat down on the bedrock that had been washed smooth by the sea. Mika went back to the boat to get his sketchbook, and on his return, was happy to find the warm sunshine had lulled Stefan to sleep. Anna-Liisa sat on the rock near him, her long legs stretched out, wiggling her toes in the water.

Without a word, Mika set to work, sketching her with firm strokes, taking in the way her hair was caught by the slight breeze. Her t-shirt revealed her small, firm breasts, so unlike the voluptuous kind he usually found attractive.

Mika didn't know why he found her so lovely. So physically perfect. He decided something had changed in the way he looked at women, and he had no idea what it was, or why it had happened. All he wanted to do was to continue drawing Anna-Liisa as she sat there, so exquisite in her simple loveliness.

He finished a couple of sketches and came over to show them to her.

She took them, looked at them, and gave them back to him without a word.

Mika was nonplussed. "So, what do you think?"

"They are good," Anna-Liisa replied. "You are a good artist."

"That's it? You don't see anything special in them?"

Yes, Anna-Liisa had seen, but she didn't want to say anything. "Well, they are very good," she repeated instead, knowing all the while she was disappointing him.

She wasn't blind. She could see he had put his heart into the drawings and she was now dismissing them with a bland comment—good. They weren't good. They were beautiful. In fact, the drawings were a statement of . . . what? His feelings for her? Because she'd felt for some time he was becoming attracted to her. Like she was to him.

"Okay. That's fine." He shrugged, slapped the sketchbook shut and stood up. "We should go for a walk. Do you think it's okay to leave Sleeping Beauty here on his own?"

"Of course." Anna-Liisa got up and stretched.

They headed down the path that circled the island,

walking slowly to take in the sparkling ocean and the flying seagulls. Mika took her hand in his and she fought the desire to leave it there. It felt so good. But it wasn't right. Everything was wrong about starting this relationship. There was Aaro, there were the children, and there was the looming date of his departure.

Under the pretext of pointing at the birds, she pulled her hand away. "Look at that seagull. It has black wings, while the others have white. I do not know much about birds but—"

"Anna-Liisa." His voice was low, almost pleading, and he reached for her hand again. This time she let it stay there, and a wonderful feeling of warmth flowed into her through the contact. Without speaking they walked on. They climbed off the path, up a gently sloping rock face where the juniper shrubbery and short, twisted pines provided a measure of seclusion. There they stopped.

Mika turned to her and, without a word, he took her in his arms. For a moment he held her against him, and she could feel the heavy thumping of his heart, while her own was betraying her emotions with its quick response.

He took her face between his hands. "Anna-Liisa," he breathed. The word mingled with the sound of the wind that was swelling and dying. It was like a prayer—like an adoration, and she melted inside as his lips came down softly on hers.

The kiss was brief, though she would have wished for it to last until forever. He took her hand again and they continued down the path. Hardly a word was exchanged between them, but Anna-Liisa knew something had changed. Their relationship had taken a definite turn and was heading down a path where it was not wise to go.

On so many fronts it was completely wrong. Aaro lurked in the background, ready to pounce when she least expected it. And the children didn't need a man in their lives who would only be there for a short while, before disappearing forever.

But as for her . . .? She desperately wanted to love again. She wanted to have a partner to share life's ups and downs. She wanted to be kissed and held, and never have to sleep alone again. She wanted to love a man who would love her back for the rest of her life.

And Mika was not that man.

They continued to circle the island, until they were back at the public dock. Stefan was already there, chatting with other boaters. When he saw them he waved.

"Where did you two disappear to?" he asked when they were close. Anna-Liisa detected a hint of jealousy in the question.

"We didn't want to wake you," Mika told him. "We figured you needed a nap after all your hard work of captaining the ship."

Stefan laughed. "Admit it. You just wanted to be alone with Anna-Liisa."

Mika joined in the laughter. "You bet I did!"

Anna-Liisa turned to look at the ocean to prevent her face from betraying her feelings.

Stefan chuckled. "I guess I have to start keeping an eye on the two of you from now on."

That sounded too much like Aaro's warnings, and she didn't find Stefan's words amusing. "I do not think that will be necessary," she said, hoping her voice wasn't too tart. "There is too much of that going on already."

For a few minutes no one said anything, while Stefan probably tried to figure out what she was talking about. "So did you get around to sketching Anna-Liisa like you wanted?" he then asked Mika.

"Yes, I did. But Anna-Liisa didn't think much of my efforts."

Stefan held out his hand. "May I see?"

"I *said* they were good," Anna-Liisa objected. She didn't want Stefan to see the drawings.

"Oh, sure you did. But with not one drop of enthusiasm," Mika grumbled. He handed Stefan the sketchbook.

The Swede studied the pictures at some length, deep in thought. "Uh-huh." He nodded, and returned the book to Mika. "Excellent. You caught her exactly right. That's how she is."

"Yes, that's how she is," Mika agreed.

Anna-Liisa had a strange feeling she'd witnessed some sort of an understanding between the two men. She suspected the drawings had revealed something to Stefan about Mika's feelings for her.

But, always the practical one, she broke the moment by saying, "We should get a bite to eat at the restaurant before we go back on the ocean. Judging from the wind, it might take us a fairly long time to get to Helsinki."

"You surprise me, Anna-Liisa. I didn't know you knew so much about the wind and such," Stefan said.

"Oh, I simply looked out on the ocean and noted the wind direction," she said and turned to walk toward the restaurant.

"So you're *not* a sailor?" Mika asked, catching up to walk beside her.

"A sailor?" she said with a short laugh. "No. I have only been out in rowboats."

"That so?" was his reply, and Anna-Liisa detected pleasure in his voice.

After they'd been shown to a table and were seated, Stefan ordered a bottle of wine. "We must celebrate Mika's first two weeks in Finland!" he proposed, raising his glass.

"Yes, and the end of my assignment as a guide. I hope it has been satisfactory," Anna-Liisa joined in.

"Yes, it has been quite satisfactory, thank you."

Mika raised his glass. "Here's to the end of your *assignment.* I hope I haven't been too much of a bother."

She thought his voice sounded more like a grumble than a celebratory toast.

And somehow she didn't feel like celebrating, either. A sudden feeling of sadness filled her.

Chapter Six

Anna-Liisa parked at the curb in front of the dorm to let Mika off but he made no move to get out. Something about this didn't feel right to him. Despite the "celebration" in the restaurant, the ending seemed too abrupt and he wanted to slow down the process. Preferably not have it happen at all, but that wasn't possible because her assignment was now irrevocably over. But he didn't want her to simply walk out of his life like that. Okay, even if she wouldn't be completely out of his life, he knew from now on they wouldn't be in this intense—almost intimate—daily contact.

"Hey, since this is the last time we're together in this guide-visitor capacity, don't you think we should celebrate? I mean, you might want to celebrate that you're rid of me." He grinned, though he felt more like mourning.

Anna-Liisa's laughter bubbled out. "Now you are being silly, Mika. I thought we already celebrated the—the end on the island." He heard the catch in her voice which surprised him. Could it be she didn't want things to end, either?

"Yes, but Stefan was there, so it wasn't *our* celebration." He knew he didn't make any sense, but luckily Anna-Liisa indulged him and went along with his lame explanation.

"All right," she said. "How should we celebrate?"

"I would like to thank you by taking you out for dinner." Mentally he crossed his fingers. Her kids could always throw a screw into any plans.

And that's exactly what happened now.

"I am afraid I have to go home to make dinner, but maybe you could buy me a coffee and a cinnamon *pulla* at the cafeteria?"

"Hell, I wanted to be more extravagant than that. But if that's all we have time for, then *pulla* and coffee it will have to be. But not at the cafeteria. How about you drive us to a nice restaurant of your choosing."

Anna-Liisa obliged and soon they were sitting under a colourful umbrella on the sidewalk patio of a pleasant little restaurant, both with cinnamon *pullas* and coffee in front of them.

Silence prevailed. As usual, it made Mika uncomfortable, but Anna-Liisa seemed totally at ease, taking in the atmosphere and the people around them. He wanted to speak with her about the kiss on the island, and ask what exactly it had meant to her, but that subject wasn't easy to bring up. He couldn't just blurt out, "So what did you feel when we kissed? Was it anything close to mind-blowing like it was to me?" And if she said it hadn't done much for her, how dumb would he feel? Better keep away from the subject and not make himself appear like some love-sick idiot.

Love-sick? Nothing love-sick about it. He only really, really enjoyed being with her. A lot.

He reached across the table to cover her hand. "Thanks for putting up with me, Anna-Liisa," he said. "If you've enjoyed our outings even half as much as I have, then you've had a great time."

She didn't pull her hand away. "Yes, Helsinki is a very interesting city," she said, obviously misunderstanding his words. "I have enjoyed going to all those places again. But you can still continue to explore it on your own, or with some friends. I am afraid my time will now be taken up with preparing my lectures and getting the children ready for school. It begins in less than two weeks. I cannot believe how quickly the summer has gone. I still have to get them some school items and fall clothes. It is already August and the university classes are starting on Monday. Did you know school in Finland begins the middle of August?"

What a tirade coming from Anna-Liisa! Was she actually chattering? The woman who never chattered.

He grinned. "No, I didn't know that." He gave her hand a slight squeeze and smiled playfully. "Are you nervous, Anna-Liisa?"

With a short laugh she pulled her hand away. "Nervous? No, I am not. Why should I be nervous?"

So she wasn't totally unflappable. And it was *he* who had now upset her equilibrium. He knew he had her and pressed on with his most charming, teasing grin. "You're nervous because you would like for me to kiss you again."

"What a silly thing to say. I was simply telling you about the Finnish school system." She gulped down the last of her coffee and wiped her mouth on the back of her hand. "Are you done? I must get home. The children are wondering why I am so late."

There was no more sign of any nervousness in her pragmatic tone but that didn't bother him. He'd got her to come unglued, and he took that as a sign she had some feeling for him.

"Yep, I'm done." Mika put the last of his *pulla* into his mouth and rose, feeling like a conquering hero.

They drove back to the university again and Anna-Liisa stopped by the dorm but didn't turn off the motor. She obviously wanted him to get out quickly, rather than sit and talk. Still feeling smug, Mika turned toward her and, reaching behind her neck, turned her head to face him.

"Bye, my little guide. And thank you." He brought his face close to hers and, hearing her catch her breath, he kissed her lightly on the lips.

Without waiting for her reaction, he got out and clicked the door of the blue Mercedes shut for the final time.

After dropping off the Mercedes at the designated parking, Anna-Liisa took the bus home. From now on she would be using public transit or her own little car when traveling to and from the university. Sometimes, if she wasn't planning to pick up groceries on the way home, she would use her bicycle.

Close to her townhouse she got off the bus and strode briskly along a sandy path, taking a shortcut through a copse of red pines on the outskirts of the townhouse complex. The front porch light was on, although it was barely dusk, and she quickly made her way up the walk toward the front door. Suddenly, out of the corner of her eye, she saw the shrubbery beside the steps move slightly.

She quickly stepped up to the top stair and turned toward the sound. "Who is it?" she asked sternly. "Is that you, Aaro?"

A man stumbled out from the shadows and Anna-Liisa stopped herself from gasping in fright. Aaro stood before her, obviously drunk and disheveled.

"What are you doing here?" she demanded angrily, forcing her voice not to wobble. Her heart drummed in her breast and she was afraid he would hear it and know how frightened she was.

"I thought I should hang around here in case the kids needed me," Aaro said thickly. "I didn't know how long you were going to be gone with your boyfriend. For all I knew you might stay out all night, screwing." The last words came out in an ugly growl.

Anna-Liisa unlocked the door, ready to dash inside. "You know you're not supposed to be around this house," she said. "If you don't leave this minute, I'll call the police."

"You do that and you'll be sorry!" Aaro growled. "I told you what would happen if you start to sleep around like a whore. There'll be consequences. And remember what I said would happen to your lover-boy? He better watch his back."

A shiver of fear ran through her. He was threatening Mika again. But she found the courage to not allow her voice to reflect her fear. "I am finished chauffeuring him around, so there's no need for you to spy on him. Or me. Go away, and don't come back around here again!" She said all that with as much authority as she could muster and dug into her sweater pocket for her phone.

It was in her purse. She swore under her breath. Not wanting Aaro to see her searching for it, she instead put her empty palm to her ear and turned slightly, hoping his drunken eyes wouldn't notice.

"There's a drunk trying to get into my house," she spoke loudly, giving her address. "Come quickly." Then she faced Aaro and glared at him, her face as fierce as she could make it. "The police will be here in no time. You better leave."

But instead of obeying her, Aaro swore and lunged toward her with a grunt. Anna-Liisa sidestepped him, at the same time giving him a push that caused him to stumble on the steps and roll off into the shrubbery. He scrambled up clumsily and stumbled off, swearing loudly.

She located the phone in her purse, but decided not to call the police. That would have led to her having to charge him, go to court, and get involved with social workers who, with the best of intentions, could cause all kinds of complications and problems for her and the children.

When she no longer could hear Aaro's grunting and swearing, Anna-Liisa sat outside on the step and took deep gulps of the cool evening air to calm herself before going inside to face the children. She hoped her actions tonight would keep Aaro away from her at least for a while, but she knew it would never be nearly long enough.

From now on she would have to ask Leila to look after the children if she was late coming home. Elina was responsible and knew not to open the door for anyone, but still, it would be better to have them stay at the Koivus now that Aaro had made an appearance again. He hadn't been around the house for so long

Anna-Liisa had almost lulled herself into believing he would continue to follow the restraining order.

Before the recent spate of phone calls, there hadn't been one for such a long time she thought maybe he'd found other interests in his life. Like maybe another woman. Obviously not.

Of course this was now happening because of Mika. The ugly threat for Mika to watch his back made her uneasy. She ought to warn him. But would Aaro really do something? Maybe now that the assignment was over, and she no longer would have any contact with Mika, Aaro would settle down again and retreat back into his cave.

Considering everything, the idea of not having daily meetings with Mika should have filled her with relief, but instead it made her incredibly sad. The kiss on the island still reverberated inside her with an echo that was almost terrifying in its intensity. And the light kiss in the car—obviously for him it had been only a teasing, friendly peck—had affected her much more strongly than it should have.

She was getting altogether too fond of the man.

All night Mika's dreams were filled with Anna-Liisa. When he awoke, he couldn't get her out of his brain. Damn! The woman wasn't just taking over his waking hours, but his dreams as well.

That did it. For some time Mika had been planning

to Skype his business partners and best buddies, Michael and Miguel, in Toronto, but had never got around to it. It was too complicated to take into account the time difference between Finland and Canada, not to mention their working hours, so he always kept missing the window of opportunity. But now he really felt the need to talk to someone about Anna-Liisa and how he should deal with this unexpected development in his life.

"So, how are things in Toronto?" he asked, happy to see Michael's face on his computer screen. "How's Shaylee's pregnancy coming along?"

Days before he'd left Canada, he had been told the happy news. "And how are Miguel and Marita coping with the twins?"

Michael laughed. "I guess 'coping' is the operative word, but I must admit Marita is relishing motherhood. She's a rosy, blooming mamma, and Miguel is as much in love with her as ever."

Mika picked up his can of *Lapin kulta* beer and took a gulp. "Yeah, he fell head over heels for that lady." He chuckled. "Almost as bad as you fell for Shaylee."

"You got that right. And Shaylee's pregnancy is progressing great," Michael told him. "We've been getting this old house ready for the baby. Nursery and all that."

"Good luck with that. Renovations aren't cheap."

Michael heaved a sigh. "Tell me about it. But luckily

the business is doing well and Shaylee has sold a number of her paintings. That wife of mine sure is one talented lady."

Shaylee pushed Michael aside and waved. "Hello, Mika. Don't listen to him. The man's just chattering."

"Hi, Shaylee. He's absolutely right. But speaking of talented ladies, I've met one little lady who's showing great promise in art. I'm going to start giving her private lessons. For free."

"Wow! That must be some pretty nice little lady."

The slightly lecherous tone in Michael's remark made Mika realize his friend had misunderstood. "She's ten years old," Mika said to set the facts straight.

"Oops, sorry. But did I hear that right? You're going to give lessons to a *kid*? Mika, what's that Finnish air doing to you? You've never been able to stomach children."

"Yeah, that's what I thought, too. But . . ." How was he going to steer this conversation to Anna-Liisa, who was the reason for this call. "Actually, the real problem is the kid's mother."

"What? She doesn't want her daughter to take lessons?"

"No. I mean yes, she does, but the problem isn't about the lessons." He ran a hand through his hair. How to explain it all?

"So why did you bring that up? I'm afraid you'll have

to be more precise," Michael said, and Mika saw him reach for a glass of red wine. "I'm ready to listen."

Mika took a deep breath and began again. "The mother—her name is Anna-Liisa—is a very nice woman."

"Okay. Nice is good. Especially in women."

"And I find myself getting attracted to her."

"Attracted to a woman. Uh-huh." Michael nodded a couple of times. "That's normal."

"Stop acting like some pseudo-psychologist." Mika exploded. "I don't need your comments. I only wanted to tell you about her so I can figure out what's happening to me and what I should do about it."

"What? And I can't comment?"

"Sure you can, but not till you've heard me out."

Michael settled back in his chair. "Understood—I think." He raised his wine glass. "Shoot."

"Okay. You know I'm coming back to Canada after Christmas, and so I shouldn't start a relationship because it'll have to end in a few months."

"Yes, that's right." Michael slapped a hand on his mouth. "Sorry, that slipped out!"

Mika ignored his friend's silly humor and went on. "The trouble is, I really *want* to be with her, and the more I'm with her, the more I want to be with her. It sounds crazy, but that's what's happening."

"Can I comment now?" Michael asked cautiously.

But Mika could see his lips twitch. His friend wasn't

taking him seriously and that annoyed him. "What?" he roared.

"I know you don't want to hear me say this, but it sounds to me like you're falling in love, my good man."

Mika sat stock still. That wasn't possible. He hardly knew the woman and he didn't believe that love-at-first-sight nonsense. "You're crazy!"

"Maybe, but from the way you described it to me, it sounds like love. What do you think, Shaylee?"

"Sounds to me like Mika's in love," came Shaylee's response from somewhere close by.

"You guys are nuts," Mika sputtered. "I don't even know her that well."

Michael laughed. "Okay, okay, we're just teasing. Let's hear some more."

"Well, she has all those kids."

"*All* those kids? How many is 'all'?" Michael asked.

"Three."

"Three?" Michael and Shaylee's incredulous voices sang out in a chorus.

"Yeah, but the youngest one, Aleksi, is cute and he likes me." Mika took a gulp of beer. "This *Lapin kulta* is great beer. I'll miss it when I get back home."

"Hey, c'mon. Canadian beer is pretty good, too. Now, about this cute kid who likes you . . .?"

"Yeah, nothing much to tell. He likes to swing and sing."

Mika heard a snort of laughter from Michael and a

giggle out of Shaylee, and tried to ignore them both. "So, as I already told you," he went on. "The girl, Elina, is a budding artist. A very nice girl. She's shy, but determined to learn. But Johannes is a problem because he doesn't trust men. Including me."

"I sense a story behind that," Michael said.

"Well, the father's an alcoholic who probably terrorized his kids. He also spies on Anna-Liisa and has threatened her that if she dates any men, he'll do something. Whatever that something is. He saw Anna-Liisa and me holding hands in an outdoor museum and now he's pissed."

"You were holding hands? This is getting complicated. Go on." Michael leaned forward, showing he was ready to hear more of this drama.

"That's it," Mika concluded. "Except that he's not really her husband, because they've been divorced for years. So what should I do?"

"You should write to Dear Abby," Michael said.

"Cut the comedy," Mika snapped, "This is serious. I don't know if I should cut and run, or jump in with both feet."

"And what exactly does 'jump in with both feet' involve?"

Yes, what exactly did he mean by that, besides wanting to be with Anna-Liisa.

"Sounds to me that despite all those kids, you want to have an affair with the mother, right?" Michael asked after not receiving a prompt reply from Mika.

Did he? Probably yes, but for some reason he hadn't actually thought of Anna-Liisa in those terms. He wasn't lusting after her, so to speak. He only wanted to be with her. Kiss her, yes. Hold her, definitely. But an actual affair? He hesitated. "I hadn't really thought about—"

Michael cut him off. "Come on, Mika, you hadn't thought of having an affair with her? What then? A platonic friendship? That doesn't sound like our old Mika. Maybe it *would* be better to cut and run before you become even more confused. Think about it. You're there for only a few months, so is it worth getting involved in this jealousy mess, with all those kids?"

Mika ran a hand through his hair in frustration. "I don't *know.* That's the whole problem. I don't know what I want." Actually he knew damned well what he wanted. He wanted to be with Anna-Liisa. It was almost like a desperate need inside him. But an affair . . .? Was it that kind of a need?

Michael was silent for a moment. "Well, if you two are going to have a sexual relationship, you'll have to confront the problem with this ex-husband. However, if you simply keep holding hands till you leave, there should be no problem."

"He's a crazy alcoholic."

"That may be true, but I repeat, unless you plan to

have a sexual relationship with this woman, it doesn't matter how crazy he is," Michael said.

"But he doesn't want her to have *anything* to do with other men," Mika explained. "No relationships at all."

"How does *she* feel about all this?" Michael asked.

Yes, how *did* Anna-Liisa feel about it? "Well, I assume she doesn't like being under his thumb, but she's always gone along with his demands. She's afraid to do anything to contradict him because of his threats."

He sighed remembering how he had stupidly promised to keep her safe from Aaro. As if he could do anything about anything.

"Sounds to me like a matter for the authorities." Michael's flippant tone had changed to serious. "I'd advise you to keep away from her and her kids. Too much trouble. You're there only till Christmas, so if you want sex, go find yourself some willing Finnish lass and forget this woman and her brood. No matter how cute they all are."

Mika didn't want to hear this, but Michael definitely had a point. It was crazy to get mixed up in this affair, and yet . . . he couldn't imagine not seeing Anna-Liisa again.

"But if I do take up with her—despite your wise words—what should I do when it's time for me to return to Canada?"

"Cross that bridge when you come to it," was

Michael's advise. "See how things evolve. If you're lucky you'll have grown sick and tired of her and her brood by then. And maybe she'll also have had enough of you, and the parting will be mutually agreeable."

"Yeah, you're probably right," Mika conceded. He thanked Michael for the chat. "Bye, Shaylee," he called to the invisible wife. "Stay healthy!"

"You too," came her reply.

Mika closed the connection and threw himself down on the bed. He was no further ahead, and still didn't know what to do. He definitely didn't consider the prospect of growing tired of Anna-Liisa as "lucky", like Michael had suggested. But maybe his friend was right. Maybe he *should* see how things evolved. Crossing bridges when he came to them seemed like a pretty good plan.

And maybe now that he wouldn't be so intensely involved with Anna-Liisa any more, he would find other women more appealing—like Arja for one.

Sex. That's what he needed. A good, old-fashioned roll in the hay.

"Cornelius Krieghoff, in the middle of the eighteen hundreds, was a very prolific painter of the Québec landscape and especially of the Québeçois themselves." Mika projected a wintry scene of a group of merry-making Québeçois on a wall-screen of the lecture hall. "Krieghoff was a man who enjoyed music, dancing and story-telling, and his paintings reflect that same love of life, his *joie de vivre*."

While his students scribbled down the information or typed it into their laptops, Mika stared at the painting and grimaced. So where was his own *joie de vivre* these days? He'd never felt so glum in his life.

He'd gone out on a few dates with a very "willing Finnish lass" as Michael had advised him to do. Arja was beautiful, sexy, intelligent and fun. And she was great in bed, just as he'd expected. Thankfully his body had co-operated fully and he'd achieved his usual mighty erections, even though his heart hadn't been in the act. It was always touch and go he didn't call out Anna-Liisa's name when climaxing.

Because he missed her. Achingly.

And yet, he didn't know if he should keep away from her, or try to start a more intimate relationship—if she was willing. His indecisiveness weighed on him heavily because neither alternative sat well with him. Starting a sexual relationship would definitely make things complicated, considering the short time-line, but in the weeks since Anna-Liisa's "assignment" had ended the need to be with her had grown into something almost unbearable. He hadn't even heard the pearls drop for so long his painting of them was the only thing that brought him comfort.

During this time they'd had very few dealings with each other and the odd hello in the cafeteria just didn't cut it for him. As for her, she showed no signs of wanting to be with him and behaved as though she didn't even remember that kiss on Kaunissaari Island. Although it had shaken him to the core, obviously it hadn't meant as much to her. Probably nothing at all. This thought only added to his depression. He had felt their relationship had changed after the kiss, but it didn't look like she felt the same.

The class was over. When the students had left, Mika snapped off the projector, shut the lights, and closed the door behind him. Deep in thought, he almost bumped into Stefan in the corridor.

"Hey!" the Swede cried. "Haven't seen you around for ages. I've heard you've been pretty busy since classes started." He winked. "With Arja, I hear."

"Yeah, I have." No use denying it. The back-fence chatter at the university sure was incredibly efficient. No wonder Aaro knew about Anna-Liisa's activities. And probably his, too.

"I've also heard some good things about your lectures. Some of my students are taking your Canadian Art as an elective, and they say they're really enjoying it."

"No kidding? In what way?" News like that had a great way of making even his glum outlook brighter.

"They say it's all new stuff they'd never heard about before, and it seems your presentations have been extremely interesting." Stefan laughed. "Some of them even said—and don't take this the wrong way, my good man—they didn't know there was any art in Canada worth lecturing about."

Mika straightened his shoulders. "And I haven't even got to my favorite part about The Group of Seven artists."

"Keep it up," Stefan said and then surprised Mika by asking, "So, I guess you haven't seen Anna-Liisa lately?"

"No, not much," Mika admitted. "Not at all, really. I've only said hi to her once in a while in the cafeteria."

"Well, the reason I asked is because I thought—if you don't mind me saying—I thought you two were kind of getting along. You know?" Stefan's voice held a hint of embarrassment.

How should he reply? Damn! He had no idea how things stood between them. Except since nothing was happening, that was a pretty clear sign of the state of things.

"Well, actually, I don't really know." He only knew he missed her and wanted to be with her. And that thoughts of her consumed his every waking hour.

Stefan's eyes sparkled and he raised a hand in a salute. "Well, I'll see you around. Keep up the good work!" He continued his way down the hall, his step almost bouncy.

With a growing feeling of hostility Mika stared after him. Was the big Swede going to try his luck again with Anna-Liisa? Damn it all! He should have been more definite in his answer and let the guy know he was still in the game.

Was he?

But more importantly, was *she*? Did she even care about him at all, or had he really been just "an assignment" to her?

Deep in thought, Mika walked slowly to his office, where he collapsed into the black swivel chair and buried his head in his arms on the desk. This couldn't go on any longer. He had to decide one way or other what to do. He missed Anna-Liisa. It was like a constant ache inside him, and he was convinced if he could only be with her, this pain would disappear. Her face was the last thing he saw before he fell asleep. And when he got up in the morning, she was his first thought, and stayed with him throughout the day.

He raised his head and raked his fingers through his hair. He had to make up his mind, because he was now wasting precious time, which he could be spending with her. He swung the chair around, got up and paced the floor.

But did she even want to be with him? Whenever they ran into each other in the cafeteria—and that seemed to be very seldom these days—she seemed happy enough to see him, but had offered no invitation for him to come to her home again.

Well, no use moping about it any longer. It was

obvious he first had to find out exactly what her feelings were toward him.

And after that?

As Michael had suggested, he would cross that bridge when he came to it.

Chapter Seven

Mika set his lunch tray on the table and sat down beside Anna-Liisa in the cafeteria. She started slightly, but then nodded and pushed her tray to one side to make room for his.

"*Hei,*" he said. "Haven't seen you around for a while. How about I take you for dinner tonight so we can catch up?" Nothing like taking the bull by the horns.

Her reply was a couple of seconds too long in coming. "Sorry, I have to be home to cook dinner for the children." The words sounded forced and not very convincing.

"So how about lunch? Maybe tomorrow?"

"I . . . I'm busy. I have a lunch date with someone."

Yeah, quick thinking, Anna-Liisa, but he wasn't buying it. "With whom?" Okay, so it was a rude question and none of his business, but—

"Oh, he's . . . a friend."

Mika felt a stab of jealousy hearing the pronoun.

Obviously a man. "Stefan?" he couldn't help probing.

"No. Someone else." She sounded very confident now and continued eating without looking up.

He hesitated. Was this for real? Anna-Liisa wasn't into playing games, so obviously it was. "Okay, sorry to bug you." He got up and picked up his tray. "See you around. Have a nice lunch."

Anna-Liisa had a date, but was "too busy" to have one with him. He deposited his uneaten food into the recycle bin and left his tray on the counter. Looked like the Snow Queen was beginning to thaw out.

Mika stomped into his office and flipped through his lecture notes for the afternoon. But all he could think of was Anna-Liisa's refusal.

Unknowingly she'd supplied the answer to his unstated question. No need to ponder about her feelings toward him any longer. He was free to continue seeing Arja with no feelings of guilt. He pulled his phone from his pocket and dialed Arja's number. Why procrastinate? No time like the present.

It was noisy in Jussin Baari. Arja leaned close to Mika so she could hear him tell about his lectures. What else was there to talk about with her? Not much. And afterward they would go to her apartment and have sex, with him half-sloshed and hoping he wouldn't embarrass himself with a case of Brewer's Droop. Somehow he couldn't ever bring himself to have sex with her while stone sober. So what did that say about his feelings for the woman?

"So, have you been talking with Anna-Liisa lately?" he asked when there was a lull in the conversation, him having run out of things to tell her. It was too painful to listen to her chatter on about shopping and finding some "darling" item of clothing, or telling him about some old boyfriend, which was obviously meant to make him jealous. He couldn't have cared less if she'd been telling about some sex orgy she'd had with the Seven Dwarfs.

"Yes, almost every day," Arja replied. "Why?"

"Oh, I heard about this new fellow she has," he said as nonchalantly as possible. "You know him?"

And why, exactly was he asking this? Anna-Liisa was off his radar screen now, and her affairs were no business of his.

Arja looked at him, puzzled. "What fellow are you talking about? As far as I know our Snow Queen hasn't hooked up with any fellow. I think, personally, she still carries a torch for her ex."

Mika was stunned. "What do you mean?"

"Well, after their separation, I know for a fact she went back to him. I mean, all you have to do is calculate Aleksi's age and you can tell they got together. At least once!" Arja laughed in a wicked way that made Mika want to cover his ears.

Served him right for having asked. All he'd wanted

to know was who the new fellow was, and instead he'd heard more than he'd bargained for.

"Lots of people do that after they separate," Arja said, as though sensing Mika's displeasure with the news. "It takes them a while to get used to being alone, or find a new partner, so they get back and have some good old nookie with the ex. I mean, why not?"

"Because her ex was an alcoholic who beat her," Mika protested. "That's why not."

"But he's good-looking—or at least he used to be—and maybe he's great at sex," Arja said casually.

Mika got up. This was much more than he wanted to hear. "Hey, enough about Anna-Liisa. Let's dance," he said.

But as they were dancing, Arja again picked up the forbidden subject. "I can't say I've heard of Anna-Liisa having a new beau. Where did you hear that?"

From Anna-Liisa herself. But he wasn't going to tell Arja that. "I forget who mentioned it. Maybe I misunderstood, or something."

It looked like Anna-Liisa had made up the lunch date, but as far as this ex-hubby of hers was concerned, Mika was absolutely sure Arja's speculations were nonsense. Anna-Liisa would never go back to him.

So, something else was going on and he was going to find out exactly what it was.

"I need to talk to you." Mika spoke low, although no one in the busy cafeteria could hear. "When can we meet?"

Anna-Liisa's response surprised him with its directness, although in a way it was vintage Anna-Liisa. Her serious eyes met his. "Can you meet me at the Senate Square this afternoon at four?"

Her voice sounded sad, and he could hardly breathe for the tightness that gripped his throat.

To add a touch of humor, he asked, "Which step of the Cathedral would you like me to sit on while I wait for you? So you'll find me among all the people that are always perched there like hens."

To his relief she smiled. "How about step number seventy-eight? That will give you some exercise."

"I'll be there."

After class Mika grabbed a coffee and *pulla* and hurried to the Senate Square. He counted the steps as he climbed up and then parked himself on step number seventy-eight in front of the imposing, white Cathedral and pulled up the collar of his jacket. The chilly autumn wind from the ocean blew a plastic bag around in circles and sent various scraps of paper flying. Several other people were using the stairs as seats while waiting for a friend, a date, a ride home, or simply having a smoke.

There she was. Mika sprang up when he saw Anna-Liisa approaching and tore down the steps to meet her.

When he reached her, he took her in his arms without speaking and just held her. With her breath against his cheek, warmth flooded through him and he no longer felt the bite of the cold ocean wind. He didn't try to figure out the feeling that filled him. All he allowed himself to admit was that something unexpected and impossibly wonderful was happening inside him as he held her.

"I'm so glad you made it," he said, reluctantly releasing her. "I've missed you."

They walked over to the imposing statue of Tsar Alexander II of Russia, and stood under the watchful eyes of several angels of victory.

"What did you want to speak to me about?" Anna-Liisa asked, looking at the flowers around the statue instead of him.

Funny, Mika hadn't thought about what he would say, except that he'd missed her. And since he'd already told her that, he couldn't very well keep repeating it. Maybe this all would lead him somewhere he wasn't ready to go, but seeing her now made him feel so incredibly happy that wherever he was headed, it *had* to be the right direction.

"Um . . . I was thinking I haven't seen the kids for a while," he blurted out. Now, where in God's name did that come from? He hadn't been thinking about the kids at all today. Except maybe a few times in passing.

"No, you haven't. Aleksi and Elina have been asking about you."

"They have?" It shouldn't have meant anything to him whether the kids had been asking about him or not, but he had to admit this thought made him feel good. Someone actually cared enough to enquire about him. Maybe he was homesick. Or something . . .

"Well, you haven't asked me over." That was stating the obvious.

"No, I have not," Anna-Liisa said and an uncharacteristic blush arose on her cheeks. "The classes have started and . . . um . . . I have been busy." Her voice faded and she looked down at her hands.

Mika was taken aback. She, who was always so straightforward, now was stammering, looking for excuses. What was going on?

"My classes have started, too, but I'm not *that* busy," he said. "I could always make time for a home-cooked meal."

She refused to bite. "So, how are your classes coming along?" It was easy to tell she wanted to divert the conversation away from the subject Mika was pursuing. "What are you lecturing on right now?" It almost sounded like she was grasping at straws.

"Well," Mika hesitated. "I started with a brief overview of the history of painting in Canada." This was definitely *not* what he wanted to talk with her about. "And now I'm lecturing about Paul Kane, a

Canadian artist who traveled among the Indians of North America in the mid 1800s."

"Oh, how interesting!" Like her blushes, Anna-Liisa's enthusiasm sounded like an obvious put-on. Which was totally uncharacteristic of her. "I am sure your students are very *keen* to learn about *Kane*."

With a chuckle Mika acknowledged her word play. "I hope they are."

For a few moments they continued to stand in silence, both looking down at the flowerbeds surrounding the statue, while Mika tried to figure out how to ask what he so desperately wanted to know.

At last he decided to go for the direct route. He took her by the shoulders and turned her to face him. "Anna-Liisa," he said firmly, "What's the matter?"

She didn't look up. He raised her chin, and saw her blue eyes were troubled. "What is it?"

"I am sorry, but you cannot come over any more," she said, and the sorrow in her eyes nearly killed him.

"Why not? Is it Aaro?" He knew immediately, from the way she looked away, he had hit it right. "Has he hurt you? Tell me, please, I have to know!"

She shook her head. "No, he has not hurt me, but I do not want *you* to get hurt."

Mika frowned. "What do you mean me? I can take care of myself. But you're terrified of him, aren't you? Is there nothing the police can do to put him away for good?" He didn't want to let go of her. He wanted to hold her and protect her from that monster.

"No they cannot. He has not done anything," Anna-Liisa slipped out of his embrace but remained standing close to him. "Breaking his restraining order once is not enough. As for the stalking, it would be his word against mine. He can deny everything, and say I only want to get him in trouble."

"How long has this been going on?"

For a moment Anna-Liisa hesitated. "Only for a while," she said. "It really was not too bad until you . . ."

Mika's hands were on her shoulders again. "Until I what?" he demanded, frowning.

Anna-Liisa gulped. It was too late to take back her words. She knew he wouldn't let the matter drop until she told him, and wished desperately she'd been more careful. Now he would find out why she'd been avoiding him since classes started.

"It started again after he followed us to Seurasaari. He had been quiet for such a long time I was hoping he would leave me alone forever."

All these years she had complied with Aaro's threats and hadn't gone out with anyone. Which hadn't been too difficult, considering there was no one she wanted to date, anyway. But since Mika had arrived, everything had changed. She wanted very much to be with him, to date him and yes, even to have sex with him. But Aaro seemed to be following her every move now, and she didn't want to put Mika in danger. Quickly she glanced around. Even now the sick man could be lurking among the crowds that milled around the Senate Square.

"So, what happened?"

"He came over," Anna-Liisa said quietly. "But I pretended to call the police and he ran off." She shook her head. "He did not hurt me, but I know he is out there keeping an eye on me."

Mika shook his head "So my presence has awakened the sleeping monster. I think you should tell the police."

"I did consider it," Anna-Liisa said. "But that would create such a tangled mess with lawyers, social workers and all those good people who want to help. It is much less complicated if I simply have no dealings with you."

She heard him draw a breath, ready to say something, but she continued before he spoke. "After all, you will be gone in two or three months anyway, and that will be the end of that. Why should I stir up a hornet's nest just because I want—"

His eyes flashed, and she realized she had again revealed more than she had intended.

"What do you want?" Mika asked, his voice a low growl.

"I . . . naturally any woman would like companionship," she hurried to explain. "I do like being with you, and if things were different, I would—"

There she was again, blurting out way too much. It wasn't only Aaro's threats preventing her from being with him. She couldn't let him know what was in her heart. She couldn't tell him that she had missed him terribly and thought about him every moment when she was alone. That she longed for him to take her in his arms and kiss her like he had kissed her on the island.

But if she didn't allow herself to become too deeply involved, then, when he left, her feelings for him would gradually grow less intense and eventually she could go back to . . . back to what? To being lonely again? To having no love in her life? To being a pawn to Aaro's threats?

"What would you like?" He asked softly and drew her against him. "Anna-Liisa, what would you like?"

She had to be careful, or she might tell him how she really felt. What she really wanted. But obviously he had already grasped at the straw she had accidentally tossed out. "You would like for us to be together?" he asked. "Is that right?"

The hope in his voice almost broke her heart.

"If things were different," she allowed herself to admit. "Yes, I would. But not now."

Mika held her at arms length and laughed happily. "That's the best news I've heard in a long time!" he exclaimed. And then he did what she'd been dreaming of since the trip to the island. He kissed her. Gently at first, but when he touched the tip of her tongue with his, sweet shivers flowed down her body.

At that moment Anna-Liisa knew Mika was more important to her than any man she had ever known. The kiss made him one with her very soul. And she knew she would miss him desperately when he was gone, because she already missed him, even as he held her close to his heart.

Should she surrender to such a temporary relationship? One that would leave her weeping on the shore like the girl in the old folk song she had sung to him? Should she?

But now, with his arms around her and his lips on hers, it wasn't the time to ask such questions, because it was impossible to tear herself away from him. She kissed him back, lovingly, eagerly, and with her urging, his kiss deepened and became more demanding.

All at once she became aware they were standing in the middle of the square. She moved out of his arms and looked around, slightly embarrassed. Scores of people were passing by but, to her surprise, no one took any particular notice of them. There were, after all, several other couples—young and old—who were greeting each other in this same manner. Perhaps some of them were also meeting after a long absence.

Yes, although she and Mika had met by chance now and then at the university, it had always felt as though they were apart. And too soon they *would* be apart.

Forever. She tried not to let the feeling of loss gnaw at her heart.

"Would you like to go for coffee somewhere?" Mika suggested.

"I have to go and pick up Aleksi from the babysitter," Anna-Liisa said. "Elina and Johannes are home already. But would you like to—" She stopped, but then made a quick decision. She drew a deep breath and went on. "Would you like to come for dinner?"

Mika's face broke out in a delighted smile. "Only if you're absolutely sure you're okay about all this."

"Yes, I am. Aaro cannot be around every minute." Anna-Liisa wished she felt as confident as she sounded.

"I mean . . ." Mika raised his chin and looked directly into her eyes. "Are you sure you are okay about *us*?"

She understood what he was asking her and for a moment she faltered. "Elina and Aleksi will be very happy to see you—"

But Mika stopped her with a gentle finger-tap on her lips. "Are you sure you are all right about *us*?" he repeated. "You and me."

If she said yes, there would be no going back. At last she nodded. "I am sure," she said quietly.

Mika let his breath out in one long sigh. "Okay, then." He reached for her hand and she slipped it into his as they joined the line of people waiting for a bus at the edge of the square. On the crowded bus they couldn't find two seats side-by-side, so they stood on the aisle, holding onto the metal bar. Reluctantly Mika let go of her hand, but claimed it again twenty minutes later, when they got off at her stop.

"Elina has been drawing every night and has been waiting to show you her work," Anna-Liisa told him as they walked along the sandy path, taking a shortcut through a small copse of pines on the outskirts of the townhouse complex. "It seems your opinions hold more sway than those of her teacher."

Mika couldn't help glancing surreptitiously around him, to see if Aaro lurked behind some tall red pine.

He grimaced. "That's a huge responsibility. I'm not sure I can meet her expectations."

"I am sure you can."

"What about Aleksi?' Mika asked.

"He has been asking when you will come to swing with him in the park, like you promised."

"Right, I did promise that, didn't I?"

"And he wants you to sing with him as you swing," she added with a laugh, and Mika realized how much he had missed hearing those pearls drop.

He joined her laughter. "Now, that's a tall order." He felt so light, so happy, it wouldn't have surprised him if he would float up to the golden tops of the tall birches.

He couldn't help noticing she didn't mention

Johannes, so finally he asked, "What about Johannes? Does he have any requests for me?" He wanted to be ready to face the sullen-faced little boy.

For a few moments Anna-Liisa didn't reply. "Johannes is not very keen to have any men in our house," she said. "I think he had enough of men with his father."

Anger flashed inside him toward this man whom he had only seen briefly, but about whom he'd heard enough. "Was Aaro abusive?"

"Not physically, but he yelled and threatened and that scared Johannes. He is a very sensitive boy and is afraid of men. He thinks all men yell. And that includes you, I am afraid."

"I don't yell," Mika protested. "Much."

"Johannes does not know that."

Great. He knew if he didn't win over her children, his hopes of having a relationship with Anna-Liisa were doomed. He'd already seen she was a mother first and woman after. And angry Johannes, it seemed, could screw up everything by not accepting him as a friend.

He would just have to try to convince the boy all men weren't like Aaro, but had no idea how to go about that. He was no child psychologist. Even as he'd taken care of his three younger siblings while his mother worked, Mika had never thought about whether his sister and brothers were having some issues. He'd been too busy going to school and helping his mother at home, while his father spent his days painting, pretending he was a great artist.

Damn the man! Mika's temper still rose when he thought about his father. Not a cruel man, not unkind to anyone, but totally irresponsible. He didn't earn enough from the odd sale of a painting to even come close to supporting his family. A man like that should never have had children. Never even marry. An artist—Mika firmly believed—should remain a bachelor. Like he was and would always remain. No family responsibilities for *him*. No matter what his income was from his art sales, no woman would ever have to work her fingers to the bone to support *his* kids.

All at once Anna-Liisa's words came back to him and his heart gave a painful squeeze. "You'll be gone in two or three months and that will be the end of that."

Was that how it was going to be? Or was he really falling in love with her, like Michael and Shaylee had jokingly said? And then what? There was no use denying he loved being with her, and felt almost like he was starving, when she wasn't near.

He wrapped an arm around Anna-Liisa's shoulders and relished the feeling of completeness that filled him. He wanted . . . needed . . . the nearness of her, and was determined to have it.

While he was here.

As soon as they were through the door, Anna-Liisa became Mother with a capital M.

"Elina, go and pick up Aleksi," she said, as she shrugged off her light coat. She breezed into the kitchen to wash her hands at the sink and addressed Johannes over her shoulder, "Johannes, put an extra chair at the table for Mika. He's having dinner with us."

Mika grinned at Elina and she gave him a shy smile as she ran out past him to fetch her brother from the neighbour's. He looked for signs of dislike from Johannes and found them. As the boy dragged a chair from the hall and pushed it in place at the head of the table, it wasn't hard to miss the dark scowl Johannes directed at him from under his brows. Mika wasn't welcome and the boy made sure he knew it.

Feeling almost chastised, he went into the kitchen where Anna-Liisa had already taken a large covered container out of the fridge.

"Can I help set the table?" he asked.

"No thank you. That is the children's job," Anna Liisa told him. "You are our guest, tonight." She took the lid off a pot and placed it on the stove. "Left-over pea soup."

"That's great," Mika enthused. Anything she placed in front of him would have been fine. "I love pea soup." He was happy just to have been invited over.

"You may go and sit in the living room," Anna-Liisa said. "I will pour you a glass of wine in a minute."

But Mika didn't want to be treated like a guest. He wanted to belong and be part of the activity. This realization gave him a start. *He* wanted to belong? In this family with *kids*? His friends in Canada would have dropped dead from shock.

The door flew open and Aleksi rushed in, followed by Elina a few seconds later. He ran right up to Mika and screeched to a halt in front of him. With his hands behind his back and his little tummy sticking out, he asked, "Are we going to swing in the park?"

Mika was taken aback and had no choice but to agree. "Okay. When did you want to go?"

"Now!" came the firm reply. "Let's go now. Is that okay, Äiti?"

Mika looked to Anna-Liisa for help, but she only nodded. "But only for a few minutes. Dinner will be ready soon."

Elina came skipping down the stairs with her portfolio tucked under her arm. Disappointment flashed across her face when she saw Aleksi slip his tiny hand into Mika's large one and pull him toward the door.

"Hey, I'll look at those later, okay?" was all Mika had time to say over his shoulder before he was tugged through the door.

Aleksi gripped Mika's hand tightly. "Can you push me more higher than Johannes can?" he asked, skipping along beside Mika.

"Um . . . I think so."

"Good."

The park was within sight of Anna-Liisa's kitchen window and Mika waved to her as Aleksi pulled him toward the swings.

"Lift me on a big swing. I want to go *high*," Aleksi said and stood beside one of the black rubber seats with long chains, ready for Mika to hoist him up.

"Push me *hard*!" Aleksi ordered and Mika did as he was told. From high up in the air the boy called, "You swing, too. Then we can sing."

And without waiting for Mika, he began to sing in a clear, high voice. *"Heilu keinuni korkealle."*

Mika grinned with surprise. The song was one he remembered from his childhood, when he had visited his grandmother. They'd sat in a red garden swing his grandfather had built, and she had taught him that very song. Mika didn't think it was a huge coincidence, because probably everyone in Finland knew this old folk tune about swinging at Midsummer.

"Sing with me, Mika," Aleksi urged him. "Sing it!"

Mika pushed himself into motion with his foot, cleared the cobwebs from his throat, and began to hum. The words were long gone, although he remembered that once in his life he'd been able to sing them all. Little by little, he started to dum-de-dum along, and by the third time around, he was able to sing the repetition after Aleksi sang the lines first.

"You sing good," Aleksi opined, and Mika was surprised how this sincere compliment pleased him. In fact, the happy memories this whole swinging and singing brought back to him, made him feel incredibly good.

They continued to swing, with Mika getting off every few minutes to give Aleksi a good push. By the time they were on their way home, Mika knew he had definitely made a good impression on Aleksi. The little hand remained tucked in his, and the incessant chatter showed the boy considered him his trusted friend.

"You know Tero Koivu? He's two, but today he pooped in his diapers," Aleksi confided with a giggle.

"Well, two-year-old kids do that, don't they?"

"Not *poop*!" Aleksi said with contempt. "Pee only."

"Okay, pee only."

"*And* he sucks his thumb," Aleksi revealed disdainfully.

Mika was beginning to feel sorry for the maligned toddler. "Don't you like Tero?"

Aleksi nodded. "Sure I do. He's funny and he laughs a lot."

Chapter Eight

At the house Elina was setting the table and glanced at Mika expectantly when he and Aleksi entered. She didn't say a word but Mika sensed it was now up to him to ask about her art. But first he went into the kitchen to see what Anna-Liisa was up to.

"Can I help?" He stood behind her and wrapped his hands around her slim waist.

Anna-Liisa glanced furtively around to see if any of the children were near. "Mika, please do not—"

"Please let my hands kiss you if my lips cannot," he whispered against the nape of her neck, before releasing her.

"My, you are very dramatic. You may wash your hands and slice the bread," was Anna-Liisa's pragmatic rebuke.

Mika gave her a playful slap on the backside. "You unromantic woman." He washed his hands under the faucet, cut up the dark rye loaf, and placed the slices into a woven basket Anna-Liisa handed him. As he carried it into the dining room, Elina was placing a spoon beside each bowl.

"So, Elina, have you been working on your drawings?" he asked. "Anything you'd like to show me?"

Elina's eyes sparkled. "Yes, I do." She hurried to retrieve her portfolio from the living room couch and began to spread the contents on the table.

"Do not spread your art on the table now," Anna-Liisa said from the kitchen. "Dinner is ready. Mika can see them after."

Mika and Elina both rolled their eyes and smiled at each other.

"Yes, Äiti," Mika said in a falsetto voice and was rewarded with Anna-Liisa's laughter.

After dinner Elina and Mika looked through the drawings and Mika was once again surprised by what the young girl had produced. She was obviously talented. He could even say gifted.

"These are very, very good, Elina," he told her.

"Thank you. But I want to make them better," she said. "How?"

Mika pointed out a few places where Elina could make slight adjustments and showed her where she could improve the shading.

"Would you like to take a few lessons?" Mika asked. "I could come over after school when I don't have an evening class, and show you some techniques."

Elina turned to her mother who was in the kitchen, filling the dishwasher. "Äiti, did you hear that? May I take lessons from Mika?"

Anna-Liisa came to the door. "Of course you may," she said. "But, Mika, are you sure you have time to spare? And of course I would pay you."

"I would only accept payments in kind," he said throwing her a bold look that sent blood rushing to her cheeks. "But seriously, it'll give me a chance to do some sketching myself on the side." And give him a chance to come to the house more often.

As he was admiring the drawings, he suddenly felt a hand thrust between him and Elina. It was Johannes, holding out a tiny boat, carved from a chunk of red pine bark.

Elina started to push her brother away, but Mika took the carving and asked, "Well, what have we here?" He hoped his voice showed intense interest.

But Johannes remained silent, his face expressionless.

The little boat was carved with great detail, and even included a pair of tiny oars. "Nice," Mika said. "Where did you get it?"

"Johannes carved it himself," Anna-Liisa called from the kitchen. "Tell Mika about it, Johannes."

Without a word Johannes reached for the boat and snatched it away from Mika's hand. Then he turned and galloped upstairs.

Anna-Liisa came out, wiping her hands in a towel. "I am sorry about that. Johannes can be a bit—"

"Did I hear you say he carved that himself?" Mika asked incredulously.

"Yes."

"But he's too young," Mika said. "How can you give a knife to a kid who's seven? He *is* seven, right?"

"He has been carving since he was about five," Anna-Liisa told him. "I found him one day with a knife, carving some pine bark, and he was doing fine. No cuts. I left him alone and he has been carving ever since."

"No cuts?"

"Of course he has had cuts, but nothing serious. No stitches needed yet. He is very careful because he knows I will take the knife away if he does anything foolish."

Mika gave his head a shake. "You have some incredible children, Anna-Liisa. Elina's great in art, and Aleksi has a beautiful singing voice, as I'm sure you've noticed. And here's Johannes turning out to be a master wood sculptor. I can't believe how talented they all are, each in his or her own way."

"Yes, I think so, too," Anna-Liisa said with a smile, and in her eyes Mika saw that special glow of a proud mother. "But of course I *am* prejudiced."

Later, when she drove Mika back to the university,

rather than pulling up to his building, Anna-Liisa parked some distance away and turned off the motor.

He was puzzled. "Why are you parking here? You think I ate too much of your delicious pea soup and need some exercise?"

Anna-Liisa didn't smile, and only shook her head. "Mika, this is serious, so please do not make jokes. I do *not* want anyone to know you are coming to my house. Not even our friends at the university. Many of them know Aaro and some are still his friends. I do not want to take any chances that Aaro might hear about this."

Mika chuckled. "Hey, let's not make this into some kind of cloak and dagger affair. Surely things can't be that—"

"Please do not think I am being neurotic." Anna-Liisa laid her hand on his arm. Her eyes beseeched for his understanding. "I do not want to put you in danger."

"Me?" Mika exclaimed. "It's *you* who is in danger from that idiot. I can take care of myself."

"Please understand, Mika, that I do not want *anyone* to be in danger. If no one knows, then the word might not get to Aaro that you are coming to give Elina art lessons."

"Or to visit you," he said, and laughed when she lowered her eyes.

"Maybe if you come on different days of the week,

Aaro will not be able to pick up on your comings and goings."

Mika snorted. "Cloak and dagger stuff!"

But Anna-Liisa's fingers clutching his arm told him how worried she was. "Please, Mika. Please do it my way."

Because he didn't want to cause her any more anxiety, reluctantly he agreed. "All right, but something has to be done about that fellow. Soon."

"Pekka, it was nice of you to invite us to your cottage," Stefan said and opened the trunk of his shiny black Volvo. "I haven't been to a cottage sauna for weeks!"

Arja climbed out of the back seat. "I haven't been to a sauna by a lake since I was at my uncle's cottage in August," she announced.

Mika unfolded his tall frame from the front seat and stretched. "Me, I haven't been to a cottage sauna for a couple of decades," he said. "Not since my grandparents sold their cottage. We used to go there a lot when I was a kid."

Pekka reached into the trunk for one of the overnight bags. He had come in his motorboat to meet them at the marina parking lot, ready to ferry them across the narrow channel to the island where his cottage was.

"It's totally my pleasure," he said.

They carried their gear to the dock, where Pekka's motorboat gurgled, tied to a metal ring. Arja quickly climbed in the back and patted the cushion beside her. "Sit here, Mika," she said.

He obliged, while Stefan nimbly got in the front with Pekka.

"You poor thing," Arja said to Mika as she snuggled closer to him. "How can you exist without a cottage and a sauna?"

"No big deal. I've survived," Mika said. It would take skillful balancing this weekend not to offend Arja, but not encourage her, either. "I'm a Finn who gets along very well without a sauna."

"There's no such thing," Pekka declared. He turned and put the boat in gear. The huge outboard tore off with a rumble.

After that no one said much over the roar of the motor as the boat sped across the channel and then sputtered to a stop at Pekka's dock.

When he disembarked, Mika looked around for Anna-Liisa, who had arrived earlier with Pekka and Sanni. There was no sign of her, but Sanni waved to them from the porch of the cottage, up on a rocky, pine-covered hill. The cottage was stained red, with white window frames, fashioned after old country cabins.

They trooped up the hill and then, at Sanni's insistence, turned to look at the view. In front of them and to the left, the ocean sparkled, dotted with a number of white sails in the distance. Beyond, on the horizon, some wooded, rocky islands rose from the misty sea. The silhouette of the city was visible to the right, and in the channel in front of them a few motorboats purred along slowly.

Inside the cottage they dumped their luggage in the bedrooms Sanni assigned for them. Mika and Stefan were billeted in the children's room, sleeping on bunk beds, while Arja and Anna-Liisa would share the guest room with its two single beds.

Again Mika looked around for Anna-Liisa, but didn't want to show his impatience by asking. Instead he waited for someone else to speak up.

Of course Stefan was the first to ask. "So, where's Anna-Liisa hiding?"

"She's wandering around somewhere along the shore," Sanni told him. "In fact, would you mind going to find her and tell her we're having coffee soon."

Too eagerly Stefan took off, leaving Mika to kick himself for not asking first. Why was he being so super careful? Okay, so he was doing his best to respect the cloak and dagger caveat Anna-Liisa had placed on their meetings, even if he wasn't convinced it was necessary. Too much like some Hollywood secret agent stuff.

This invitation to the cottage had come as a pleasant surprise. Since Mika had missed being in Finland for the Midsummer celebrations, Pekka and Sanni had decided to invite him for a mini-midsummer, albeit three months after the fact, to relax for a weekend and enjoy a Finnish sauna and a bonfire. Anna-Liisa, having been his guide, had also been invited, as well as Arja and Stefan. Mika, of course, would've been happy to have only Anna-Liisa there, and not have to watch Stefan make his moves on her without being able to interfere.

Like now.

Stefan came strolling up the hill with Anna-Liisa, the two of them apparently deep in conversation. But did he have to hold his head so close to hers?

During the coffee, served in the sunroom, Stefan confided with a chuckle that he'd overheard Pekka speak about this weekend and had asked to come along.

"I didn't want to miss out on a sauna," he said. "So I just kind of invited myself."

And Sanni had invited her good friend, Arja, to keep the numbers even. "You know—boy, girl, boy, girl, boy, girl," she now said laughing and pointed to each in turn.

"But you better remember you're *my* girl," Pekka said fiercely, putting his arm around Sanni, who giggled like a teenager.

"So, who's *my* boy?" Arja asked, looking around. "Mika? Stefan?"

For a moment the air became strained when neither man volunteered.

"Don't everyone jump up at once," Arja said with a pout.

Pekka had brought his bushy-tailed spitz with him for the weekend, and it was sitting by Arja's foot, panting and waiting for crumbs to fall off the table.

Arja patted the dog's head. "Reksi?"

They all laughed, and the awkward moment passed.

Mika laid his dainty porcelain cup on its matching saucer. "I'd like to take a coffee with me down to the beach, sit on a rock and drink in the scenery along with the caffeine," he said. "But carrying these cups and saucers would be kind of dangerous. Don't you guys have any mugs?"

Sanni rose, laughing. "Of course we do. I just wanted to be more formal for our Canadian guest. I'll get you a mug."

"Please bring one for me, too," Anna-Liisa said. "I would like to show Mika around. That is my assignment, you know."

"I thought the assignment was over by now," Stefan put in with a raised eyebrow. "Or has it been extended?" He was obviously trying to be funny, but succeeded instead in sounding jealous.

Anna-Liisa smiled. "You know what they say, 'Once a guide, always a guide'."

Mika rose from the table, satisfied that Anna-Liisa

had understood his intention. "You know I'm always happy to have a pretty guide to show me around," he said cavalierly making a great show of his pleasure.

Carrying their mugs of steaming coffee, Mika and Anna-Liisa wandered down to the shore and circled left, around a promontory, where the ocean opened up before them.

Mika's arms ached to hold her but he wasn't sure if they were still visible from the cottage. "You also serve coffee from those tiny cups and saucers," he said by way of small talk, although he would rather have told her how much he wanted to kiss her. "Seems to be the Finnish way."

"Yes, I think it is." Anna-Liisa stopped and sat down on a smooth bedrock that sloped down to the sea. She slipped off her sandals and wiggled her bare toes.

Mika stood beside her gazing out at a fishing boat that motored toward the channel. "Well, that's certainly not my way. I don't even own a cup or a single saucer, never mind a matching pair."

"I guess we are more civilized around here," she said smugly.

"Or pretentious." Mika sat down beside her and took in deep breaths of the salty air. "Even coffee tastes better by the ocean. Have you noticed?"

"Umm." She took a sip from her mug.

"I wonder how kisses would taste." He grinned and wiggled his eyebrows lecherously. "You game for an experiment?"

Anna-Liisa placed her mug on the rock and turned to him. "I thought you would never ask." He could hear the longing in her voice.

Mika swept her into his arms, and pressed his lips on hers. The kiss, which began softly, soon deepened as his hunger for her grew. He found Anna-Liisa's desire matched his own, and with a groan he laid her down on the smooth rock. His hands caressed her slim body, feeling every curve under the light summer dress. She yielded against him as he pressed her closer, sending his brain into a dizzying maelstrom of joy. She wanted him, as much as he wanted her. If there had been any doubt in his mind about that, it had now vanished.

Anna-Liisa's breathing became faster. "Mika," she whispered against his neck. "Mi-ka."

The word came out in a sob that made him stop and look down at her. Her eyes were brimming with tears.

"What is it, darling?" he asked, puzzled.

Anna-Liisa sat up and pulled her knees against her chest. She waited until her breathing was calm before answering. "We cannot do this, you know."

Mika gave a short laugh. "I didn't intend to, not here."

But she remained serious. "I do not mean that. I mean I cannot have you put your life in danger. We can never know what Aaro might do."

"Please don't worry. If he tries anything stupid I'll call the police," Mika said. "There are laws, you know. He'll be locked away."

"But what if it is too late? If he gets a gun and—" she stopped and buried her face in her arms.

"Let's not think guns," Mika said. "This isn't America."

But she was obviously frightened and he didn't want to let her think he took her fears lightly. He sat and gazed out on the ocean. Aaro hadn't been pestering her before he came on the scene, because she had always complied with his demands. But now . . . He didn't want her to live in constant fear that Aaro might find out about them. She would never rest easy, the way things were.

Damn the man! If only there were some way to get him behind bars. Locked up forever, if possible. There had to be a way.

With his thumb Mika wiped the last of the moisture from her eyes. "Let me think about this," he said. "I'm sure I can come up with something. But in the meanwhile, you're absolutely right, it's best if no one knows about us." He brushed his lips softly on her cheek and trailed kisses down to her neck. "It's going to be difficult, though."

"You must not do anything rash," Anna-Liisa warned him.

He stood up and pulled her to her feet. "Listen,

darling, I'm not the heroic type, believe me. But Aaro can't be allowed to hold people hostage with his threats. I'll think of something."

She raised his hand to her lips. "I do not want a hero. I only want you. To be safe, I mean," she quickly added. "But we better get back before someone comes looking for us."

For a September day the weather was incredibly warm and they all spent a deliciously lazy afternoon drinking wine and beer, eating whatever Sanni conjured up, and taking walks along the shore.

As the sun started its slow descent, Pekka went to heat up the sauna, a small log building close to the shore. The men carried wood from a nearby woodpile and Pekka used birch bark to start a fire in the sauna stove, under the *kiuas*, which was a large pile of rocks in a barrel.

"I hope, Mika, you're okay with the Finnish way of doing things," he said and blew into the fire to make it roar.

Mika stood watching the procedure. "Which is . . .?"

Pekka straightened up. "We all go in the sauna together. Women and men."

"Of course. Why not?" Mika agreed. "That's sounds much better than just hanging out with you guys."

"In the nude," Pekka clarified. "Think you'll be comfortable with that?"

Mika tried not to show his surprise. "Sure," he said

and gave a short laugh. "That sounds even better." Of course he'd heard this was sometimes done, but hadn't expected to experience it.

Sanni came up with an armful of towels and laid them on the bench on the covered porch. "There's no hanky-panky," she warned him. "When the kids are with us, we always go in the sauna together as a family. And when we're socializing and have other couples over, it makes sense if we all go in at the same time. *Saunominen*—that's what the whole process is called— takes hours. It would defeat the whole purpose of the visit if the women waited two hours while the men were in the sauna, and then the men waited for the women to do their *saunominen*."

"Yeah, I can see that," Mika agreed. "And I guess no one goes in the sauna in a bathing suit?"

"You got *that* right!" Pekka said with a chuckle. "That would be considered totally indecent."

Mika hooted. "Back home we'd consider it indecent for mixed couples to go in the nude. Go figger."

An hour later the sauna was hot enough so they all trooped into the dimly lit room and climbed onto the top bench. Sitting in the corner by the wall, Mika felt surprisingly at ease. His only complaint was that Anna-Liisa was the farthest away from him and hardly visible in the darkness. But he took heart in the fact that she was only a few bare bodies away. Stefan sat next to him, and then Pekka and his wife. Arja was next and Anna-Liisa sat in the corner. Seated cozily side by side, like chickens on a roost, they were able to carry on a conversation without difficulty.

Pekka was in charge of the water dipper and from time to time he threw water on the rocks of the *kiuas*, producing hot steam that circled the room. After about fifteen minutes of this, Arja bounced down off the bench and headed for the door. "I've had enough of the heat. You guys go ahead and throw more water, but I'm going for a swim."

She was beautiful with her rounded hips and full, perky breasts, but Mika couldn't keep his eyes off Anna-Liisa's slender body as she followed Arja out the door. Say what they might about no sex allowed in a sauna, at this moment Mika was glad the room was dim and his thoughts—among other things—weren't visible.

"Don't you guys get all macho and make the sauna too hot," Sanni called as she followed Arja and Anna-Liisa out the door.

The night had fallen, with only a sliver of a moon in the dark sky. While Arja and Sanni frolicked close to the shore, Anna-Liisa headed toward a small rocky shoal that stuck out of the water about twenty meters away. The cool water felt pleasant as it washed over her heated body. She rolled onto her back and delighted in how the light from the sauna window shone on the water and splintered into diamonds as it hit the wake she left behind her.

"Hey, don't you go out too far!" Sanni shouted.

"No, I won't. Don't worry, I'm a good swimmer," Anna-Liisa called back. When she reached the shoal, she pulled herself up on the rock and sat, arms wrapped around her knees for warmth, enjoying the stillness. But the breeze from the sea was cooler than she had anticipated and soon her skin was pricked with goose bumps.

She saw the light glisten on the wet bodies of Mika, Stefan and Pekka as they came running out of the sauna. They entered the water with whoops and splashes. So much for silence.

"Where's Anna-Liisa?" she heard Mika ask.

"She swam over to that rock," Sanni told him. "I think you should go out there and swim back with her. I don't like her to be out that far on her own, especially in the dark."

A few moments later Anna-Liisa heard a swimmer approaching, and soon Mika pulled himself up onto the rock beside her.

He pushed his wet hair back from his face with both hands. "I was sent to rescue a fair maiden in distress," he said. "You seen any around here?"

"No. There is no one here but me," Anna-Liisa replied. "Maybe you have the wrong rock."

"No, I'm sure they said twenty meters from the shore. But since I can't find a fair maiden, I'll rescue you, instead."

Mika reached out to take her in his arms and, feeling her prickled skin under his palms he exclaimed, "You're freezing. Let's get back before you're stiff with cold."

They slipped into the water, which felt warmer than the air, and swam toward the shore. But before they had gone more than a few meters, Anna-Liisa felt Mika's hand on her back. She turned to face him and the next moment he was holding her hard against his slick body. She could feel every intimate muscle and hair on his body and, as he slid his hands along her curves, the blood surged in her with such force she was sure the ocean water had reached hot tub temperatures.

As they floated and swirled in the water, she blindly caressed him, touching whichever part her hands happened to reach. His hard body against hers sent waves of starving need through her, and she had to quell the moans that pushed up from deep within her. Sounds carried easily across the water, and she was thankful for the splashes and laughter from the shore.

"Anna-Liisa, you're wonderful," Mika whispered, before his mouth covered hers in a kiss so passionate she almost went limp with desire. He cupped her breasts and then slid his hand down to touch her intimately, murmuring his pleasure as they continued to twist and swivel around each other, treading water with their feet.

"Hey, are you guys okay out there?" came Pekka's voice across the water, and reluctantly they parted and resumed their swim toward the shore.

"We're good," Mika called back. "A nice shot of brandy for Anna-Liisa would be great, though. She's freezing."

"I am *not*," Anna-Liisa whispered to him. "I think I have not been this hot since the summer." She laughed, because for the first time in years, her body felt totally alive. Never had she felt this much happiness being with a man.

And right now she didn't even want to think that he wasn't going to be around much longer. Why shouldn't she take happiness when it was offered to her on a silver platter?

"I love your laughter," Mika whispered. "I'll want to hear it forever."

But Anna-Liisa understood no matter what loving words he said to her now, he wasn't talking about forever. And that was fine with her.

Almost.

She sped up her stroke and beat Mika to the shore.

Everyone went back into the sauna and the ritual of alternating sauna with swimming and drinking cool beer or wine went on as the darkness slowly fell.

At last Sanni told the men to stay out. "We ladies are going to wash up now."

So while the men were in the water, the women scrubbed themselves with loofas, offering to wash each other's backs as was the custom. After rinsing off, they wrapped themselves up in big, fluffy towels and sat on the open porch to cool down, while the men went into the sauna to get soaped up.

Before the men were done, Sanni had gone to the cottage and now returned with open-face sandwiches of smoked salmon on dark sour rye.

Mika remembered how his grandmother had bought some *ruisleipä* from a local Finnish bakery when he was a kid.

"My Grandmother always told me rye bread puts strength into your *muskels*," he told them as he chewed and chewed on a slice of the dense, almost black, buttered bread. It wasn't something you gulped down in a hurry.

"That's what we say, too. Strong *muskels*," Sanni mimicked and everyone laughed.

"And now for the crowning touch!" Pekka came out of the sauna with a large packet wrapped in foil. It had been sitting on top of the rocks on the *kiuas* for a few hours and when he opened it up he exposed a fat, round sausage that sizzled deliciously. It had burst its skin and now, sliced up and spread with mustard and accompanied by plenty of beer, it was quickly devoured.

Mika was sure he'd never tasted anything so delicious.

Or maybe it was because everything tonight seemed so perfect.

Pekka and Sanni had collected wooden scraps and dry branches near the water in preparation for the *Juhannus* bonfire. When the meal was over, they got dressed and gathered around the huge pile of rubbish, which Pekka had doused with fire starter. He lit some birch bark and soon the flames were crackling and reaching higher and higher into the night, accompanied by loud cheers.

"Ah, we have a talented pyromaniac among us!" Stefan exclaimed.

Pekka brought out some lawn chairs and they settled around the fire to watch the sparks explode against the black night sky like tiny fireworks.

Moving as casually as possible, Mika managed to get the chair beside Anna-Liisa before Stefan could usurp the spot. He couldn't help thinking it was almost comical how two grown men were vying for the attention of this woman but, dammit, he wasn't going to sit somewhere on the other side of the bonfire, where he wouldn't even be able to see Anna-Liisa through the flames, while Stefan sat beside her.

To his dismay, Arja came to sit on his left and immediately hooked arms with him in a chummy way. But then she leaned over in front of him and began a conversation with Anna-Liisa about some aspect of the Finnish curriculum. Finally Mika gave up and suggested he and Anna-Liisa trade spots to make it more convenient for the women to talk. So much for a romantic bonfire, but at least he was still sitting next to Anna-Liisa.

Soon Stefan, sitting next to Arja, joined in the conversation, and the three of them probably would have gone on talking shop all night, if Sanni hadn't given a shrill whistle to put a smart stop to it.

"It's supposed to be *Juhannus*, remember? Not some staff party. We should sing!"

"It's too dark for a Midsummer party," Arja grumbled. "The sun is supposed to stay up all night."

Sanni shrugged. "Sorry, but I couldn't arrange that." She began to sing the Midsummer favorite, "*Heilu keinuni korkealle*".

Thanks to Aleksi, Mika was able to join in and impress everyone with his pronunciation.

"Hey, we'll make a Finn outa you yet," Pekka shouted. "Here's to Mika!" He raised his beer can. "Great singing!"

But as the bonfire turned to embers, the effects of the sauna, food and alcohol began to show and the singing turned to yawns.

"Off to bed, you party-poopers!" Sanni cried and began to collect the dishes into a large basket. Arja and Anna-Liisa offered to help, but she shooed them off. "We'll clean up in the morning. Pekka will douse the fire. It's almost dead, anyway."

The sleeping arrangements weren't exactly what Mika would have preferred, so while Pekka and Sanni cuddled in their own double bed, he had to sleep on the top bunk, directly above the snoring Swede, while Arja and Anna-Liisa were comfortable in the guest bedroom.

Chapter Nine

The next morning Mika could hardly wait to see Anna-Liisa again. He had fantasized she was lying in his arms and, with images of her floating in his head like the proverbial sugar plums, it hadn't been easy to fall asleep. And snoring Stefan hadn't helped the situation, either. Finally he'd dozed off, and dreamt of her slender naked body in Stefan's arms.

He was bitterly disappointed when, right after breakfast, she waltzed off to pick mushrooms with Stefan, having barely said good morning to him.

"There's several varieties of edible mushrooms in the woods behind the cottage," Pekka had told them the day before, and this morning Anna-Liisa was keen to get some to bring home with her.

"I'll go with you!" Stefan had cried before Mika had a chance to volunteer. "To scare the bears away."

"Yeah, you'd scare anything away," Mika had remarked, trying to be funny, but sounded more like a grumpy bear himself.

Stefan and Anna-Liisa went off with their woven birch baskets, leaving Mika to nurse his coffee and his bad temper. He picked up the morning paper that had been delivered to the cottage by a motorboat. Why hadn't he been fast enough to offer to go with her? Being in the forest with Anna-Liisa would have given them a wonderful opportunity for . . . anything.

"I can't imagine going into the forest to be eaten by mosquitoes," Arja said with a shudder. "I don't love mushrooms *that* much." She seated herself beside Mika on the porch bench and pulled the newspaper from his hands. "This is not the time to be catching up on world news. We came here to relax and get away from that sort of thing."

Mika stretched his arms above his head. "It's in Finnish, so I can't read it anyway," he said. "I was only looking at the photos and trying to guess what the news story would be. Since it was delivered all the way here, I thought someone ought to read it."

"Don't worry, Pekka will later," Arja said. "Here, have some more coffee." She filled his cup from the thermos carafe that stood on a side table and snuggled closer to him.

Obediently Mika took a gulp. He was in no mood to banter with Arja and put up with her flirtation. He was about to set her straight but, remembering Anna-Liisa's wishes, he obediently accepted Arja's coquetry.

But something had to be done about Aaro. The man had no right to control Anna-Liisa's life like some puppet-master. But what? He'd thought about it when he'd lain awake last night, listening to Stefan's snores, but hadn't been able to come up with any brilliant ideas.

"You're awfully preoccupied," Arja remarked. "Something bothering you?"

"Hey, not at all!" Mika cried, brightening up. "I think I'm just slightly numb from all that *saunominen* and beer. I'm not used to such things, you know." He forced out a laugh. "That sauna experience sure was something else. It was great of Pekka and Sanni to arrange it."

Arja snuggled even closer on the sunny bench and sighed. "Well, if you're so tired, why don't we relax here together. Just close your eyes."

Any man should have been delighted to have a woman like Arja sit beside him, giving clear signals she was game for more snuggles. What could he do but comply, for rejecting Arja would have made her think—correctly—that his interests lay elsewhere.

"Yeah, sure." He put an arm on the backrest behind her and Arja rested her head on his shoulder.

And, of course, at that precise moment Anna-Liisa and Stefan emerged from behind the cottage, their baskets brimming with mushrooms. Before Mika had time to jump up to greet them, he saw a look of dismay flash across Anna-Liisa's face. It disappeared as quickly as it came, and was replaced by a smile of pride as she held up her basket.

"Look everybody. Are they lovely or what."

Pekka and Sanni came from the cottage to admire the mushrooms.

"Look at them all!" Stefan crowed. "And it took us no time at all. The forest is chock full of them."

Mika got up and fingered a mushroom in Anna-Liisa's basket. "Are you sure these are edible?" He knew absolutely nothing about mushrooms. "I don't trust mushrooms unless they come in a plastic tub from a grocery store."

"Oh, I know my mushrooms," she retorted, and the slight barb in her voice made him happy. She was jealous.

Anna-Liisa told herself that seeing Arja sitting so cozily with Mika didn't bother her, because she was sure it wasn't his idea. Or at least she *hoped* it wasn't. But still . . . She made a quick exit from the porch into the kitchen with her basket.

As she rinsed off the mushrooms in the kitchen sink with a soft brush, she talked sense to herself. After last night's sex play in the water it was natural to feel resentful to see him cuddling with another woman, even if it didn't mean anything to him. But could he not have tried to avoid it?

She heard Sanni come in, but kept on cleaning the

mushrooms.

"Some of these will make a nice addition to our lunch," Sanni said and started to make fresh coffee. "I'm so glad you decided to go and pick them. Me, I'm too lazy, but Pekka often goes mushroom picking in the autumn."

"I love it," Anna-Liisa ventured to say, hoping her voice didn't reveal the indignation still sizzling inside her. "It's better than picking berries. The basket fills up so much quicker with mushrooms."

Sanni laughed. "I hear you."

The laughter helped Anna-Liisa feel better, and she knew she would be able to look calmly at Mika, even with Arja clinging onto him.

As her thoughts went back to last night in the water with Mika, the brush slipped from her hand and clattered into the sink. She glanced at Sanni but the woman was too busy measuring coffee to notice.

Anna-Liisa picked up the brush and resumed cleaning the mushrooms, but her heart beat faster and she could feel her face heating up. It was no use fooling herself. She wanted him. She had dreamed about having sex with him for . . . how long now? It almost seemed he had filled her thoughts forever.

But during the day she was forced to look on with dismay as Mika dealt gallantly with Arja's attentions. She knew it was because he was trying to live up to the "rules" she, herself, had set for them, and was doing his best not to raise anyone's suspicions. So, on her part, she kept up the pretense that she was keenly interested in everything Stefan was telling her. Which didn't make it the greatest day, even though all they did was eat, talk and relax.

Mika spent considerable time taking photos of the beautiful but barren Finnish archipelago landscape for use in future paintings. Anna-Liisa would have loved to accompany him as he wandered around the island but had to contend herself with walking along the shore with Sanni, while Arja went with him instead. As Arja's laughter rang out, she wondered if Mika thought it, too, sounded like pearls falling into water.

Late in the afternoon the guests prepared to leave. After they had packed up, Anna-Liisa helped carry some of the luggage to the shore and just by chance "happened" to walk down beside Mika.

"I have missed being with you," Mika murmured. "This whole day has been a terrible waste."

"Yes, you are right. It has been a *lovely* day," Anna-Liisa countered brightly, as Pekka passed them, carrying a cooler.

"But I wanted so much to kiss you and hold you in my arms, I had to keep my hands in my pockets to keep from reaching out to touch you," Mika said when Pekka was out of ear-shot again.

"I missed you, too," Anna-Liisa admitted and touched his bare arm. Even that felt good, but it wasn't enough. She needed him, and her whole body trembled at the thought of making love with him.

Pekka took Arja, Stefan and Mika in his motorboat to the mainland where Stefan's car was waiting in the marina parking lot. Anna-Liisa and Sanni waved them off and then turned to walk up the hill to the cottage.

"This has been a lovely visit," Anna-Liisa said to Sanni. "At first the children were quite disappointed when I told them they would have to stay with the Koivus, but when I said it was going to be all university people, they decided it would be a pretty dull weekend."

Sanni laughed. "I can understand."

"Well, it wasn't dull for us!" Anna-Liisa said. Swimming with Mika had been anything but dull. She turned to look out on the ocean at the receding motorboat and blew an invisible kiss to him.

"It'll be a shame to close up the cottage for winter," Sanni was saying. "We like to come here with the kids as long into the fall as possible. And these days the weather has been cooperating so nicely, we may continue to come right into October."

"That would be pushing it, don't you think?"

"Maybe, but we don't want to close it up yet." In the cottage, Sanni clicked the coffee maker on. "The winter is so long and it always seems like spring will never come."

Anna-Liisa stiffened. Now was the time, but did she

dare? Yes. She forged ahead before losing her nerve. "I was thinking, Sanni, that if you aren't closing the cottage yet, maybe I could rent it for a day?"

"Sure, of course," Sanni exclaimed. "But don't even mention renting. You can bring the kids here and enjoy yourself. Unfortunately it'll have to wait for a couple of weeks, because we're having my parents over next weekend, and Pekka's brother's family wants one more kick at the can before the cold weather sets in. But let's hope it stays warm till the end of October. You can let us know when you're coming, so we won't barge in on you."

"That's fine, Sanni. I'll let you know." Anna-Liisa remained calm and went into the cottage. It wasn't the kids she was thinking of. It was Mika. And finally making love with him.

The date was set. Now all she had to do was talk to Mika about it.

How would he react to her proposal? Would he consider her too forward? She didn't think so. Surely any man would be delighted to be invited to spend a day on an island with a woman, making wonderful love. The sweet kind of love she'd always dreamed of, after suffering through Aaro's rough treatment. And even rape.

Now, if only Aaro weren't looming like a terrible specter over her life, she would have been even happier. And if only Mika weren't leaving at the end of the semester, she would have been totally ecstatic.

Yes, and if wishes were horses . . .

But since none of these things was likely to happen, she might as well grab happiness when she could.

In only two more weeks.

Anna-Liisa picked up the incoming phone call as she was hurrying down the corridor, heading for her class. The growly voice in her ear stopped her in her tracks. Aaro had never called her during her working day.

"So, how was the weekend with your lover-boy?" His sneering words sent a convulsion of fear through her. Of course Sanni and Pekka, being a very popular and sociable couple, would innocently have spread the word to a whole host of people, among them Aaro's friends and drinking buddies. They would have filled him in on who had gone, and now Aaro was on the warpath.

"We had a very nice time," Anna-Liisa said, striving to keep herself calm. "But since that is none of your business, I will not discuss it. Do you have something you wish to say?"

"Damned right I do!" Aaro roared. "Remember, I've told you if you start screwing around, you'll have to face the consequences!"

This might not have been the best time or place to do so, but Anna-Liisa suddenly found the courage—or was it foolishness?—to confront him about his threats. She looked around quickly to make sure the corridor was empty before speaking. "No, I don't remember, because you've never specified what would happen." Her bravado was diametrically opposite to how she felt inside. "Supposing you spell it out for me." She was hoping, when push came to shove, he would reveal his hand and show his threats were only empty blather.

But he was an alcoholic and unpredictable.

"I'm warning you, there'll be consequences!" Aaro roared.

Anna-Liisa held the phone away from her ear as anger and loathing flashed through her. "You know what, Aaro? I am not going to live my life being ordered around by you. From now on I will do whatever I please and associate with whomever I wish. Do you understand me?"

There was a moment of silence at the other end. Then Aaro growled, "Yeah, you go right ahead, but tell that lover-boy of yours to watch his back. And that's all I'm going to say to you!"

Anna-Liisa used the brief pause to deliver her final blow. "If I wish to screw around, as you so elegantly put it, I will do so. And with a dozen men if I please."

She snapped her phone shut and stood, trembling violently. What had she done? She leaned against the wall to steady herself. What, in God's name, had she done? Now Aaro would explode and in a violent fit could do all kinds of horrible things. First of all, she would have to make sure the children were never alone in the house. Then she would have to warn Mika and tell him what a stupid thing she had done. With her stupid, defiant words she could have endangered all their lives.

God, she was an idiot. Aaro hadn't been *too* horrible before Mika came on the scene, not after the restraining order had been placed on him. And if she had just held her tongue a few more months until Mika left, she and Aaro could have continued their master-slave relationship till one of them died.

But was that what she wanted? Did she want to be a puppet on a string under Aaro's commands for the rest of her life? Never daring to associate with any man? No, she did not. Now that Mika had awakened her sexual desires, perhaps—after he was gone—she would want to have a relationship with someone. A loving, sexual relationship.

She ran a hand across her eyes. She didn't want to even think of loving anyone else. But maybe, as the years passed and the memory of Mika grew dim, she could find someone— No. She took a deep breath. She didn't ever want to forget him. No one else could ever take his place in her heart.

Mika, she whispered to the empty corridor. *I don't remember a time when I didn't love you. And there will never be a time when I don't love you. You are in my soul.*

But she would have to warn him and tell him about what she had just done and the danger she had put him in with her careless words. Aaro was unpredictable and Mika should be careful. Of course he would laugh and say she was neurotic, but she couldn't rest until she'd convinced him to look out for himself.

Anna-Liisa glanced at her watch and straightened up. Time to go to her class and face her students. On the way she slipped into the ladies' room to make sure her face revealed nothing of the emotional upheaval she'd just gone through.

"So what do you think I should do?" Mika was Skyping with Michael again—his "Ann Landers". "I have to do *something* about this Aaro problem."

"Because . . .?"

"Because Anna-Liisa is worried sick and doesn't want people to see us together while this Aaro is lurking around. She called to warn me the guy had said I should watch my back. This thing has to be resolved somehow."

"Yes, sounds like it's getting serious."

"I'm not worried for myself, but poor Anna-Liisa can't rest for fear the bastard will shoot me or something." He got up to pace the room in his frustration.

"I can't see you, when you run around like that,"

Michael stated calmly. "So this isn't only about sex?"

Mika returned to the screen. "Of course it's not only about sex. I care for her deeply. And I don't want her to be worried. And I want to be with her. I mean . . . I don't want to be *without* her." Did his valiant attempt at an explanation make any sense? When she wasn't around things just didn't feel good. Not right.

Michael smiled. "That's good. I was hoping you'd say that."

Mika thought he could hear Shaylee clapping in the background. "He's hooked," he heard her say with glee. "At last the man's in love."

"Cut it out, Shaylee!" Mika shouted. "I never said that."

"Well, I'm saying it. Love, love, love," Shaylee sang.

"Go ahead and sing all you want," Mika muttered. "But make sure you don't sing that word in a same song with my name."

"Enough, you two," Michael interjected. "So, if you don't want to be without her, I guess you'll have to get this Aaro-fellow removed from the picture. Right?"

Mika was glad his friend was starting to take the situation seriously and didn't crack jokes, because he didn't find this the least bit funny. When Anna-Liisa had told him about Aaro's phone call, she had told him what she had said to Aaro. In a very uncharacteristic state of emotional turmoil, she had pleaded with him to be careful and vigilant and make sure Aaro didn't get anywhere near him.

"As I said, I'm not concerned for myself, but I'm worried he'll do something to Anna-Liisa, or even to the kids," he said. "As far as I know he's never threatened the children, but—"

"You're right, you have to get rid of the guy. But how?" Michael mused.

"I'd love to throw him under a bus, or push him off the dock and—"

Michael hooted. "Hey, don't get too violent here. We don't want *you* locked up for the rest of your life. It's *him* you have to get rid of, remember?"

Such a long silence followed that Mika thought Michael had got distracted by some TV program. "Hey, are you still thinking about my problem?"

"I am," Michael said. "And I think I have an idea. You probably won't like it though."

"Any idea is better than no idea."

"Well, supposing you kind of baited the guy so he attacks you, and—

"You're right. I don't like it."

"Listen, will you. Just so he attacks you, but doesn't get a chance to do anything because you call the police and he gets arrested."

"Nice plan, except for two things. What if the police don't come in time? I could get beaten up. And they won't hold him for very long, anyway, so is it worth getting a bloody nose for a few days of no Aaro?"

Michael snorted. "Some hero you are!"

But Mika wasn't amused. "I'm serious. That's a joke, not a plan. If you can't think of anything reasonable, just forget it."

"Well, it's hard to think of something that's not illegal. Your plan about pushing him under a bus is starting to sound better and better."

"Right. Thanks anyway, but I think I'll pass on that one, too."

After wishing Shaylee a healthy pregnancy, Mika closed the connection, but continued to stare at the dark screen.

What could he do about that damned Aaro?

After dinner, Elina and Mika were poring over her drawings, which were scattered all over the dining table.

"Drawing something that is coming straight at you is very difficult," Mika said.

"I know. I always mess that up," Elina said.

"It's a matter of drawing what you see in front of you, not what you *think* you *should* see. Like the tips of fingers coming at you are kind of like little round cherries."

"Cherries!" Elina laughed and Mika noticed how much she sounded like her mother.

Pushed off to one corner of the table, Johannes was doing his homework. Mika was aware of the frustrated sounds that were coming from him, but pretended not to notice.

At last the boy angrily swept his textbook off the table. It hit the floor with a thud. "I can't do this stupid math!" he shouted and dropped his head into his arms on the table.

"What seems to be the problem?" Mika asked cautiously.

Anna-Liisa emerged from the kitchen, holding a dishtowel, but kept her distance.

"I'm pretty good in math," Mika said. "You think I could take a look? Maybe I can help."

"Show Mika your book, Johannes," Anna-Liisa said calmly.

With his mouth pouting in frustration and his shoulders hunched, Johannes slid off his chair and retrieved the book from the corner. He plunked it on the table in front of Mika.

He turned to a page and pointed to the part that had obviously made him lose his cool. "See?"

"Right." Mika quickly tried to figure out what could have caused the outburst. "I see apples and numbers and—"

"Yeah, that's right," Johannes cried. "Apples. I don't see *how* three plus an apple can add up to five. That is *so* dumb. What is that *apple* doing there?"

"Yes." Mika was beginning to see what the problem was. The lesson was beginning algebra and the apple was supposed to be a place holder. Like the good old x or y in his high school math book.

Johannes continued his tirade. "Math is s'posed to be numbers, not stupid fruit."

So using the apple as a placeholder was confusing Johannes. "Well, let's see if we can get this straightened out." He took three of Elina's pencils and placed them in a row. "The question is, how many more pencils do you need so you'll have five pencils?"

"Two, of course," Johannes said indignantly. "Everyone knows that. We need two more pencils."

"Do you have any apples, Anna-Liisa?" Mika asked, and Anna-Liisa hurried to get a few from the fridge. Mika took one and placed it beside the pencils. "This apple is sitting here, holding the place of those two pencils you say we need. So now take away the apple and put the two pencils there instead. Three pencils plus two pencils adds up to five pencils."

"That was easy," Johannes gloated.

"Too easy for you, buddy. Now, let's put seven pencils here. The question is, how many more pencils do you need so you'll have ten pencils? Let's put this apple here to hold the place of that number while you figure it out."

Johannes leaned his chin in his hand as he sat and thought about this for a while. Then working furiously with his fingers, he came up with the answer. "Three more pencils."

"Correct. So now we can take away this apple and put the three pencils there instead. The apple was just holding the place for those three pencils till you got it figured out."

Johannes brightened up and there was no sign of the sullen kid from a few minutes ago. Mika saw the lesson was working. After a few more examples using pencils and apples, Mika suggested they use a banana instead of an apple. They did a few more examples, using a banana for the placeholder, after which Mika suggested they use one of Johannes' trucks.

They continued on, now using real numbers on paper, and Elina helped by drawing an apple or a banana as a placeholder each time.

"It doesn't matter what we use to hold the place of the number, because once you've figured out what the number is, you can take the placeholder away and put the number there," Mika said.

After a while Johannes got up from the table. "Okay. I will go and do my homework now. *By myself*!" he added proudly.

"Say thank you to Mika for helping you," Anna-Liisa reminded him.

"Thank you, Mika," Johannes said obediently and ran upstairs to the room he shared with Aleksi.

"Do your kids ever walk up those stairs?" Mika asked when the sound of thumping footsteps had faded.

"Hardly ever," Anna-Liisa said, smiling. "It is good exercise." She held out a glass of wine for him.

Mika took the glass from her and together they moved into the living room.

A feeling of happiness filled him as he sat back on the leather couch and looked around him at the cozy home. Anna-Liisa sat down beside him—but not too close—while Elina collected up her drawings and went upstairs to do her homework. Aleksi was lying down on the floor, his chest propped up by a cushion, watching cartoons. Mika smiled. Hearing Bugs Bunny and Elmer Fudd feuding in Finnish sounded strange.

"Bugs sure is good at languages!" he exclaimed. "I didn't realize he spoke Finnish."

"So does Daffy Duck," Aleksi told him. "They all do."

Mika laughed. "Amazing!"

This had been another wonderful evening. Anna-Liisa had prepared dinner and afterward he'd gone to the park for a few minutes to swing and sing with Aleksi. He'd taught Elina about foreshortening and now, to Mika's great satisfaction, he seemed to have broken through Johannes's wall of sullen attitude. At least he hoped he had.

Mika exhaled a long, contented sigh. Sitting here beside Anna-Liisa, in this peaceful house—at least when the kids were upstairs—a feeling of completion filled him. It was like his quest was over. Like Johannes, who had solved his math problem by finding the missing number, Mika had also found the missing puzzle piece in his life. For years he'd been trying to find the answer to the feeling that he was missing something. And now he knew. All those years, while he'd been searching for something nameless, he'd actually been searching for this woman. That missing something now had a name—a beautiful name he never tired of saying to himself—Anna-Liisa. There were days when he was so filled with happiness he wanted to shout the name from his balcony for all the university to hear. All of Helsinki.

He felt complete. Almost.

Because this feeling brought with it an urgent need to be with her. Completely. Skin to skin, bone to bone, with nothing between them. To stare honestly into each other's eyes, with nothing to hide, at the moment of coming together and joining as one. This he also wanted to shout out—his deep longing, his crying need for her. This need for completion. For total fulfillment.

How much longer would he be able to live like this, close to her but still apart?

He turned to look at Anna-Liisa beside him and wanted to reach out to bring her close against him, so he could hear her breathing, feel her heart beating against his ribs, smell her soft hair.

But she would never allow this when the children were in the house. And they were always here. After the children were in bed she would come to him and send him over the moon with her kisses. But she would never go beyond that.

"Anna-Liisa," he spoke low so Aleksi wouldn't hear over the TV. "When you drive me back tonight, will you come up?"

Anna-Liisa shook her head. "Please do not ask me that, Mika. You know I will not." She reached over and briefly grasped his hand. "But I have something to tell you . . . later."

"What?" Aleksi piped up. "What are you going to tell him?"

Mika and Anna-Liisa looked at each other and burst out laughing.

"The proverbial little pitcher with big ears," Mika muttered.

"I am going to tell him about . . . about a secret," Anna-Liisa said quickly.

"Äiti!" Aleksi whined. "That's not fair. You have to tell me, too."

"Then it would not be a secret, would it?" Anna-Liisa was obviously playing for time.

"But why should Mika know it and not me?" Aleksi persisted.

"Because it is a grown-up secret." Anna-Liisa laughed at the boy's pouting face. "Now go upstairs and brush your teeth. Time for bed. Leila will be here in a few minutes to look after you while I drive Mika back to the university."

Later, in the car, Mika asked, "So what grown-up secret do you have to tell me? Or was that a ploy to stop Aleksi from asking questions?"

"Both," Anna-Liisa replied and smiled. "I do have something to tell you, and I expect you will be all right with it."

"As long as Stefan isn't involved," he said, causing her to burst out in the most beautiful pearly laughter he'd heard in a long time. It made him laugh, too.

"No, it is just us. You and me."

That sounded promising. Like he was going to hear something very good.

He did.

"I asked Sanni if I could have the cottage for a day," Anna-Liisa told him.

Mika exhaled one long breath. "No kids?" Mentally he crossed his fingers.

"No kids."

Chapter Ten

The October day was sunny, but on the cool side. Mika got off the bus at a roadside stop and put down his backpack. Anna-Liisa's red Honda was supposed to be waiting to pick him up at about ten, but it wasn't here yet. She had wanted him to meet her by the highway, because she didn't want to be seen picking him up at the university. He stood at the side of the road and admired the impossibly tall, straight birches growing on the edge of the farmers' fields that stretched out along both sides of the road. The trees reached high into the blue sky as though, with their leafless branches, they were trying to grab the clouds floating by. The crops of barley and rye had been harvested long ago, and the fields were yellow with stubble. Everything around him was still. Not even a chirp from a cricket broke the silence, making the wait for Anna-Liisa almost bearable.

At last Mika saw the red car in the distance and he

picked up his backpack in readiness. As the car got closer he hitched up his thumb.

Anna-Liisa stopped and rolled down her window. "I am sorry. I never pick up hitchhikers." And she continued down the road, leaving him to stand by the roadside.

Several yards on she did a u-turn and returned to where Mika was waiting. "But you look like a harmless fellow so I will make an exception this time," she said.

Mika opened the door and threw his backpack in the back. "I'm glad you don't ever pick up hitchhikers," he said. "With this exception, of course."

She put the car in first gear and took off. Mika wanted to ask her to stop the car so he could take her in his arms and kiss her. Instead, during the twenty-minute ride to the marina, he kept up a casual conversation to prevent himself from reaching over to touch her.

"I've started to lecture about the early twentieth century Canadian painters," he told her. "I've been showing Maurice Cullen's work to the class. He depicts light on snow in a most inspired way." He knew his voice sounded low, thick with want for her, and he swallowed.

"Sounds wonderful," Anna-Liisa commented. "You will have to show me his paintings some day."

Did she feel his presence as intensely as he felt hers? Nothing in her voice gave her away, while he suspected he sounded like a lovesick moose.

He coughed before going on. "He and a bunch of other very talented artists started the Canadian Art Club. Guys like Edmund Morris, James Morrice, Homer Watson and . . . and others." He faltered as desire filled him. "I want to hold you, Anna-Liisa," he at last blurted out.

She reached over and took his hand and through his fingertips he could feel her quickened pulse.

"We are almost there," she said softly.

The slight break in her voice told him her desire was as strong as his.

After the short motorboat ride, during which Mika was able to show off his almost non-existent skills with an outboard motor, they climbed up the hill to the cottage. Mika carried the cooler with food Anna-Liisa had brought with her. She unlocked the door and was about to pick up her bag when Mika suddenly swept her up in his arms.

Anna-Liisa shrieked and then giggled in surprise as, without a word, Mika pushed open the door and carried her over the threshold like a bride. He deposited her on the floor but continued to hold her and she could feel his heart hammering against her breast. This was what she wanted, what she'd been waiting for. So when he kissed her, she responded with all the pent-up yearning and hunger that had filled her for weeks.

Mika groaned and his kiss became harder and his tongue thrust deeper into her mouth. But then his actions became rough, almost savage, as he pushed the jacket off her shoulders and groped her breasts through her blouse. Unzipping her jeans, he slipped his hand in and cupped her mound. Anna-Liisa whimpered her objection as he pushed a finger into her through her panties, but he ignored her and pushed her against the wall. He cupped her buttocks, pulling her against his hard erection, and all the while he ravaged her mouth with his, thrusting his tongue deeper into her.

This was not the way it was supposed to be! Images of Aaro forcing himself on her flashed through her brain. She panicked, pushing him away with all her might.

"No, Mika, stop! I do not want this. Stop, Mika!"

His breath came in heavy gasps and he stared at her, his eyes dark and unfocused. "What?" he gasped. "What is it?"

"I do not want it to be like this."

He released her so suddenly, she almost lost her balance.

Anger flashed in his eyes and his breath came out in loud gasps. "What? You don't want sex?" he ground out through clenched jaws. "Isn't this why you asked me to come here?"

Anna-Liisa shook her head. "No," she gasped. *"This*

is not why I asked you to come here. Not *this*." She leaned back against the wall and tried to calm her breathing. This was not what she had envisioned when she had asked Sanni for the cottage. This brutish man was not the Mika she had expected to make love to her. He was not thinking of her and her needs. Only of himself.

She wanted to tell Mika about Aaro. About how he raped her. About how Aleksi was the result of that horror. But she couldn't. She had never told a living soul, and was afraid if she breathed a word to anyone, the knowledge could somehow leak out and reach Aleksi's ears. Aleksi must never know his father raped his mother. After the pregnancy began to show her mother had chastised her for sleeping with a man who had treated her so terribly, but Anna-Liisa had simply swallowed the accusations. Why endanger Aleksi's innocence? And there was no reason why Mika should know anything about this. He would soon be gone.

Slowly his breathing became calm, although his eyes still remained puzzled. He collapsed into a rattan chair.

"Okay. So why *did* you ask me to come?" He leaned forward, elbows on his knees, waiting for her reply and from his clenched jaw she could tell he wasn't going to be very receptive to anything she would say. "I feel I'm owed an explanation."

"I asked you to come because . . ." What could she

say? Because she loved him and had been hungering for him for weeks and had wanted him to make love to her. That was all true but it was not what she wanted to tell him because she knew his come-back would be, *That's exactly what I was doing.*

"No, you were *not*," she said firmly, in answer to her own thoughts.

Mika frowned, puzzled. "I wasn't what? What are you talking about?"

"You were *not* making love." Was she making any sense, even to herself?

"I wasn't? Excuse me for being slightly confused, but—"

The sarcasm in his tone hurt. She didn't want to continue this, but she did owe him an explanation.

"You were . . . you were almost like . . ." she swallowed and her eyes filled despite her best efforts to keep cool.

"Almost like what?" He sounded a bit less angry now and she was able to continue.

"It was almost like you were . . . you were like . . . " But she couldn't say the word '"rape", because what Mika had been doing couldn't even begin to compare with Aaro's brutal actions. "Like you were forcing your-self on me."

Mika was on his feet. He took her hands into his and pressed them against his breast. "I'm sorry. I did-n't intend to. It's just that lately I've been thinking of nothing but making love to you."

"I have been thinking of that, too," Anna-Liisa confessed. "But I imagined you would first caress me gently." She looked up at him, suddenly feeling shy.

"I'm so sorry. I guess I was too eager and didn't take note of your feelings." He kissed her fingers.

Anna-Liisa shook her head. "No, it is I who should apologize. I should have told you of my expectations. Of course you would be eager. And naturally you thought that I would feel the same, since I initiated this." She shook her head. "I do not want to think about it."

Confusion flashed in his eyes. Of course he didn't understand it was Aaro she didn't want to think about.

By now they were both calmer, standing, facing each other rather awkwardly. Anna-Liisa knew she'd spoiled something very special and regret tore through her. Passionate love-making was what she'd been dreaming of, imagining, but somehow when the moment came, she wasn't able to erase the memory of Aaro's groping hands on her, forcing himself on her, with her fighting back silently, while upstairs Elina and Johannes were sleeping.

Anna-Liisa shuddered. "I am chilly," she said. "I think we should heat up the sauna."

Was she stalling for time to keep him at bay?

Whatever it was, Mika was fine with that. He sensed there was something behind her behavior she wasn't willing or ready to share with him. From now on he would let her call the shots, so he could see exactly what it was she wanted from him. He didn't plan to mess up again by making any wrong moves.

They went down to the shore bringing their towels with them. Mika carried a few loads of wood into the little room where the *kiuas* was situated, and lit the fire under it to heat up the stones. Anna-Liisa made sure there was water in the metal hot water tub attached to the *kiuas*.

While the sauna was heating, they made their way back up the hill to the cottage. As they walked, Mika took her hand in his and kissed her palm. He was determined not to let whatever had gone wrong earlier spoil the whole day.

Anna-Liisa smiled up at him. "I asked you to come here so we could make love, and we will."

Her frankness never ceased to amaze him. "Yes," he said. "For sure."

Inside the cottage Anna-Liisa headed for the kitchen. "I will make us some coffee."

Mika laughed as she poured water into the coffee maker. "Coffee is the answer to everything, isn't it? Did you bring any *pulla*?"

"What is coffee without *pulla*?" Anna-Liisa retorted. "And I also brought bologna for sandwiches. Fine Finnish food." Out of a bag she pulled a round dark rye loaf and proceeded to slice it thin. She buttered each piece and put slices of bologna on each.

When the coffee was ready, they carried their steaming mugs and plates with sandwiches and slices of *pulla* down to the shore. Although it was already October, the stone face was warm from the sun that had been pouring on it all day. They settled down on the smooth rocks that slid into the sea and the silence around them was almost unreal. Except for a couple of brave sailors that glided silently by, there was no boat traffic, and the neighboring cottages were empty, most of them closed for the season.

Anna-Liisa munched on her sandwich and wiggled her bare toes in the water. "I think I could go for a swim. Are you game?"

"It's *October*!" Mika yelped. "That water's not exactly body temperature."

"Chicken!" Anna-Liisa chided him. "It will be bracing."

Mika shuddered. "You mean freezing, don't you?" He dipped a slice of *pulla* into his coffee and slurped it into his mouth.

"I meant after the sauna," she amended.

"Oh, that's better." Mika laughed, relieved. He didn't want to play macho and dive into the freezing sea.

When the sauna was hot they undressed on the covered patio. Mika didn't even try to keep his eyes off Anna-Liisa's slender backside, because that would've been impossible. It was also impossible not to touch her. Standing behind her, he reached out and put his hands to her waist and then slid them down along her hips. He heard her catch her breath and felt a shiver run through her.

"I know there's not supposed to be any hanky-panky inside the sauna," he said. "But how about out here on the patio? Is that permissible?"

She didn't turn, but her body yielded and softened under his hands.

"I think the rule also goes for patios," she said softly.

He reached up and cupped her breasts. "That's a terrible rule," he murmured against the back of her neck.

"Yes," she whispered. "It is."

"We can't break it?"

Anna-Liisa shook her head and slipped out of his arms.

In the dim sauna room, they sat side by side on the top bench. Mika threw water on the stones and the soft heat wrapped them in warmth. Her arm brushed against his, and although this made him want to touch her more intimately, he made no move to get any closer. That wasn't done in a sauna.

Damn!

A few minutes later, glistening with perspiration, they ran out and plunged headfirst into the cool water. Anna-Liisa shrieked and Mika hooted with laughter as they emerged, spluttering, up to the surface.

"You were right, this is definitely *not* body temperature!" she cried. "Brr."

"But it certainly is bracing," Mika called out over their splashing. "I don't suppose you want to swim to the rocky shoal this time?"

"What I want is to go back in the sauna," Anna-Liisa replied, her teeth chattering. With a few strokes she was back on shore, making a dash for the sauna, with Mika chasing after her. He caught her at the door and picked her up in his arms.

"What are you doing?" she screamed, laughing.

Without a word he carried her back to the shore and unceremoniously dumped her back into the water off the dock. "That's for calling me a chicken!" he shouted, and dove in after her.

Anna-Liisa escaped back on shore and this time she made it safely inside the sauna. Mika followed fast on her heels.

"Isn't it customary to wash each other's backs?" Mika asked when they were done taking heat. "That's what I was told, anyway." He had been dying to touch her again, to run his hands down her glistening body, but had refrained with great difficulty.

"Yes, it is," Anna-Liisa replied. She got down from the top bench and began to mix some hot and cold water in two plastic tubs for washing. "Would you like for me to wash your back?"

"Please." He handed her the long-handled brush

and sat on the lowest bench. She soaped the brush with fragrant pine soap and gave his back a thorough scrubbing, rinsing off the suds with a few dipperfuls of warm water.

"My turn," he announced. He took her loofa and carefully soaped it with a natural soap while she lay down on her stomach on the middle bench. He began to rub her back, slowly moving the loofa up and down her spine and shoulder blades.

"Ahh, that feels so good," Anna-Liisa sighed.

Hesitantly Mika brought the loofa lower, and gently massaged her buttocks, all the while expecting her to tell him firmly this was *not* done in the sauna.

But she didn't. So he continued to enjoy himself, rubbing her slender body with the loofa until it became obvious she was thoroughly scrubbed and he was only doing it for his own pleasure.

"You don't want your front washed, too?" he asked, hopeful, but not very optimistic.

"No, thank you. Please rinse me off now," Anna-Liisa said.

Mika poured water down her back with a dipper and ran his palm over her smooth skin to rinse off the suds—as well as for the pure enjoyment of caressing her. She didn't object.

When the *saunominen* was over, they sat on the patio, wrapped in thick towels, breathing in the autumn air that had turned cooler as the day wore on.

Mika exhaled with satisfaction, his body relaxed and his mind at peace.

It was still afternoon, but the sun was already getting lower in the sky, getting ready to set by six. The shortening days signaled not only the approach of winter, but also the end of his tenure at the university. This thought always caused a sense of panic to rise inside him. Was he really going to go away and leave her?

But not now. At this moment he felt totally indolent after the relaxing sauna, the bracing swim, and with Anna-Liisa sitting beside him, both of them wrapped only in towels.

Anna-Liisa brought him back to more practical matters. "Ready for some sauna coffee?" she asked.

"I'm ready for something, but it's not coffee," Mika said and stood up. Slowly he pulled away the towel from around his loins and stood before her, naked. He held out his hands for her.

"Anna-Liisa" he said, when she didn't move.

Like that very first time when he kissed her, the word sounded to her like a prayer. It was then she had known he would become someone very important in her life. She just hadn't known how important. As she reached out and gave her hands to him, her towel fell to the patio floor. He drew her against him and they stood, skin against skin, holding each other. He was warm against her and she didn't feel the wind from the sea.

"I have waited for you a long time," she said.

"Me too," he choked out against her hair. "All my life I've been waiting for you to come to me. You complete me, like a missing puzzle piece that I found at last."

Her heart beat with anticipation as he picked her up in his arms and carried her up the path to the cottage. She had been dreaming of this, waiting for someone like him. And now that he was here—he would soon be gone. Anna-Liisa pressed her face against his neck to banish the thought from her mind. He was here now and that was all that mattered.

In the cottage sunroom Mika laid her down on the daybed and knelt on the floor beside her. She trembled as he looked deep into her eyes and kissed her gently on the mouth, running his tongue softly over her bottom lip.

His movements were slow and deliberate as he caressed her breasts, kissed her stomach and slid his lips over every inch of her until she was completely on fire. She felt him sheath himself, and then he took his time entering her. Each slow, sensuous stroke sent her moaning with the incredible beauty of it all. It was like nothing she had ever experienced, and she wanted to relish every second of it. But soon she needed more, and urged him with her hips to set a faster rhythm. As his thrusts quickened, so did her breathing, and she dug her fingers into his shoulders to brace herself.

When her climax came, he came with her, crying out her name.

Shuddering, he collapsed on her. Spent with the sweet pleasure of it all, Anna-Liisa caressed his back. He softly kissed her face as their breathing slowly calmed down. This had been everything she'd dreamed it would be, but had never expected to experience.

As the afternoon wore on, they made love again. And then again when the autumn day turned to dusk. Anna-Liisa, feeling sated and still glowing inside, languidly began to tidy up the cottage, while Mika went down to the shore to check up on the sauna and lock it up.

As night fell they motored back, with the lights of the city showing the way to the marina, sprinkling the water before them with diamonds.

"I hope Sanni never asks the kids how they liked their day at the cottage," Anna-Liisa said. She knew it had been very unwise of her to throw caution to the winds and take the chance of being discovered. But it had been more than worth it. If there was a price to pay, she was willing.

Mika tied up the boat in its spot at the wharf, and they carried their belongings to Anna-Liisa's car, the only one waiting in the parking lot. During the summer the place would have been full of vehicles, but now, as the cruel autumn winds began to blow, the cottages had lost their charm.

But not for her. Not today.

A short distance from the university Anna-Liisa parked at the curb and shut the motor.

Mika turned to her, his forehead puckered in a deep frown. "When can I see you again?"

The question had been on his mind all the way home but he hadn't wanted to spoil the relaxed feeling of euphoria that filled him during the ride. Somehow he wasn't expecting a favorable reply.

And he didn't get one.

Anna-Liisa shook her head. "It will not be easy to arrange another private meeting. If I asked for the cottage again, especially now that autumn is here, Sanni and Pekka would wonder what is going on. And I cannot keep imposing on the Koivus to babysit for me too often. Leila knows about you, but she has her own family to take care of. I do not want to take advantage of her friendship. Now that I cannot leave the children on their own, she is kind enough to look after them once in a while if I have to work late or have a meeting."

They sat silently for a few minutes. Mika tried to think of some plan, but came up empty-handed.

He clenched his jaw. Damn that Aaro! He was calling all the shots while Mika was cursing impotently and putting up with it. He flinched as he remembered Michael's taunting words, "Some hero you are!" What kind of a man was he, anyway? Why wasn't he doing something about the situation? Why was he letting some drunken bully dictate their every move?

Damn, damn! The whole situation made him feel like some no-account weakling. He couldn't even touch Anna-Liisa here because Aaro might be spying on them. Or someone who knew Aaro might see them.

He looked at Anna-Liisa sitting beside him at the wheel. It was dark, but a streetlight shone into the car. He knew she wouldn't let him take her in his arms and kiss her good night.

So what was he going to do about it? When he left Finland, could he honestly leave Anna-Liisa and the kids in the clutches of that drunken bastard? Could he ever live with himself if something happened to any of them?

The answer was obvious. Before he left, he had to do something.

But what?

Chapter Eleven

The first term was almost over. Mika and Anna-Liisa were both busy with the last few lectures and preparing the final exams. Aside from the times he went to give Elina art lessons and received a meal in return, Mika saw little of Anna-Liisa. Of course she wanted it that way, but he was far from content. After that wonderful day at the cottage, his body yearned for her and the brief kisses and hugs only made the fires burn more intensely inside him.

But despite the agony, he was happy because he could visit the home where he felt like a part of the family. Yes, Elina was something else, all right, and Mika enjoyed working with her and seeing her progress. The girl was shy and didn't say much to him, yet he knew she absorbed everything he told her. Each time he came back, he could see she'd been practicing whatever he had taught the previous time. Her diligence touched him deeply, and he found himself growing more and more fond of her. Maybe she didn't talk a lot, but her quick wit and whimsical sense of humor came out through her drawings, and sometimes had him laughing out loud at some of the images.

He was happy to go to the park to swing and sing with Aleksi, even though the cold winds blew through the bare trees and he had to wear gloves when holding onto the icy chains. And he was relieved that Johannes was more comfortable with him in the house and no longer scowled at him from under his brows. The boy showed Mika how to carve little objects from bark or soft wood, and Mika was amazed at the boy's dexterity with the knife.

But with each passing day the end of his time in Finland was getting closer and closer. If he thought about it, it almost felt like a death sentence, so he closed his mind to it as much as possible. Why cause himself a huge pain in the gut? Why not just enjoy the time he had left?

But Aaro never left his mind, and he spent many a sleepless night thinking of what he could do about the man. But the only thing he could think of was to simply go and talk with him. He didn't much hope that this would take him anywhere, but he had to try.

Mika stood on the sidewalk in the early evening darkness, waiting for Aaro. It was only 6:30 but the sun had already set. He was getting used to the early arrival of darkness as winter approached.

This was probably a stupid, insane plan, but he didn't know what else to do. He'd found out which shelter Aaro usually went to for the night, and now he stood near the door, hoping the man would show up.

Several other rather scruffy-looking fellows were standing around, smoking and talking in guttural Finnish. They cast sidelong glances at him, because, Mika knew, he didn't look like he belonged in the scene. His clothing wasn't rumpled and even though his hair was longer than most, it was clean and brushed back.

After an hour of standing around, waiting, he was ready to give up for the night. He had decided he would keep coming back here, whenever he wasn't at Anna-Liisa's doing what he liked best—singing with Aleksi, or tutoring Elina, or learning from Johannes how to carve.

Mika had just decided he would walk back to the university rather than take the bus. It would be quite a hike, but he had time.

"Hey, you!"

The gravelly voice came from a dark, narrow alley close to Mika and stopped him cold. Although he had never heard Aaro talk, somehow he knew that's who was addressing him.

Mika turned toward the alley and peered into the

darkness. "You talking to me?"

"Yeah, you."

Aaro spoke English, which didn't surprise Mika. Most people did, especially those with higher education.

A disheveled man emerged from the shadows and Mika could see as well as smell he was totally intoxicated.

"You waitin' for me?" Aaro asked, slurring his words heavily.

"If you're Aaro, then yes, I was waiting for you. I want to talk to you."

The man had probably been hiding in the alley the whole time while Mika had been waiting in front of the shelter.

"Can we go somewhere? A cup of coffee maybe?" Finns never turned down a cup of coffee and Mika hoped that would help sober the fellow a bit.

"Beer," Aaro said instead.

"Sure, beer's good. Where should we go?" Mika hoped the place wouldn't be a total dive, but in his situation he didn't have much room to barter.

"C'm here." Aaro turned and led him a few doors down to a fairly decent-looking bar, at least from the outside.

Inside the noise-level was deafening and Mika knew it would be impossible to talk in this atmosphere. "Listen, I want to talk to you, so maybe we could do it outside on the sidewalk instead. What do you say?"

But Aaro had already signaled a waiter to take them to a table.

"*Olutta*," he told the fellow.

"*Kaksi*," Mika said, holding up two fingers. What the hell, might as well be as friendly as possible. His plan—if he even had one—was to be non-confrontational. But he wasn't going to have a friendly chat, either. He wanted to let Aaro know in no uncertain terms he would use the full force of the Finnish law to stop him from harassing Anna-Liisa. Not that he had any idea what the Finnish law said about these situations, but if Aaro didn't co-operate, he was ready to hire a lawyer.

The waiter set two glasses of foaming beer in front of them.

Aaro took a long gulp and put his glass down with deliberate slowness. "You like my wife." It was a sneering remark, not a question.

"Do you have a wife?" Mika asked in return.

That didn't sit well with Aaro. From under his brows he glowered at Mika, his eyes two ugly slits. "She is my *wife*!" he stated, and slammed his fist on the table.

"You two are divorced," Mika said evenly, but that infuriated Aaro even more.

He now hit the table with both palms, causing nearby heads to turn. He rose, leaning on his hands, hunching forward toward Mika. "I'll kill you," came a low, guttural threat.

So much for a non-confrontational meeting.

"Right. That's what I want to talk to you about," Mika said. "Let's go outside. Too much noise here." He took a drink from his glass, wiped his mouth on the back of his hand and got up. "Let's go." He dropped a few Euros on the table. "Coming?"

For a few seconds Aaro hesitated and then he moved, knocking over his chair.

Outside the bar a few men were still hanging out, leaning against the wall, smoking. Mika stopped to wait for Aaro, who stumbled as the door hit him in the face.

"*Perkele*!" Aaro shouted. "*Saatana!*" He struck the door with his fist and turned to confront Mika, ready to take his anger out on him.

"Take it easy," Mika said, raising his hands to calm him. It didn't seem like the best moment to have a conversation. The fellow was not only roaring drunk, but he was now mad as a bull. He even looked like one, swaying there with his shoulders hunched.

Suddenly, without warning, Aaro lunged. Mika saw a flash of steel in his hand and quickly dodged out of the way. Aaro went flying onto the street. There was a sound of a horn and a deafening screech of brakes, followed by a sickening thud as the car hit the body.

"Someone call an ambulance!" Mika shouted.

Damn! Was 911 the emergency number in Finland?

"How is he?" Anna-Liisa rose quickly to meet the doctor who approached them.

She and Mika had spent the better part of the night in the waiting room, expecting at any moment to hear the news that Aaro was dead. Dawn was breaking and she saw Mika's eyes drooping from lack of sleep.

"Are you his wife?" The doctor asked in Finnish.

"His ex-wife," Anna-Liisa said. "This is my friend, Mika Laine. He was there when it happened."

"I'm Dr. Heikkinen." He extended his hand to each of them in turn. "Sorry I can't give you very encouraging news, but I'm afraid it's still too early to tell how this will turn out. Does he have any immediate family? Children?"

"The children are young," she told him. "He has no one else."

The doctor shook his head. "Well, I'd bring the kids here if they want to see their father alive, because we don't know if he'll make it. One thing we do know is that several vertebrae in his spine are crushed and even if he makes it, he'll never walk again."

Anna-Liisa's hand flew to her mouth. "Oh, God," she breathed. "He'll be in a wheelchair?"

"If he makes it. Yes."

From the corner of her eye she saw a puzzled, questioning look in Mika's eyes. The conversation was in

Finnish and she knew he hadn't understood any of it.

"But the fact that his liver looks like Swiss cheese obviously isn't the result of the accident," the doctor went on.

"He's an alcoholic," Anna-Liisa stated the obvious.

"Yes. Which makes his recovery all the more uncertain. He is in a coma but you may go and see him." The doctor and Anna-Liisa shook hands, and he nodded to Mika before walking off.

Mika looked at Anna-Liisa and cocked his eyebrow. "Not good news, is it?" he asked.

"No. But we are allowed to go and see him," she said and picked up her coat and purse off the chair.

Mika stretched. "To be honest, I have no desire to go and count the tubes coming out of his orifices." He rubbed the back of his neck. "It's late. We should go."

"But I must first go and see him," Anna-Liisa insisted.

Mika frowned. "What the hell for?"

She couldn't just walk away. "He has no one else who cares if he lives or dies," she tried to explain, but realized too late how her words sounded to him.

"And you do?" Mika's voice rose in disbelief.

He didn't understand. "He is a human being—" Anna-Liisa began but Mika stopped her.

"Only barely. Besides, you don't owe him anything."

She was too tired to think. "I know I do not, but he has no one else—"

"Technically, he doesn't even have you," Mika said. His cold voice sent chills down her spine. He looked deep into her eyes. "Or does he?"

Anna-Liisa sighed with exhaustion. She was too tired to argue. "You do not understand. I'm his wife and—"

Mika's eyes narrowed into angry slits. "I believe you're his *ex*-wife. Or have I misunderstood this whole thing?"

She had never seen him like this and it alarmed her. She put a restraining hand on his arm. "Mika, of course I meant his *ex*-wife. But he *is* the father of my children. I cannot walk out on him when he could be dying."

"Well, he's all yours. And I hope he makes a full recovery. You say he's your husband. I guess he always will be." He turned on his heel. "I'm outa here!"

Was she really hearing this from Mika? Her mouth opened to protest, but he was gone.

She heard the loud echo of his heels on the marble floor as he marched down the empty hall. With a quiet whimper she crumpled down into the chair and covered her face with her hands, too exhausted and distressed even to cry.

He should have stayed away, but a few days later something pushed Mika back to the hospital again. Did she love her ex-husband? She couldn't. Everything she'd ever said about him assured him she definitely was not in love with the man. And Anna-Liisa was honest. He would have staked his life on her honesty, and that feeling couldn't change overnight.

Every morning at the cafeteria there was talk about Aaro's condition. Some people defended Anna-Liisa's actions, while others considered her crazy and wondered why she would drive to see him each day. And Mika wondered about the same thing. *Why*? He remembered the look of anguish in her eyes when the doctor had told her about Aaro's condition. Did she really care that much for the guy?

Mika had to go and see for himself. He had to find out if this was the end for them, or was there some slim hope he'd misunderstood everything.

With trepidation in his heart he took a bus to the hospital when he knew she would be there. He found Anna-Liisa sitting by Aaro's bed knitting while he slept. Knitting, for God's sake, like a dutiful little wife! She looked up, obviously surprised to see him but said nothing.

Anger boiled inside him. The cozy domestic scene made him loose his cool. "How very idyllic!" he sneered without greeting her. Probably not the best way to start the conversation.

He was right on that.

"Mika, I want you to leave," Anna-Liisa said firmly. Not "Please leave", or anything like that. She wasn't *asking* him to go, she was *telling* him to get the hell out of there.

"Yeah, I guess two lovers in the same room is a bit much for you, isn't it? But there must be something pretty special about the guy for you to go back to have sex with him even after he beat you up." Mika's mouth twisted in a smirk. "It didn't take much to figure out Aleksi was conceived *after* you two split up. Arja told me, and I wondered about it, but this explains it all. Sorry I meddled in your affairs and caused this to happen to him, but I honestly thought you wanted to be rid of the bastard."

Anna-Liisa stood up. "Leave right now," she pronounced firmly.

But he couldn't go, not before he'd got the answer to the question that had been festering inside him since the night of the accident.

"So you really love him?" There was no other conclusion he could draw from this. She was still his wife. Maybe not lawfully any more, but certainly in her heart, because her actions were obviously those of a wife.

Anna-Liisa looked up at him, much too calmly. "He is a human being. He has no one else. What more can I say?"

"You can say you love me." What made that come out? Love? That word had never been mentioned between them.

But since it was out, he waited for her reply with bated breath. It never came. She simply sat down again and picked up her knitting.

"Thank you," he pronounced evenly. "*Kiitos.* That's all I wanted to know." He started to walk out but turned back at the door. "But I would like to know why you asked me to come to the cottage. Were you that starved for sex or what? And Aaro was too drunk to deliver?" Even to his own ears, his burst of laughter had an ugly, grating sound. "Would you believe—" He had to swallow and start again. "Would you believe I actually thought it was because you cared for me?"

He turned and left, his stomach roiling. In the corridor he had to lean against the wall for a moment to steady his shaking legs. He felt like he was going to be sick right on that shiny granite floor.

"Michael. I've made up my mind about things," Mika said firmly to his friend on the computer screen. "I'm out of here at the end of the semester."

Michael's eyebrows shot up. "Oh? What happened to wonderful Anna-Liisa? I thought you couldn't live without her."

"I thought so, too, but—" He related the events of the last couple of days.

Michael gave a low whistle. "I didn't think you'd really go through with this confrontation with Aaro. Too bad it ended the way it did."

Mika leaned his forehead on his fist. "Yeah. She's totally committed to him and I haven't got the stomach to hang around and watch."

"I mean too bad for *Aaro* it ended that way," Michael said.

"Yes, Mr. Sympathy." Michael just didn't seem to get it. The situation wasn't bad because Aaro was injured, it was bad because Anna-Liisa was out of his life. "It's better it all came out now that she still has feelings for him. I was an idiot, and was taken for a ride." That's what he kept telling himself. But he couldn't help thinking—when the need for Anna-Liisa overwhelmed him—that he wished he'd left well-enough alone and not gone to confront Aaro.

"It's lucky for you there were witnesses around to see how Aaro got hurt," Michael said.

Damn! Michael didn't seem to get on the same page with him. It was the loss of Anna-Liisa that Mika wanted sympathy for, not for that bastard Aaro.

"You could've been charged with attempted murder, when it became known there was this love triangle going on," Michael went on.

"There never was a love-triangle, because as far as Anna-Liisa was concerned—no matter what she led me to believe—for her it always was only the two of them. She visits the hospital almost every day after work and sits with him, like a dutiful little wife."

"But you told me they were divorced."

"They are. At least on paper. But it seems neither of them is ready to give up on the relationship. He kept calling her his wife, and the other day she said he was her husband. She *meant* to say her ex, but I'd call it a Freudian slip, because she's certainly behaving like he's the real thing."

"Yeah, I've heard of couples like that who can't seem to get over each other no matter how ugly their relationship was," Michael said. "But it's weird how the last time we Skyped, you were talking about throwing him under a bus or pushing him off the dock. And then this happened. That was almost prophetic."

"You *know* I didn't mean any of that!" Mika yelped. "I was only trying to talk with him, not cause this to happen."

"I know, but still . . ."

Obviously he wasn't getting anywhere with Michael.

"Anyway, I'm just letting you know I'll be back by Christmas, so don't forget to buy me a gift."

In dismay Mika closed the connection, and slumped down on his bed. If he'd never gone to talk with Aaro, Anna-Liisa would still be his. Although, stupid him, she never *had* been his. Aaro had been dead right when he called her his wife. Maybe on paper they weren't married any more, but emotionally she still was his, and that was all that mattered.

Mika heaved onto his back and flung an arm across his eyes. So, actually it was a good thing this accident happened, or he would never have known how much she still cared for the guy. When push came to shove, that's when people usually showed their true colors, like Anna-Liisa had now shown hers.

Mika flipped over onto his stomach again.

But that was perfect. He'd never wanted a wife in his life, anyway. Nor kids, for that matter. He'd had enough of taking care of his brothers and sisters before and after school and every bloody weekend while his mother worked. Changing diapers and carrying the babies around. Spooning food into reluctant mouths and holding grubby little hands on the way to the park. Finding the time to do what *he* wanted to do had been nearly impossible. Being seven years older than the next brother, he'd had no choice but to help out his mom. But sometimes he couldn't help wondering what the hell had happened to birth control all of a sudden. Had they run out of money to buy condoms, or what?

So now, not having to deal with Anna-Liisa's brood was a relief. Or it *should* have been. He didn't have to try to be friendly to that sullen Johannes. Although lately he'd been pretty friendly. And giving him math lessons was interesting. Made Mika think about algebra in a new way. And he had to admit he loved giving art lessons to Elina. It was rewarding seeing the quick progress she was making. And finding his singing voice after all those years, while swinging and singing with Aleksi was kind of fun. Satisfying. Sometimes he even sang in the shower now, which he hadn't done for years.

He cleared his throat and tried to hum a few bars of "Home On the Range", but it ended in a deep sigh.

He wanted back the home he'd almost had with Anna-Liisa and the kids.

Mika sat, tense and uneasy, beside Arja, as she steered her car from the university parking lot into the early evening traffic. Funny, how he'd always felt totally at ease beside Anna-Liisa, and had never stopped admiring her facility with the gearshift. Arja didn't have the same smooth moves. So obviously it wasn't the marvelous Finnish driving schools that had made Anna-Liisa so competent at the wheel, contrary to what she'd told him. Damn! Even sitting here in the car with Arja he couldn't help thinking of Anna-Liisa.

People were out Christmas shopping, and on Kaisaniemenkatu the traffic was snarled. Mika read the street name and smiled, remembering how Anna-Liisa had laughed when he'd tried to pronounce that long word.

"What's so funny about this?" Arja frowned, seeing his smile. "We're not moving anywhere."

"I was remembering something," Mika said. "No big deal." Yes, remembering again. He was always remembering. There didn't seem to be any way to avoid it.

"I think we should've left the car at the university

and taken the tram," Arja said. "Though they don't seem to be going much faster."

"We have all evening," Mika said. Today he'd given his last lecture, and exams would be starting next week. So much for "Art in Canada". He only hoped he'd been able to convey to his students his own love for The Group of Seven painters, because in his opinion their art symbolized the very essence and spirit of Canada. In their oil paintings you could see the vast Canadian forests, the beauty of snow, the primeval power of mighty rivers, and the gnarled, stubborn pine trees clinging to rocky crags above sparkling lakes. If only he could take Elina to Canada one day and show her all that, and so much more. He could only imagine what this gifted child-artist could do with it all.

"Hey, Laine!" Arja poked him on the arm. "I was talking to you. What are you dreaming about?"

Mika jerked himself back to reality. "Oh, sorry. I think I'm just worn out after putting my best effort into my last legendary, prize-winning lecture." He gave her a lopsided grin. "Wanted it to be the crowning legacy of my time here, you know. So what were you saying?"

"I suggested we abandon the car on some side street and walk to Jussin Baari, for a drink and maybe grab some pub fare, instead of trying to make it to some fancier establishment. We can celebrate the end of lectures with a dinner another day."

Jussin Baari. He hadn't been there since that first

time with Anna-Liisa. Did he want to go there? And re-member.

"Sure. That's fine with me." Mika tried to lace the reply with enthusiasm. It wasn't possible to avoid every place in Helsinki where he'd been with Anna-Liisa, so he better just get used to it. And he would be leaving before Christmas, anyway, so that shouldn't prove too difficult. He'd been out with Arja a few times the last couple of weeks and, although she'd made it plenty clear she would like for them to be intimate like they'd been before, he just couldn't bring himself to go for it. Arja was a nice woman, but she wasn't Anna-Liisa.

Hell, why should it matter whether she was like Anna-Liisa or not? With Arja it had only been casual sex, the kind he couldn't have with Anna-Liisa. He could never think of Anna-Liisa in those casual terms because her laughter enchanted him, because every-thing about her enchanted him, and he cared for her—way too much.

But by now he should be more than ready for a tumble with Arja. So what was stopping him?

It was that one, wonderful day at the cottage with Anna-Liisa. A sigh of longing rose from deep within his chest.

Damn. Looked like Anna-Liisa had spoiled every other woman for him, and until the enchantment she'd woven around him wore off, he had to deal with the fact that he didn't want anyone else. It might take a month, it might take a year, but he was confident eventually he would be free of her.

Though so far the magic hadn't shown any signs of waning. He missed her and needed her as much as ever.

Jussin Baari, like he remembered, was dimly lit and full of noise. The waiter led them to a table by the window.

"*Kaksi pilsneriä*," Mika said to the waiter and grinned at Arja. "Are you impressed with my Finnish?"

Arja laughed. "After all this time in the country, I don't consider it a huge feat that you are able to say two beers. In fact, I'd expect you to be able to discuss something more intellectual than that."

"Intellectual! What could be more intellectual than knowing how to order beer and sausages?"

"Sausages. That reminds me," Arja said. "I hear you and Anna-Liisa went to Sanni and Pekkas's cottage in October. Together."

Mika's jaw dropped. "How did you know?" What kind of a spy system did the university have in place?

To Mika's dismay, Arja's laughter sounded slightly lecherous. "Word gets around."

"How?"

"Well, Sanni told a few people that Anna-Liisa had asked for the cottage. And Stefan asked Anna-Liisa's kids if they'd enjoyed being at the cottage. I think he was driving them somewhere—I'm not sure—and they told him they hadn't been to the cottage. So he put two and two together, and since no one had seen you around that day either—"

"Yeah, okay, so we were at the cottage." He couldn't start disputing facts that were obviously common knowledge.

"Nice time?" Arja's hand slid across the table to caress his fingers.

Mika had to swallow. Nice time? Hell, it had been the most wonderful day of his life. "Yeah, nice," he choked out.

"Wow! That good, eh?" Arja's laughter definitely did not sound like pearls dropping into pristine water.

Mika's face flamed with anger. Not at himself, but at Arja. She was making that beautiful day at the cottage sound like a cheap tryst.

"I guess nothing's sacred at the Helsinki U," he sneered and knocked back the rest of his beer in one huge swallow. How could he get the hell out right now?

He couldn't.

"But I hear you two are no longer a number," Arja continued and Mika didn't bother to ask how she knew this. Probably from Stefan, via some circuitous route.

"I didn't realize we were ever considered a number," he said, trying to keep the irritation from his voice.

Arja's laughter was starting to grate on him. "Oh, yes, everyone knew you were visiting her on a regular basis."

"I was giving art lessons to Elina," he began. "And—"

"Oh, sure you were!"

Mika knew she was trying to be funny and not offensive, but it didn't come out that way. He was disgusted with the insinuations and had to finish this off as quickly and painlessly as possible. A few couples were gyrating on the dance floor in front of the disc jockey. Maybe if they danced a couple of numbers he could suggest a quick exit and he could return to the blessed solitude of his room.

"You care to dance?" he asked and got up, showing he wasn't looking for a refusal.

Arja's eyes sparkled. "Looks like I do," she said and slipped her hand into his.

It didn't feel right.

Unfortunately it was a tango which, Mika knew, was a favorite with many Finns and required for couples to dance pretty close. At first he tried to be cool and danced apart from her, but obviously that wasn't what Arja had in mind.

"This is a tango, not a jive," she said and snuggled against his chest, pressing her hips against his pelvis.

"Sorry, I'm not the greatest dancer—" Mika began, but Arja pooh-poohed away his apologies.

"You're doing just fine," she purred.

They stayed longer than he wanted, because he didn't know how to call it an evening without being rude.

Arja was obviously enjoying herself immensely and downing more than a few beers along the way. As the evening wore on, she became louder, and her talk became laced with more sexy innuendos, until Mika couldn't stand it any longer.

He went to call a taxi, and when Arja was safely stuffed in the back seat, he gave her address, and paid the driver.

"I'm going to walk back to the dorm," he told her before he slammed the door shut. He wasn't sure if she heard him or not, and didn't care. He needed fresh air.

Chapter Twelve

Again Anna-Liisa sat by Aaro's bed. She'd been dropping in on him most days for a few minutes, and today she'd again brought along her knitting. The nurses had told her he was coming along amazingly well for someone who, only recently, had been at death's door. She wanted to stay today till he woke up, to see if he was getting more responsive. The last time he'd recognized her and they had exchanged a few words.

Her thoughts, as always, went to Mika's visit the week before—if one could call it a visit. He'd asked if she loved him.

She'd relived that scene a thousand times in her mind and each time she'd imagined herself running into his arms, shouting, "Yes, I love you, Mika, with all my heart!" How she wished she could have told him that, but she couldn't. Maybe if she never said it out loud, it wouldn't hurt so much when he left. Maybe she wouldn't feel like the maiden singing sad songs on the shore.

Anna-Liisa glanced up from her knitting and saw that Aaro was staring up at her. Today there was something different about the way he squinted his eyes, but at the same time, it was very familiar. That was the old Aaro scowling at her, and it made her afraid. Like before.

"I want vodka," he said gruffly. "You bring me some?"

"You can't have alcohol in the hospital," she said calmly and put the knitting down, ready to deal with whatever was coming. "Here's some juice the nurse has—"

"I said I want a *vodka*!" His voice still wasn't strong, but it had all the same growly ugliness as before. "Vodka, not bloody juice!"

She stuffed her knitting into the cloth bag, and got ready to leave. "No drinks allowed here," she said firmly.

"Then get me outa here!" he wheezed. "I'll get it myself!"

"You can't leave the hospital." That was a mistake. Her negative words were only making him more and more agitated.

"The hell I can't. I'll show you, you useless bitch." He yanked at the IV tube attached to the back of his hand.

Quickly Anna-Liisa pushed the emergency button. "Don't do that, Aaro!"

She heard hurried footsteps approaching, but before the orderly had entered the room, Aaro had grabbed a stainless steel water pitcher from his night table and flung it at her.

She had no time to duck. The bottom edge of the metal container hit her squarely on the forehead and she fell sideways, into the arms of the orderly.

When she woke up she was lying on a gurney in the corridor, her head bandaged. Leila Koivu was bending over her, a worried look on her usually cheerful face.

"You're awake," Leila said. "Thank goodness."

Anna-Liisa felt her forehead. "I assume they had to stitch me up?" She was surprised there was no pain or throbbing in her head. Probably the freezing.

"They said twenty-three stitches," Leila confirmed. "The edge of that metal pitcher did a great number on your forehead. A very deep cut, they said."

"What time is it?" Anna-Liisa sat up, alarmed, but sudden dizziness made her sink back onto the pillow. "Where are the children?"

"Stefan has them. He's taking them for some burgers and fries for dinner."

Anna-Liisa closed her eyes, "You're both such great friends. I'm so lucky to have you."

"Yes, but you're also lucky Aaro didn't do something more serious to you," Leila said severely. "For the life of me I can't understand why you've been coming here all this time to see him. I mean, what has he ever done to deserve your kindness?"

"Please don't lecture me, Leila," Anna-Liisa said with a tired sigh. "I had to come. He's the father of my children, after all, and I couldn't ever face them if they knew their father had died alone and friendless. He has nobody."

Leila snorted. "And he has only himself to blame for that."

"He's a sick man, Leila." But Anna-Liisa knew she was talking to someone who, despite her kindness, didn't believe alcoholics were sick.

"We could argue about that all night," Leila retorted. "He does *not* deserve your kindness. Not any more. You've done your Guardian Angel bit and now, my dear friend, you are *not* coming here to see him again!" Leila shook her raised finger to emphasize her words. "I *forbid* you!"

Leila was right. It was obvious Aaro had learned nothing from this experience and was still as cruel as ever. Even without alcohol.

Ann-Liisa opened the oven door and as the heat hit her face, she quickly jerked herself back. Although a dressing covered her forehead, the wound was very heat-sensitive. She pulled two baking sheets from the oven, each with a dozen *riisipiirakka* and placed them on the stovetop.

Anna-Liisa snorted. The stitches would be removed in a couple of weeks, but probably not before the staff Christmas party. Too bad it wasn't going to be a costume affair, because she could have gone as an accident victim. Which she was. If Aaro's deliberate actions could be considered an accident.

The crisp rye crust of the rice patties smelled delicious and the rice pudding in the centre was slightly golden. Perfect. These treats were a favorite of her kids and would be devoured in a heartbeat, unless she put them in the freezer till Christmas.

Before they had even cooled, she grabbed one *riisipiirakka* and threw it onto the breadboard. She blew on her burning fingers and proceeded to spread butter on the steaming rice pudding, where it immediately melted.

Anna-Liisa poured herself a cup of coffee, sat down at the kitchen table, and as soon as the *riisipiirakka* was cool enough to handle, she bit into the delicious rye crust. She should have made them more often, but the process was too time-consuming to do by herself. Sometimes she and Leila teamed up to bake them, but somehow lately life had got in the way.

Anna-Liisa sighed, wiping the melted butter off her chin with the back of her hand. Mika loved the *riisipiirakka*, too. If he would come over again, she would gladly have baked them for him every week. But she'd burned her bridges when she'd chosen to go and visit Aaro. It didn't matter, because what difference did a few more weeks make? He would soon be gone anyway. She could have called him up and tried to explain her motives for the hospital visits, but why bother? What good would the explanations do except maybe make her appear less of an idiot in his eyes? Back in Canada he might amuse his friends by telling them about one crazy woman in Finland who went to visit her drunken thug of an ex-husband in the hospital.

So what?

Visiting Aaro was something she had simply had to do, even if to the children he was only some distant stranger whom they sometimes heard mentioned. In the family albums, which they sometimes flipped through, he *was* their father, although Johannes never wanted to look at his photos. Elina always had questions about him, and wanted to know how he was related to this or that aunt, uncle, or long-gone grandparent.

Eventually Anna-Liisa would have to guide them through the relationship they would be forming with him—if he lived—and she didn't want her own actions to reflect uncaring. Their father used to be a good man who now was sick, and that's what she wanted the children to know and remember.

She had removed all photos of him that depicted him in an unpleasant light, both from the computer files and the albums. Whether the children kept contact with him or not would be up to them, but she wanted them to know their mother did not judge his worth as a human being.

Anna-Liisa took another bite of the patty, making the rye crust crunch. So Mika was keeping company with Arja these days.

Crunch, crunch. So be it.

And if she had thought about these things with her brain instead of her heart, she would have had to admit that despite their one wonderful day at the cottage, their relationship would soon have ended anyway. Only now it had ended a bit sooner. Brushing away the moisture from her eyes, she took a gulp of coffee. It made no difference at all. No difference at all. It was all good.

She got up to remove the *riisipiirakat* from the baking sheets and through the window saw Aleksi sauntering home from the park. It had been snowing the night before, and as he trudged along, he picked up snow and threw it into the air. Anna-Liisa made a face as she saw him suck on his woolen mittens, caked with clumps of wet snow. Yuck! She could still remember the taste of soggy mittens and the tiny bits of wool that got into her mouth when she'd done the same thing as a child. It had been almost impossible to spit out the tiny wool threads.

Aleksi burst through the door and wrinkled his nose

with delight as he sniffed the air. "*Piirakoita!*" He threw off his boots and snowsuit and dashed into the kitchen.

"Hang up your snowsuit and put your boots side by side against the wall," Anna-Liisa said and he quickly complied with only a small whimper.

Aleksi sat at the table and slurped the butter off the warm patty. "Nobody swings in the park any more," he observed. "I don't know why. The swings are still there."

"Maybe it is considered a summer activity," Anna-Liisa said and slipped another two baking sheets into the oven.

"I think it's because Mika doesn't come any more," Aleksi said. "When he came, we always swinged. When he doesn't come, we don't swing any more."

Anna-Liisa's eyes misted. "Can you not swing without Mika?"

"No." Aleksi took a crunchy bite of his *riisipiirakka* without explaining.

But it wasn't only Aleksi who asked about Mika. Even Elina had shyly told Anna-Liisa she would like it if Mika came and worked with her again on her art.

"Do you think maybe sometime he will?" the girl had asked, her quiet voice cautious with hope, but ready to accept the inevitable.

Even now, waves of pain shot through Anna-Liisa when she thought of that conversation. Elina was so eager to learn.

"Mika has final exams to mark," she'd said. "Like I do. And then, he'll be leaving."

"Yes, I know."

The sad resignation in the girl's response had stabbed right through Anna-Liisa's heart.

But what surprised her most was Johannes. One day he showed Anna-Liisa his newest pine bark creation and remarked, "Do you think Mika would like this? See the way I got the dog's tail to stick out and curl up? It didn't even break off."

"I'm sure he would like to see it very much," Anna-Liisa said. She knew Mika would have been pleasantly surprised to see this excellent likeness of a curly-tailed spitz. But he never would.

"You think you could take it to him so he'll have it when he goes away?" Johannes asked.

Anna-Liisa didn't want to show her surprise. "Yes, I will," she said, trying not to let him see her lips quiver.

Johannes handed her the tiny figurine, which later she carefully wrapped in tissue and tucked into her purse.

And now she had no choice but to deliver it.

A couple of days later, after class, she drove reluctantly to the dorm and took the elevator to the fifth floor. It was almost five months ago she had taken Mika up here to show him his room, and she hadn't been back since. She could recall every second of that moment. The way he had stood behind her as they had looked out at the glimmering ocean, with her being conscious of his every breath. Had she already then been so attracted to him that those few minutes spent with him here were forever etched in her heart?

She hadn't called to tell him she was coming because she half-hoped he wouldn't be in. Along with the little carving, the package she carried contained a framed watercolor painting of a Christmas scene from Elina, and a picture, drawn by Aleksi, of him and Mika swinging in a snowy park. Aleksi had covered the top of the picture with black sticks, each with a black ball dangling at the end.

"Those are the notes we're singing," he had explained earnestly.

And from her, she had included a few *riisipiirakka* wrapped in foil. She'd debated about that, because she didn't want him to interpret them as a gift, and make him feel he had to reciprocate. She intended them simply as a token of their friendship. If one existed any more.

She knocked, and when there was no answer, for a moment she couldn't tell if the feeling inside her was one of relief or disappointment. She left the package hanging from the door handle and turned to go. As she waited for the elevator, she took in deep gulps of air, which could have been gasps of relief, except for the moisture that filled her eyes.

"To some party animals *pikkujoulu* is even more important than Christmas itself," Arja explained to Mika as they got out of the taxi. "They shouldn't really call it 'Little Christmas', considering what a big deal it is nowadays."

Mika laughed. "Party animals like you?"

Arja slipped her hand under his arm as they walked up to the front steps. "Darn tootin'. I love *pikkujoulu* parties."

The department party was held, like Mika's welcoming party in July, at Sanni and Pekka's home. But, naturally, this time everyone stayed indoors and, because the house wasn't too spacious, it didn't take long before the atmosphere was very cozy. Mika noticed no one had brought kids, and it was soon clear why. Alcohol ruled, and was the reason most people had arrived by taxi or by public transit.

On Sanni's instructions Mika carried their coats into a bedroom, designated as the cloakroom, and threw them on top of a growing pile on the bed. How many people had Sanni and Pekka invited? But, more importantly, would Anna-Liisa be there? And even more importantly, would she come by herself or with Stefan?

Through the grapevine—mainly Stefan—he'd heard she no longer went to see Aaro because somehow the man had managed to hurt her even while lying half-dead in the hospital bed. Filled with impotent frustration for being unable to do anything about it, Mika had asked for the details. When Stefan filled him in, he'd felt a sharp stab of shame in his heart. Here he was, the big hero who'd vowed he would protect her from Aaro, and instead had lambasted her while she sat by that bastard's hospital bed.

It was no use trying to deny she still had an immense effect on him, and it was more difficult than he'd ever believed to get over her. He couldn't figure that out, because he'd been in and out of affairs several times in his life and had gotten over each one in a week, maybe two in more serious cases. Or when he'd snagged himself another sexy, beautiful woman, whichever came first.

But not now. There was no comparison between those so-called affairs and the intense emotions Anna-Liisa had aroused in his heart.

When he'd opened the package she had left at his door the previous week, a maelstrom of warmth and tenderness had washed over him. Elina's beautiful painting, Aleksi's picture of the two of them swinging in a snowy park, and the dog Johannes had carved. He'd sat on his bed, fingering the gifts on his lap while his eyes had misted.

But it had been the rice patties from Anna-Liisa that had caused the worst heartache to grip him. The baking made him miss not just her, but the total package—her, her calmness, the children, the home. It was the honest earthiness of the gesture that came through in the baking, which had totally unnerved him, and he had allowed the sadness and the longing for everything he was leaving behind to flow out unchecked from his eyes.

It didn't take long for the party to get loud. People jostled past each other on their way to and from the bar and the snack table. Christmas *glög* was a popular drink this early in the evening, but Mika didn't care much for the hot mulled wine. Instead he poured himself a glass of dry red, and carried it with him as he chatted and mingled with everyone. All the professors and many of their spouses were now his friends, not like in July, when they'd been only a sea of faces and strange names to him. Like always, they now accommodated him by speaking English, so he didn't feel left out.

But still, something was missing.

Anna-Liisa hadn't come.

Loud music thumped through the house, and made Mika long for the silence of the outdoors where snow was softly falling. The songs were modern versions of traditional and new Christmas tunes, set to a strong beat that made them suitable for dancing.

"Sa-aanta Claus is coming to town, Sa-aanta Claus is coming to town," people sang or shouted more or less in tune.

Stefan hadn't come yet, either.

Mika resisted the urge to ask Sanni whether the two of them had accepted the invitation. So he waited. And waited.

The area rug had been rolled up and carried out of the living room, and the occasional tables and chairs had been pushed against the wall or taken into one of the bedrooms to make room for dancing.

Arja pulled him by the arm onto the crowded floor where there was hardly room to move.

"I like this," Arja whispered in his ear as their bodies were pressed together by the crowds. She gave a suggestive wiggle of her full, round hips against his groin. Lately there'd been an increasing number of such moves by her, but Mika had always countered them with humor, so as not to hurt her feelings.

Sanni rang a very loud cowbell to get everyone's attention. "You like my tinkling sleigh bell?" she quipped and then announced, "The buffet is now officially open. There's all the Christmas foods your mother always made, from liver casserole with fresh lingonberry sauce, all the way to rice pudding with fruit sauce. Any questions?"

"Do I get dessert if I skip the liver casserole?" Harri asked.

"What's the general opinion?" Sanni wanted to know. "Does he get dessert if he doesn't eat the liver?"

"No way!" everyone roared. "No dessert for him!"

Just then the door opened and Anna-Liisa entered, followed by Stefan. This produced more loud, raucous banter.

"Hey, where have you two been?"

"Were you trying to melt the Snow Queen on the way, Stefan? Is that why you're so late?"

"Any success?"

Mika didn't join in the teasing. He couldn't. All he saw was the bandage on Anna-Liisa's forehead. He hadn't known the wound was that extensive, but seeing her now, pain gripped his heart.

When Stefan passed by him with his and Anna-Liisa's coats on his arm, Mika had the urge to trip the guy. He'd looked so smug, coming in with Anna-Liisa, like he'd won a prize for having as his date the most coveted woman in the department.

"Hauskaa pikkujoulua!" Stefan greeted him with a self-satisfied grin pasted on his face. Mika grunted his reply, which Stefan might interpret as a garbled version of "Happy Little Christmas." Or something less courteous.

While Stefan was gone, Mika elbowed his way toward Anna-Liisa. He had a perfectly good excuse to speak with her. After all, he had yet to thank her for the rice patties.

At last he stood behind her and was filled with an urgent need to wrap his arms around her. "Hello,

Anna-Liisa," he said, almost choking on the words.

She turned around. "Hello, Mika."

She looked totally composed. He didn't see a flicker of emotion on her face, while he felt like a stuttering idiot, hardly able to speak. He couldn't take his eyes off her bandage and involuntarily his hand went up to gently touch her forehead.

"You're hurt," he said, fighting to get the word out.

"I had the stitches out just yesterday, but did not want to show the ugly scar at the party." She smiled. "Female vanity, I guess."

Like that first time at the airport, her wide smile and full, pink lips made Mika want to kiss her. But, like then, he couldn't, even though in the intervening time they had exchanged something much more intimate than kisses.

For a few moments they simply stood there, and Mika forgot why he had fought his way up to see her. Being this close to her felt so incredibly wonderful. And when the jostling crowds pushed them even closer, it was even better.

Finally he remembered. "I wanted to thank you for the package you left at my door. It's the nicest gift I've ever received."

"You are welcome," Anna-Liisa said. "I will tell the children you liked their gifts."

"Tell Aleksi I love the drawing of us swinging," Mika went on. He kept hoping Stefan, who was now standing at the bar waiting for his turn, would be detained for about two hours.

"He asked me why no one ever swings now," Anna-Liisa told him. "He is convinced it is because you do not come any more. For him it has nothing to do with the fact it is winter and people do not swing in the park in the winter."

Mika wanted to say that even if it was winter he would come and swing with Aleksi. But he couldn't. He knew Anna-Liisa wouldn't ask him to come over any more. After the accusing, ugly words he'd flung at her at the hospital, he couldn't blame her if she never wanted to see him again. It was a wonder she even spoke with him now.

"And tell Elina her painting is beautiful," he said. "I'll hang it on my wall every Christmas for the rest of my life." That sounded slightly too dramatic, but that's how he felt, and he wanted Elina to know that.

"I will tell her," Anna-Liisa said.

"And please tell Johannes he did a super job with the dog. The tail curls up so realistically. And I was amazed how he was able to carve the legs without breaking them."

Now Anna-Liisa's smile broadened. "I will let him know. He will be so happy you noticed the way the tail is curling. He was sure you would."

Mika put a hand on her shoulder. "They're great kids!" And then, because he couldn't help it, he gripped her other shoulder and pulled her close. "And thank you for the *riisipiirakat*," he whispered in her ear over the noise. "They were delicious."

He desperately wanted to feel her arms around him, but they stayed down by her sides.

"You are welcome, Mika," she said.

He would have given ten years off his life just to be able to kiss her. Or even to hold her for the rest of the evening.

But Stefan tapped him on the shoulder and cleared his throat. "Excuse me, you two, but here's Anna-Liisa's drink."

"I was thanking her for the rice patties she gave me for a Christmas gift," Mika explained. He had to let her go then. Feeling lost without her in his arms he turned away and saw Arja making questioning contortions with her face from across the room.

"What's up?" she asked when he finally reached her.

"Oh, nothing. I was just thanking Anna-Liisa for some stuff the kids made me for Christmas." He turned to the buffet table so she wouldn't see his eyes. He was afraid they might be glistening with moisture.

The food looked and smelled delicious but Mika didn't have the stomach for any of it. Dutifully he collected a spoonful of each dish on his plate—including the compulsory liver casserole—but all he wanted to do was get the hell out of there. The sight of Stefan having his arm around Anna-Liisa's shoulders was too much to take. It should have been *his* arms around her. Holding her close.

When only dregs remained on the buffet table, Sanni rang her huge cowbell again. "Time for *joulupukki!*" she shouted. "If all the good little boys and girls find a place to sit or stand, *joulupukki* will bring you whatever you deserve. I hope you've all been good."

"What about the bad ones? What happens to them?" someone yelled.

"They go and sit in the corner, of course," Sanni replied. "But I hope there aren't any bad boys or girls here tonight."

"I don't know about that!" Harri yelled. "Anna-Liisa and Stefan came here so late, I wonder what *joulupukki* will say about *that!*"

Through the good-natured hoots and hollers Stefan preened like a hero, while Mika stared darkly at him. Anna-Liisa, he saw, took it all in good humor and only gave a short wave of her hand to dispel any silly ideas.

Eventually everyone found a place along the walls, some of the women sitting on the knee of one gentleman or another. The room became quiet as they all listened for the jingle bells and banging at the door that would announce the visitor.

Soon Pekka came blustering in, carrying a huge burlap sack over his shoulder. He wore an old fur coat, probably Sanni's, and his face was covered by a scraggly, moth-eaten beard that had seen better days. On his head he wore a huge wolf-fur hat with earflaps, and on his hands he had enormous reindeer-hide gloves. He heaved the sack onto the floor and stomped around the room with his big, black rubber boots, banging his cane on the floor, making as much racket as possible. He was bent over and, like all good Finnish Santas, held his aching back with one hand, lamenting the weight of the sack he was carrying. All this was greeted with shouts and laughter.

"Now we must sing to *joulupukki*," Sanni announced and to Mika's amusement, the whole room broke into a rousing, off-key rendition of the traditional children's song to Santa. And to his surprise, he remembered the first couple of lines from his childhood.

"Joulupukki, joulupukki,
valkoparta, vanha ukki!"

A couple of women with red elf hats appeared from the kitchen to help the "old, white-bearded *joulupukki*" distribute the gifts Sanni had prepared for everyone. They were mostly silly gag gifts, but when Mika opened his, he found a book, *Finland in Pictures,* signed by the whole department. There was a bookmark directing him to a particular page, and when he opened it up, he knew why Sanni had put it there. It was a photo of one of the rocky islands in the archipelago around Helsinki, much like the one where the cottage was. Sanni had written a message on one corner of the page, "Always remember our cottage, Mika, and the friends who will keep you in their hearts."

As if he could ever forget that day with Anna-Liisa. After they'd gotten over the unfortunate start, they had made love—such wonderful, passionate love like he'd never experienced in his life. The whole day had been so warm and loving he couldn't figure out if the memory of it gave him more pain or pleasure. But the knowledge it would never happen again brought such an unbearable ache into his heart that to think about it was like stabbing himself.

And he had spoiled it all with his abominable behavior at the hospital. He felt like his insides were one big lump of regrets and he wanted to go and ask Anna-Liisa to forgive his stupidity. Would she even consider it? But with every inch of space between them occupied by someone, it seemed like they were doomed never to get near each other tonight.

When his burlap sack was empty, *joulupukki* said, "Let's give Sanni a big hand for all her hard work, in helping me prepare all these presents. And now, my reindeer and sleigh are waiting outside!" With a final *"Hauskaa Joulua!"* he stumbled out, slamming the door shut behind him.

Everyone wished each other Merry Christmas and shook hands with those closest to them, before the drink glasses were picked up and the music started again. Mika went to thank Sanni for his gift and then took the book into the bedroom and wrapped it in the folds of his jacket.

He was glad Arja was a popular dance partner. One after another the men came to ask her, leaving Mika to either stand and watch the dancing, or ask some other women. But what he really wanted was to hold Anna-Liisa in his arms again. When he'd held her against his heart a while ago, it was as though he had received some fabulous elixir that had miraculously relieved the constant, deep ache inside him.

But now, watching her dance with Stefan, the pain returned. Like an addict hungering for relief, he made his way toward them. After a dozen "excuse me's" he finally reached them and tapped Stefan on the shoulder.

"Mind if I cut in?" he asked, knowing full well Stefan *would* mind. He would mind a great deal, but Mika didn't care.

Looking slightly annoyed, Stefan politely moved aside and Mika claimed his prize. At this moment he didn't want to think about Anna-Liisa's feelings toward Aaro. This was about his own urgent need. His body's cry for help to ease the pain that was eating at him.

His arms went around her and with a groan he buried his face against her neck. "Anna-Liisa." He didn't care if she didn't love him. At this moment, all he cared about was the sweet feeling of relief brought on by holding her close. He didn't want to let her go. Ever.

Then, miraculously, her arms slipped around his

neck, and they simply stood in one spot, gazing at each other, not even moving to the music.

She looked directly into his eyes. "Mika," she said, her voice very low. He had to strain to hear her over the noise.

"There is something I want to tell you before you leave Finland. It is something I should have told you before, and I know this is not the time or place, but I want to tell you that . . ." She lowered her head.

Mika raised her chin. "Tell me what?"

She took a deep breath as if to give her courage. And when he heard her words, he knew why she'd needed that.

"I didn't go back to Aaro. He raped me."

When the words were out she looked relieved, as though a huge weight had been lifted off her shoulders.

And smashed right onto his, with the weight of a cement block. "What?" he rasped. Had she really said what he thought?

Around them the dancers were laughing and stomping to the rhythm of a schottische and the noise level was through the roof. Mika led her down the hall, into a corner of the back porch.

"What did you say?" he croaked. "Aaro raped you?"

It was quieter here, but she still had to speak directly into his ear to be heard. Her words came out in a rush. "Yes. That was the last time he ever—And little

Aleksi was born as a result of that horrible act." She smiled ruefully. "So in a way I have to thank Aaro for raping me, because I cannot imagine my life without Aleksi."

They stood still, and Mika still held her close, while trying to digest this information. "And here I thought you had gone back—" he began, but she interrupted.

"Yes, so did my mother, and so did everyone else. I could not tell anyone what happened because I did not want Aleksi to ever find out how he was conceived. I did not trust anyone, not even my mother because it would have been such a juicy bit of gossip to share with her friends. But since you will be gone soon I wanted you to know I did *not* go back to him. And I wanted you to understand why I reacted the way I did at the cottage to your ardent love-making. It was not fair of me to react like that, after inviting you there, but I could not help it. I wanted to apologize for my re-action." Her eyes begged him to understand.

Mika buried his hands in her hair. "My poor darling. And here I was accusing you of . . . of . . . can you ever forgive me and forget my ugly words at the hospital? I don't blame you if you can't, but I was jealous and angry. I had no right to speak to you like that." He gripped her shoulders. "Anna-Liisa, please forgive me?"

The noisy, raucous schottische was over and the couples were dispersing. Glasses clinked and talk and laughter rang out again in the living room.

"Yes, I forgive you," she said. "You did not know. And do you forgive me for not telling you?"

"Yes," he sighed, and held her against him, pressing his cheek against her soft hair. He must not think sad. He must not think end.

Chapter Thirteen

"Excuse me, you two. I hate to interrupt, but I've been searching all over for you, Mika. Can I see you for a minute?"

Mika turned, and couldn't hide his irritation. It was Jaakko Mäntysalo, the department head, tapping him on the shoulder.

"I won't keep him very long," Jaakko reassured Anna-Liisa with a playful wink. "So you and Mika can get back to whatever you were . . . um . . . discussing."

With a nod to Anna-Liisa, Mika followed Jaakko into the spare bedroom where all the coats were piled on the bed.

Jaakko flipped on the light and closed the door on the party noise. "Did you enjoy teaching the class?" he asked without preamble.

"Yes, I did. Very much," Mika replied. Where was this leading?

"I got some really favorable reviews from your

students," Jaakko continued.

"Yes, Stefan told me about them. That was very rewarding to hear."

"Well, I'll get right to the point so I won't keep you from . . ." He grinned and indicated with his head toward the door, "from more important matters. Do you think you'd be willing to sign up for a spring session and teach it again? There's been a lot of interest."

Mika took a step back. "Wow! This is quite a surprise."

"I imagine it is," Jaakko said. "But a pleasant one, I hope. So think about it. Talk it over with your partners in Canada and see how they feel about it, and whether it fits into the overall business plan for your company. If you're agreeable and things work out, we could see about extending the contract into the fall term."

With a pat on the back, Jaakko left Mika leaning against the pile of coats, digesting the news. Stay in Finland? There definitely would be no problem with Michael or Miguel as far as the spring session was concerned, because he hadn't yet completed his year of sabbatical.

But staying here would make no sense unless Anna-Liisa loved him. He had already asked her once, at the hospital, but she had remained silent. Could he survive another knock in the teeth if he asked her again?

Well, there was only one way to find out. And if she

said no, he would just get on the plane and bid a fond *hyvästi* to Finland.

He came out of the bedroom and stood at the door, searching for Anna-Liisa. The white bandage around her head made her easy to locate in the crowded room. She was chatting with Arja, but looked upset. What the hell was Arja saying to her?

Mika jostled his way through to them as quickly as he could.

"Hello, ladies," he said jovially. "Having a little *tête-à-tête*?"

Arja turned to him and slipped an arm around his waist, which he immediately, but gently, removed.

She stuck out her lower lip in a pout. "Mika is always so unromantic," she complained to Anna-Liisa.

Without further explanations, he took Anna-Liisa by the arm. "Excuse us, Arja, but I have to talk to Anna-Liisa."

Arja shrugged and turned to chat with the person beside her, while Mika steered Anna-Liisa away.

The only place where they could have a conversation without shouting at each other was the bedroom where Jaakko had just given him the news. They entered and Mika flipped on the lights, closing the door behind them. He stood in front of Anna-Liisa, hands in his pockets, to hide his crossed fingers. He had to speak now, before he lost his nerve. Everything depended on her answer.

"I once asked you if you loved me and you didn't reply. Do you remember? At the hospital."

"I remember," she now said, and looked down at her hands. Mika saw they were trembling, the only visible clue to her emotions. She clutched them together and waited.

"If I asked you now, what would your answer be?"

When she remained silent, Mika went over to the pile of coats and came back with the book *joulupukki* had given him. He flipped over to a particular page and handed the book to her.

"Remember this?" he asked.

"Oh!" Her eyes flew open as she saw the picture of the rocky ocean shore.

"I can't help wondering why you asked me to come to the cottage." Mika spoke softly, not wanting her to think he was accusing her of anything. "Since you obviously don't love me, so then why—?"

"I never said I did not love you!" she cried. Her hand flew up to her mouth as she realized what she had said.

Mika's face broke into a wide grin. "So you *do* love me!" He grabbed her and swung her around in the small space, causing some coats to slide off the pile.

"Yes, I do," she stammered. "But . . ."

She loved him. As the wonderful words sunk into his brain, he took her face in his hands and kissed her over and over again. "That's all I needed to hear!" he rejoiced. "Because I love you too, my darling, with all my heart!"

For a few precious moments she allowed him to rejoice, before she put her hands against his chest and pushed him away.

"Please, Mika," she said, shaking her head. "This does not mean anything because . . . because you are still leaving."

But he joyfully heaved her up on the pile of coats. "Yes, it means something. Because Jaakko has just asked me to renew my contract, at least for the spring session. And since you love me, I will say yes to him. I am not leaving."

Anna-Liisa slid off the coat pile and back into his arms. This time his kiss was deep and full of passion, demanding her to respond. And she did. It left them both gasping. He wanted her right now, and from her response he knew she wanted him. Her eyes, gazing up at him, were dark with desire.

"I need you, Anna-Liisa," he murmured, holding her face between his hands. "And kissing you only makes it worse. But I still want to kiss you."

"I know."

He felt the rapid pulse on her temple and as he kissed her again, she trembled under his hands.

At last Anna-Liisa broke free. "People might be coming for their coats."

Mika grinned at the ever-pragmatic Anna-Liisa as

they picked the fallen coats from off the floor and dug out their own.

A wordless agreement passed between them. They would be together tonight. Somewhere.

But first Mika would have to take Arja home. And since Anna-Liisa had come with Stefan, they would also have to deal with that.

"I better take Arja's coat while I'm at it," Mika said.

"And I will have to talk to Stefan," Anna-Liisa said as they left the room.

In the hallway they passed Harri and Pirkko coming to get their coats.

"You're leaving, too?" Harri said to Anna-Liisa. "We'd love to stay, but duty awaits at home. She's called the mother-in-law."

"Same with me," Anna-Liisa said, and Mika smiled inwardly at the way she was trying to sound innocent. "I hope Stefan is ready to go."

"But what about you, Mika? You and Arja don't have any kids at home," Pirkko exclaimed. "Why not stay and enjoy the party? You might never be at another *pikkujoulu* again."

Mika grinned. "Oh, I think it's probably time to run," he replied vaguely. Before things turn ugly, he finished in his head. He knew Arja had tossed back more than a few drinks during the evening.

Anna-Liisa went off to find Sanni and Pekka to thank them, while Mika looked for Arja. When he finally located her, he was pleasantly surprised to find her standing with Stefan, hanging possessively onto his arm.

"Would you believe, Mika? Stefan and I have known each other for years, but we've only discovered each other just now!" Arja crowed with a slight slur. "I simply *love* this guy. I hope Anna-Liisa won't kill me for stealing her beau."

"Anna-Liisa's a pretty generous and open-minded woman," Mika said. "Hey, listen Arja, I'm pretty tired and was going to suggest we leave."

"Gee, Mika, I hope you don't mind if I stay," Arja said. "Stefan and I have a lot of dancing and talking to do yet." She looked up at Stefan with hooded eyes.

That was the best news Mika had heard all evening. Except for the job offer. And Anna-Liisa telling him she loved him. Okay, third best news. "I don't mind at all," Mika assured her. "And you can stay and enjoy yourself, too, Stefan, because Anna-Liisa said she wanted to call a cab and get home. Her babysitter's waiting."

Confused, Stefan looked at Anna-Liisa, who joined them with her coat slung over her arm. "But I thought you said—" he began but stopped short when Arja poked him in the ribs.

"Yes, I was going to let them stay the whole night at the Koivus but I thought better of it," Anna-Liisa said, and Mika could see her blush. Not a very fluent liar, it seemed. "I think I am imposing on my neighbors too much," she finished.

Mika went to throw Arja's coat back in the bedroom and, after thanking Sanni and Pekka for a great party, he stood in the hall waiting for his taxi.

"I cannot get a cab," he heard Anna-Liisa tell Sanni. "Looks like all of Helsinki is celebrating *pikkujoulu* tonight."

"Mika, you got one, didn't you?" Sanni called to him. "Couldn't you ask the driver to go around to Anna-Liisa's house after dropping you off?"

Perfect. He could have kissed Sanni for suggesting this.

"Of course," Mika said. "That okay with you, Anna-Liisa?"

Again he saw her cheeks flash red and could hardly hear her whispered reply. "Yes."

Sanni hurried away to fulfill her hostess duties, having no idea how thankful Mika was to her. Some day he would have to buy her a bouquet of roses.

Mika and Anna-Liisa sat in the back of the dark taxi, their arms only occasionally brushing against each other, but Mika could feel her as though she'd been pressed, naked, against his side. The electricity sparked through her overcoat, up his arm, and right into his heart. He wanted her so much he could taste the desire in his mouth and had to gulp it down. In the darkness he also heard her swallow and knew she was feeling the same.

But their talk circled wide around this topic.

"I didn't ask where the kids are tonight," he said.

"Elina is having a sleep-over at her girlfriend's house and Johannes and Aleksi are at the Koivus for the night," Anna-Liisa told him. "Sometimes these parties go late, so . . ." Her voice faded and she swallowed again.

"That's good," Mika said. He knew his voice sounded thick. All he wanted to do right now was take her in his arms and kiss her. Deeply and completely.

When the cab pulled up in front of the dorm, Mika reached for her hand. "Will you come up?"

"Yes," she whispered without hesitation.

His heart soared.

The tail light of the taxi disappeared into the darkness. Mika felt the sharp chill of the night air hit his exposed skin and beside him Anna-Liisa shivered. He unlocked the outside door and they took the elevator to the top floor. The hallway was empty and quiet as they made their way to his door. In his hurry he fumbled with the lock, dropping the keys, and heard Anna-Liisa's quiet giggle as he snorted his impatience.

Inside his room she pulled off her boots, and Mika came up behind her to remove her overcoat. He hung it up carefully in the closet, to signal he expected her to stay the night, and then took her in his arms.

"At the cottage I think we were just two people who wanted to have sex," he said. "But now—"

"I have to confess something," Anna-Liisa said, "I invited you to the cottage because I already loved you. It was not only for some casual sex, as you obviously thought."

Mika held her tightly. It felt so wonderful to hear her say that. To know she'd loved him all along. Like he'd loved her, without acknowledging it to himself.

"And it was far from casual for me, too. I loved you, I think, from the moment I saw you at the airport. There was something about you that enchanted me from the first get-go." He kissed her. "Do you think now that we're alone at last, you could enchant me some more?"

Anna-Liisa laughed. "I am afraid I left my magic wand at home, but I will see what I can do."

"I'm so relieved that now I'll be able to hear you laugh. Forever. One of my goals in life will be to keep you so happy that you'll laugh many times every day."

"Just keep thinking up more lame knock-knock jokes," Anna-Liisa quipped.

"Right now I have other things on my mind," Mika rumbled and went to turn off the ceiling light. He snapped on the dim bedside lamp and dug a condom out of his pocket. He placed it on the night table and once again drew her against him. He kissed her soft lips, like he had first wanted to do at the airport, and her mouth opened to receive him, making him groan with want. His kiss became hungrier, deeper and he felt her tongue slip in to tangle with his. Her fingers buried in his hair and she pulled him closer.

"Mika, I love you," she whispered. "It is so wonderful to be able to say it to you."

He picked her up in his arms and carried her over to his bed, narrow and single like all the beds in the dorm. But that's all they needed, because Mika wasn't planning for them to sleep side by side. He laid her down and lowered himself down on top of her. She shifted under him so the weight of his body settled between her legs while he caressed her through her blouse.

She held his head between her hands and raised it, and he saw a smile glimmer in the blue depths of her eyes as she asked, "Do you think we would make more headway if we took off our clothes? Just asking, because I have wanted you all evening at the party."

Her direct words surprised him although they shouldn't have. There never was anything phony or coy about her. Not even in lovemaking.

"*All* evening?" He couldn't help teasing her. "Even when you were dancing with Stefan?"

"Yes. That is when I wanted you the most. I wanted *your* arms around me, not his."

These words were like an aphrodisiac and he devoured her mouth with a kiss that left her whimpering and pushing herself up against him. Quickly they divested themselves of their outer clothing and proceeded to lovingly remove the last remaining garments off each other. Standing, facing her, Mika slowly took off her bra and cupped each exposed breast. With murmurs of appreciation he savored the hard nipples, circling them with his tongue, before skimming his hands down her sides. Her skin was smooth and soft and he traced the curve of her waist and hips with his palms as he pushed down her panties. She wiggled out of them and then slid her hands down his hard stomach to feel him through his underwear.

"Mmm," she murmured, obviously impressed, and pushed his shorts down.

He again laid her on the bed and sheathed himself. Then, holding himself over her, he ran his mouth over her neck and throat causing her to moan with pleasure.

Anna-Liisa opened herself to him. "Please," she whispered and Mika entered her in one deep stroke that made her gasp. Her urgent movements set the rhythm, and almost drove him to distraction. But he managed to keep himself in control until, within moments, her rapid breathing turned to gasps and he pushed in response to her demands. It was only when she convulsed with a sharp cry of ecstasy that he allowed his own climax to explode inside her. She clung to him, pressing herself against him, and he heard her cry out his name as blissful darkness momentarily overtook him.

Spent, Mika lay on her and he felt her relax under him. As her breathing slowed down to a long sigh of contentment he eased himself off her and lay on his side. He held himself up on one elbow and tried not to fall off the narrow bed.

She turned to face him and smiled. "That was nice," she murmured.

Mika chuckled. "A typical Finnish understatement. We, in Canada, would have said something like 'stupendous' or 'mind-blowing'."

"Or awesome," she added.

"Well, I thought it was," he said. "Pretty awesome."

"Nice," she insisted with a laugh. "It was very nice."

Mika grabbed her and bit her shoulder. "I guess I wasn't as successful as I thought. Now I have to show you awesome!"

In one smooth move he flipped her over onto her stomach and climbed up behind her. "Here comes awesome," he cried and, raising her bottom up, he parted her thighs. He thrust himself forcefully into her, making her cry out in surprise. Soon she was helping him by arching her back, so he could get in deeper. Because of his fast rhythm, it didn't take long before her breath turned to panting and he knew her climax was close. He continued to increase the speed of his thrusts, until finally her body shook with spasms of fulfillment. He felt her clenching rhythmically around him, which sent him into a blinding release.

He collapsed against her back, still deeply imbedded, while she held herself up on her elbows, breathing hard.

When he could speak again, he asked, "So, was that awesome?"

"It was different," she said and he could feel her shoulders shake with laughter.

"I don't want to let you out of my arms," he said. "But unfortunately this bed isn't that great for two people to sleep on, unless they're one on top of the other."

Anna-Liisa made a move to get up from under him. "No, it is not, but I did not complain, did I, even though I am the one underneath? But I have to go now to call a taxi so I will be there in the morning when the children come home."

Mika clasped his arms around her, hugging her from behind. He didn't ever want to wake up in the morning without Anna-Liisa beside him.

"Couldn't we spoon here for a few hours? Like till daylight? It's only two o'clock. Too early for you to leave."

"No, we could not. You know very well daylight doesn't come till after eight," Anna-Liisa replied and extricated herself from his embrace. "My boys will be running home from the Koivus before that," She got up and went to get her phone from her purse. "I will call a taxi."

Stretching lethargically Mika got off the bed and

approached the window. With the late November sunrise it would still be dark for another several hours.

"But first, come here," he said and held out his hand to her. He was looking out, beyond the dark city, to where the lights reflected on the black waters of the harbor. And far out on the ocean, they blinked red, yellow and green directing the ships around the maze of islands.

"Isn't it a beautiful sight?" he said, holding her hand. "And on a rainy night, it's even more beautiful. I'm so glad you got this apartment for me. I've often stood here, thinking about you, and how I'd like to bring you up here to share this."

"And here I am," Anna-Liisa said and leaned her bare back against his chest. "It is lovely."

"Not awesome?" Mika joked.

"Never."

"I want you to see my painting of it. And something else." He went to the closet in the corner, pulled out a few large papers, and held up a watercolor of the scene from the window on a rainy night.

"That is beautiful," Anna-Liisa said. "It looks like the city is crying, but the tears do not look sad. They are very colorful, so maybe they are tears of joy?"

"Maybe now I can think of them like that, but I must confess, as I painted it I was almost in tears myself, thinking how I'll be leaving you soon."

He held up the second paper. "What do you think I was thinking about when I painted this?"

Pearls were falling into a pool of clear water, each pearl a perfect study of reflected light. And the tiny splashes of water droplets were almost like shiny pearls themselves."

Anna-Liisa laughed. "Is it what I think it is?"

Mika smiled. "Yes. Your laughter is like this to me, like precious pearls." He put down the painting and once again took her in his arms. "Just like you are, *kulta*. So very precious."

Her hand caressed his cheek. "As you are to me, my *kulta*."

The winter dawn was still hours away when Anna-Liisa got out of the taxi at four. She made her way up the sidewalk and unlocked the front door. The house felt empty without the children, for even as they slept, she always was aware of their presence.

She took off her boots and hung up her coat in the hall closet and went into the kitchen to make herself a pot of coffee. As she munched on a very early morning snack of rye bread, bologna and cheese, she thought about this night. It had been one whirlwind of happenings—all happy ones—and she was still trying to sort through it all.

Mika was staying in Finland for the foreseeable future and, depending on how things worked out, perhaps forever. And they were in love. That was now indisputable. And although they hadn't had time to talk much about it with all that had happened at the party—and especially afterward—their talk had been slanted in the direction of an eventual marriage. She hugged herself and smiled as the wonderful memory of their lovemaking still warmed her. Tonight there were no poignant thoughts in her mind about parting, because all obstacles to their love had miraculously been lifted. She still couldn't believe it was true.

But even in her own joyful euphoria, she couldn't help thinking back to when they had left the party. As she had turned at the door to wave bye to her friends, she had seen Arja looking after Mika. Despite what Arja had said about being crazy about Stefan, her eyes had been filled with sadness and longing. At that moment Anna-Liisa had realized it was Arja who was left behind on the shore like the girl in the folk song.

She placed her porcelain coffee cup on its matching saucer and admired the lovely floral pattern. Aunt Justiina had given six of them as a wedding gift to her and Aaro.

Aaro. No longer would she have to worry about him and his threats. It was a relief to be able to sit here and not feel he was lurking behind the window, and yet she couldn't help feeling pity for him and his sad state. He would soon be transferred to a nursing home, and it made her sad to think that a man who was only in his late thirties would have to live in an institution for the rest of his life. She could only hope that he would eventually come to terms with his situation. Although, according to the doctor, his organs were in such a sad state that his long-term survival was doubtful at best.

But she could not allow thoughts of Aaro to get in the way of her own happiness and her future with Mika and the children.

Yes, the children. How would they react to this sudden change in their lives? She knew Elina would welcome Mika in her quiet, accepting way. And Aleksi would more than likely jump for joy because now Mika would be around forever to swing and sing with him. But what about Johannes? Lately he had become quite friendly toward Mika. Hadn't he even given him the little wooden dog? But would he accept Mika as his father? Any mention of a daddy—anyone's daddy—always made him clam up and shudder. He seemed to hate and fear the very word.

Anna-Liisa knew she would have to tread gently with him.

Mika sat in front of his computer, Skyping his partners. He had asked Miguel to join the session, so they could talk about the implications of him staying in Finland past his one year sabbatical.

"How's my favorite godson doing?" he asked Miguel.

"I hope he's thriving and growing bigger than his twin brother."

"I believe they're about the same weight," Miguel told him. "Alexander was the first born and may be a bit heavier than André, but you'd have to ask Marita about that. She's the one who knows all the tiny details about their growth."

"I probably won't be able to tell which one is my godson," Mika said.

"Probably not. The boys are like the proverbial two peas in a pod," the proud father said.

"But to get back to our discussion," Michael broke in. "I think we have several options. I, for one, don't see Mika staying in Europe to be a problem, as far as the company is concerned."

"I agree," Miguel said. "We don't have to dissolve the partnership. In fact we should take this opportunity to expand into Europe. We have the latest technology and our North American advertising can offer the European market something new and different."

"That's something I was thinking about when Shaylee and I were in Europe last year," Michael said. "And Mika living there will make that all the more feasible."

"You can always fly here if there's some pressing issue that can't be settled by long-distance conferencing," Miguel added.

"Yes, and I can give art classes here in Helsinki,"

Mika put in. "Most young people here speak English. And if I learn a few basic Finnish sentences, I should be okay even if there's a non-English speaker in class. Listen to this—*pensseli*. That means brush. I'm almost there already!"

"Sounds more like a pencil," Michael said.

"But as for your painting, you can do that any-where," Miguel put in. "I'm sure Max will be ecstatic to receive your art for his gallery. I think the only big change will be that we won't see your ugly face around here that often." He laughed. "And that can be considered a relief!"

"Except for this damned Skype!" Michael added with a chuckle. "Couldn't we do phone conferences with only audio?"

Mika grinned. "Thanks a lot, buddies. Nice to be appreciated. But now I won't have to put up with you bugging me about finding a woman. I've found the most perfect woman this side of heaven!"

"Except for the one I found," Michael countered. "Shaylee is looking forward to seeing your Anna-Liisa and the kids here in the not too distant future. So when will you be able to bring them to Canada?"

"That's what Marita was asking," Miguel put in. "*My* perfect woman is dying to meet *your* perfect woman."

"Maybe we'll come to Canada in the spring to get married," Mika mused. "I'd like for both of you to stand up with me."

Miguel laughed. "You're afraid you'll need to be propped up, right? Sure, we can do that."

It was great to kibitz with his old college buddies. Not seeing them at the studio would be something he'd miss, for sure. But life was full of trade-offs, and he wouldn't trade Anna-Liisa for anything. Not even for a place in heaven.

Chapter Fourteen

Dinner was over. Mika and Elina had finished their art lesson and the children were upstairs doing their homework. Even Aleksi was learning to print his letters under Elina's patient tutelage, getting ready for pre-school.

Mika dried the last of the plates and put it into the cupboard. "I was just thinking," he said and hung up the dishtowel on a doorknob.

"Thinking is good, " Anna-Liisa said, nodding, and gave the counter one last wipe.

He came to stand behind her and put his hands around her slim waist. Nuzzling her neck, he breathed in her sweet smell. "I have neglected one huge thing."

"What have you neglected?" She leaned her head back against his shoulder.

"I haven't proposed to you yet," he said.

"That is true. You have not."

He continued to hold her. "And here I've been

assuming all along we're going to get married."

"You have? Now why would you assume that?" She tried to step out of his arms but he held her fast.

"I have been assuming that because I love you so much."

"Yes?"

He softly caressed the back of her neck with the tip of his tongue and could feel the shiver that swept through her. "And I thought maybe you'd like to get married, too."

"Goodness. Why would I want that?" she exclaimed and finally gave up the struggle to free herself.

He turned her to face him. "Because you love me." He kissed her, softly at first, and then more deeply when she responded.

The kiss ended and she drew a long breath. "So are you going to propose, or am I going to have to do it?"

Mika chuckled. "My ever pragmatic Anna-Liisa!" He fell down on one knee. "Please, my darling, will you marry me?"

"Not when you behave like an idiot," she declared and turned to leave the kitchen.

Mika was up in a flash, blocking her way. "Please marry me!"

"Well . . ." she drummed her fingers against the door frame. "Okay, I will," she said at last. "On one condition."

"Anything!"

Her face turned serious. "That you will not say any-thing to the children until I have first had a talk with them. After all, you will become their daddy and that is—"

"No!" The shrill, desperate cry made them both start. Mika whirled around to see Johannes run down the hall, to the front door. The slam shook the pictures on the walls.

Mika was baffled. "What just happened?"

"He ran outside without a coat. Or boots." Anna-Liisa cried, ready to rush out after her son.

Mika stopped her. "You stay here. I'll go find him." At the door he reached for his jacket, grabbed Johannes's boots, and snagged his snowsuit and mitts from the wall hooks. Then he dashed out after the boy.

It had been snowing for most of the day and so it wasn't difficult to see which way Johannes had run. Mika followed the tracks left by the boy's slippered feet. He saw that at one point Johannes had slipped and had fallen on his stomach. His bare fingers had left their prints in the snow as he had struggled to get up. Poor kid would soon be frozen.

The tracks led Mika into the park playground and it didn't take him long to discover Johannes crouched inside the plastic playhouse at the top of the big red slide.

"Johannes, come down and put your snowsuit and

boots on, " Mika said quietly but firmly.

"No," came the obstinate reply.

The boy was sitting on the cold plastic, holding his knees up against his body for warmth.

"Okay, then I'll come up and bring them to you." And with that Mika started to climb up the ladder to the playhouse. He didn't get very far before Johannes sprang up and slid down the slide and took off again, running.

Mika swore under his breath as Johannes scrambled away in the ankle-deep snow. Mika sprinted after the boy and, with his long steps, soon caught up with him. He picked him up and tucked him under his arm where the boy's kicks and struggles could do the least damage.

"Let me go!" Johannes cried in frustration. "I'm telling Mommy you're hurting me!"

"If you stop kicking I won't have to hold you so tight," Mika said calmly. "And if you promise you'll put on your snowsuit and boots I'll let you down."

The struggling became calmer as Johannes obviously thought about his options. Besides, he was probably freezing.

"Okay," he finally muttered.

Mika lowered him to the ground and helped him get dressed. Then he slipped the woolen mittens on the boy's hands and pocketed the slippers.

"There. Now you can stay outside and run around

all you want." He turned and began to walk back home, hoping Johannes would follow.

He did, shuffling behind Mika like a puppy.

"Why did you yell like that?" Mika asked over his shoulder. "You nearly made me jump out of my skin."

Behind him Johannes giggled. "Did I? Make you jump out of your skin?"

"Almost. But why did you do that?"

"I don't want you to be a daddy in our house!" the boy declared angrily. "Daddies are bad."

"Not all daddies."

"Yes, they *are*," was the adamant reply.

They trudged on in the snow, one behind the other, in silence.

"Was your daddy good?" Johannes asked unexpectedly.

The question stopped Mika in his tracks. What was his father like? He hadn't yelled or threatened his kids. He hadn't beaten his wife. But he definitely hadn't been a good father. So how should he answer? He didn't want to lie to Johannes, but felt if he told the truth, it would only reinforce the bad impression the boy had of all fathers.

"Well, he was . . . kind of okay, I guess. But I didn't like him very much when I was a kid," he finally confessed and started to walk on again. Tentatively he held out his hand for Johannes, and in a few more steps he was gratified to feel the boy's mitten slip into his bare hand.

"Yeah. I don't like my daddy, either." Johannes spoke as though Mika was his confidante, a comrade in arms.

"Why not?"

"Cause he yelled all the time. He scared me."

This wasn't going right. His plan had been to reassure Johannes daddies were okay, and that he would be a good father to him. Instead he was telling the boy about a man he had hated as a kid. Now that his father was gone, he didn't really think about him much. Not as a father-figure, anyway. What was past was past.

Snow crunched under their feet and Johannes's snowsuit made swishing sounds as the boy trudged along beside him.

"Why didn't you like *your* daddy?" Johannes wanted to know.

"Well, he was a—" Mika stopped again. If he said his father was a self-centered, uncaring artist it could ruin his chances of getting Johannes to ever trust *him* to be a good father. He was an artist, too, after all.

"What was he?" Johannes's voice piped into his thoughts.

"My daddy didn't yell or scare me," Mika said, playing for time.

"So why don't you like him?" Johannes asked as they started to trudge on again. Johannes stumbled in the deep snow and Mika's gripped his hand tighter to steady him.

"I guess it's because he didn't take care of his family too well."

"Yeah." Johannes sighed, sounding old and wise. "I know."

Mika knew he had to say something positive or this conversation would have the opposite effect to what he was hoping for. "You know, Johannes," he began tentatively. "I think every man starts out wanting to be the best daddy in the world."

"So why aren't they?" Johannes looked up at him with big, sincere eyes that wanted to understand.

"Stuff happens. People change."

"What kind of stuff?"

"Well, in your daddy's case, he started drinking alcohol and it changed him." Mika wasn't sure how much he should be telling a seven-year-old child. And he was more than slightly apprehensive about what Anna-Liisa might say about this conversation.

"Yeah. Mommy told me he drinks vodka," Johannes said. "That's why he's scary."

Mika breathed a little easier. He wasn't saying anything the boy didn't already know.

"What stuff happened to *your* daddy?" Johannes wanted to know.

"He . . . um . . . he got too many kids and he didn't know how to take care of us all."

"I *hate* my daddy," Johannes declared with so much vehemence it surprised Mika. "Do you hate your daddy, too?"

And then Mika knew what he had to say. He had resented his father for most of his life and this resentment had poisoned his way of thinking about being a husband and parent. It had made him feel that he, like his father, would be unsuitable for those roles. So he'd shied away from relationships that could have led to marriage.

But now he knew he wouldn't be like his father. He would be a good father to Anna-Liisa's kids, because he sincerely wanted to. He didn't have to worry about one day becoming selfish and self-centered like his old man because he had Anna-Liisa's love, and he dearly loved her children. He would give his life for any and all of them.

But with the hatred Johannes was already carrying inside him for his father, the boy might go through life with a twisted idea of fatherhood that could ruin his chances of finding a loving mate and establishing a family.

If he could only give the boy a happy version of Aaro to carry in his heart it might replace the violence he had experienced. Mika racked his brain for ideas.

He had to try.

"When you were born," Mika began, "I think your daddy was really happy to have a little son to love." So what if the man was a rip-roaring drunk. History wasn't always accurate, and family histories were especially susceptible to inaccuracies. They depended on people's recollections, and on stories passed from one person or generation to the next. It made no difference when, exactly, Aaro started drinking.

"You think so?"

The faint hope in the boy's voice almost made Mika's eyes fill up. "Yes, I think he was a loving daddy until alcohol changed him," he said with as much conviction as he could muster. "The way I see it, when your daddy was yelling, he wasn't angry with you. He was actually angry with himself, because he knew he was letting his family down."

Like his own father. Mika remembered when his mother had become ill with cancer and, instead of being caring, his father had become angry. Mika had been surprised by this reaction, and it had taken him years to figure out his dad had been worried about his wife, and angry with himself for being unable to help her. He was raging at the illness consuming his wife, but had shown it in a most inappropriate way, making his children think their father was angry with their mother.

"Well, it sounded like he was yelling at me," Johannes stated, looking doubtful with Mika's version of events.

"Yeah, I'll bet it *sounded* like that, and I can imagine

it was scary for you. But I'm absolutely sure he was angry at himself, not at you." Did Johannes understand anything he was trying to say? "You know, grown-ups can sometimes be pretty illogical."

"What does that mean?"

"Illogical. Like they say things that don't make any sense," Mika tried to explain.

"Yeah, I know." Johannes sighed again, shaking his head, like he knew all about adults and their lack of logic.

"And I believe he still loves you, deep inside him. Like he's loved you all along, but he didn't know how to show it. So he yelled instead."

"That's so dumb. He yelled when he should have been nice."

"I know. It sounds totally illogical. But it happens."

They continued on in silence, while Mika tried to think of how he should proceed.

"I know you were very young, but can you remember a time when your daddy *wasn't* mean?" Mika asked and crossed his fingers, hoping there'd been such a time. Even once.

He saw the way Johannes looked away, pursing his lips together, that perhaps he remembered something, but didn't want to tell.

At last the boy looked up. "He carved me a horse once. From wood."

"Did he?" This was a great revelation, something to

build on.

"Yeah. Äiti told me he carved it for me." Johannes sounded reluctant, as though he didn't want to credit his father with anything positive.

Mika wondered if Anna-Liisa had also changed family history by telling her son something she hoped would make him feel less fearful of his father.

"Did he do a good job?"

"Yeah. Guess so."

"So that's why *you*'re so good!" Mika exclaimed. "You take after your daddy."

"Yeah. Guess so."

"So he wasn't all bad, was he? He was a good carver and he made a horse for you. And now you know how to carve, too."

"Yeah. Guess so."

"So where is this horse now?" Mika hoped it was still around.

"In my room."

"Do you think I could see it?"

"Yeah." Johannes was starting to sound slightly more affirmative.

"That shows your daddy wanted to be loving, but he was so mad at himself for drinking, he yelled and scared you instead." Was he making any sense to this boy who listened to him with such big, sincere eyes? "He *wanted* to do the right thing, but alcohol made him do bad things."

Johannes kicked at a clump of icy snow lying on his path. "Alcohol is really bad stuff, isn't it?"

"It can be," Mika said and didn't elaborate. He had a few beers himself now and then, and enjoyed a glass of wine with his dinner, but at this point Johannes probably saw alcohol as black and white—bad or good. That was something to address in the future.

They had almost reached the house.

"You think my daddy loved me? Even though he yelled a lot?" Johannes sounded hopeful.

"Yes, I think he loved you." Mika hoped to God he was telling the truth. But as long as it made the boy feel good, what the hell. "And I was wrong not to like my daddy," he confessed. "He wasn't a bad person. He just saw things differently."

Yes, maybe his own father simply had his priorities screwed up. Maybe he sincerely believed he could make it as a professional artist if he put his everything into it. Could you fault a man for having big dreams? Making wrong choices didn't necessarily make him a bad person.

"So you think I shouldn't not like my daddy?"

"No, you shouldn't not like him. He has a sickness that makes him do bad things. You can't help him, but you shouldn't hate him. It's okay to hate the sickness, though."

Just before they'd reached the house, Johannes suddenly asked. "What kind of a daddy will you be?"

The positive slant in the question made Mika's heart give a joyful leap. Maybe a while ago that question would have jolted him, but today he had an answer. "I'll be the very best daddy I can possibly be, because I love you and Elina and Aleksi." He grabbed Johannes by the waist and hoisted him high up in the air. "And I love your äiti, too."

The boy squealed with laughter as Mika caught him and put him back on his feet.

Mika picked up a handful of snow and rolled it into a ball. "See who can hit that tree!" He flung the snowball at the straight trunk of one of the nearby red pines at the edge of the park. It smacked right on and the snow splattered around.

Johannes quickly made himself a snowball and threw it at the tree. In his eager, happy rush he missed by a mile.

"We gotta work on your accuracy, young man," Mika said. "Stand with your feet like this and aim carefully. Stare at the spot you want to hit."

After a few attempts, Johannes managed to hit the tree more by accident than skill, but Mika praised him profusely.

"Yeah, I think you'll be a good daddy," Johannes declared as they walked to the door. "You teach me stuff. Like math, too."

A lump rose in Mika's throat. "Thank you," he said hoarsely.

They took turns brushing their snowy boots on the spiky hedgehog by the front steps. "Should I make my daddy a Christmas present?" Johannes asked. "I don't know if *joulupukki* visits hospitals."

Mika knew he'd succeeded, and his heart swelled. "Let's ask your mom and see what she says." He opened the door and Johannes bounded in, landing in Anna-Liisa's waiting arms.

Soft snow fell on Christmas Eve as though someone had ordered it especially for the night—big, fluffy flakes that had sent Elina, Johannes and Aleksi outside before dinner to dance around and try and catch them on their tongues. The streetlights had been on for a few hours already, making the snow sparkle in the night.

Mika stood by the kitchen window, an arm around Anna-Liisa's waist, and watched the frolicking children. Her head rested on his shoulder and he still had a difficult time believing the happiness that filled him whenever she was near. She was his home. Instead of pushing all that away, he finally dared to admit this was what he'd been missing in his life—probably been longing for since he was a kid living in his dysfunctional family. But now his search was over. The missing piece had fallen into place and her name was Anna-Liisa.

"Anna-Liisa," he said softly against her hair. Saying

her name was almost as good as kissing her.

"Yes?"

"Nothing. I just wanted to say your name." He knew that would bring out the pearls of her laughter.

Mika nuzzled the back of her neck that smelled of the pine soap she'd used in the Christmas sauna earlier in the afternoon. This was the first time he'd been invited to the "holy sanctum", located down the hallway that led to the back door. He'd wanted so much to go in with Anna-Liisa, but she and Elina had gone in together. He'd gone with the boys and had helped wash Aleksi, and made sure Johannes remembered to scrub behind his ears, as had been Anna-Liisa's instructions. Mika looked forward to the day he and Anna-Liisa would be able to go to sauna together, and he already imagined how he would wash her from top to bottom. And she would return the favor.

"Knock-knock," she said, out of the blue.

"Who's there?"

"Meh..."

"Meh who?"

"Orange or cranberry?"

"What?" Mika frowned.

"Meh-who. *Mehu*. That means 'juice' in Finnish. I thought you knew that. Now my joke is spoiled."

"That's what you get for doing a bilingual joke. At least my Plato-joke was understandable in only one language."

"But mine requires more brain-power than your simple one."

Mika laughed and gave Anna-Liisa a slap on the bottom.

"Simpleton that you are, you should be out with the children catching snowflakes on your tongue," she said mischievously. "They are so over-excited about *joulupukki* coming, it is good they are wearing off some of their energy outside. I hope they will be able to settle down for dinner in a couple of hours."

The Christmas ham sizzled in the oven and smelled so delicious that Mika knew he wouldn't miss the North American turkey one bit.

"It was nice of Jussi Koivu to offer to be *joulupukki* for them," Mika said.

"Yes, and you will have fun being *joulupukki* for the Koivu children. It is only your first Christmas in Finland and already you get to play that important role."

Mika made a face. "Sure. I don't even know what a *joulupukki* is supposed to do. How come no one thought to ask me, before I was so cavalierly volunteered for the job by *someone*?" But he gave Anna-Liisa a kiss on the cheek to show he didn't mind.

"Because if I had asked you, you would have declined," Anna-Liisa said. "But what better way to get into the Christmas spirit than by being *joulupukki*?"

"You're right. But good thing I'm only going across the courtyard, because I'd hate for people to see me walking around the city in a red suit with a pillow stuffed into my pants."

"There are lots of *joulupukkis* walking around on Christmas Eve," Anna-Liisa told him. "No one would think you were ridiculous."

"Well, I would."

They continued to watch the children, who had been joined by the three Koivu kids. The snow muffled the sound of their laughter.

"I assume Aaro never played Santa?" Mika asked, hoping he wasn't stirring up bad memories.

The hospital had called a few days earlier with the news that Aaro's alcohol-damaged organs were failing and he wasn't expected to live much past the New Year. Anna-Liisa hadn't told the children yet, so their Christmas wouldn't be affected.

"When Elina was little, he did," Anna-Liisa said, but didn't elaborate. "But now I want to look forward to our life. I just want to be happy."

Mika knew she'd gone to visit Aaro and had brought him the Christmas gifts the children had made. Elina had gone with her mother, making Mika wonder at the girl's ability to forgive. Although Aaro had caused the child such unhappiness over the years, Elina never talked about it, and didn't seem to hold it against him. Was she wise beyond her years, or was she like her mother, who believed no human being should be left to die alone?

Later, after the dinner dishes had been washed, the left-overs refrigerated, and everything had been tidied up, Mika answered the pre-arranged phone call and left to "help Jussi with some car trouble", as he told the boys. In the carport he struggled into the Santa outfit waiting there for him. He stuffed a pillow into his pants, and went across the courtyard to deliver the sack of gifts waiting in the Koivus' carport.

He rang hand bells and banged loudly on the door as he'd been instructed, and the over-excited Koivu children opened the door for him. Anna-Liisa had taught him the appropriate words to say in Finnish and had reminded him over and over to make sure he made his voice sound different.

Mika had been apprehensive about this performance, done entirely in Finnish, but it worked out better than he'd hoped. After enquiring if there were any good children in the house, he listened as the kids sang the welcoming song to him. He proceeded to hand out the gifts, reading each person's name from the gift tags. They were all so excited with their presents he didn't have to say anything else till it was time to leave. The children sang him the thank-you song and he told them their singing was *hyvä, hyvä*. Relieved that he'd done a credible job, he left, calling out, *Hauskaa Joulua!*

"Whew!" he whispered to Anna-Liisa who met him at the door. He'd left the Santa suit in the Koivu's carport for Jussi's performance. "You would've been proud of me. Next year I think I'll get a job as a mall Santa and make some money."

"We don't have mall Santas," Anna-Liisa informed him.

"What's a mall Santa?" Aleksi asked. He'd once again come up unnoticed behind them.

"A *small* Santa," Mika said quickly. "Your äiti said there are no small Santas in Finland." He grabbed Aleksi and tossed him up, almost to the ceiling. "That's how tall Santas are here!"

Aleksi shrieked with laughter. Mika brought him down and sent him off with a pat on the bottom. He grinned at Anna-Liisa and pulled her against his side, planting an affectionate kiss on the top of her head. This was all so wonderful and new—this woman, these kids—soon to be his family.

They entered the living room where the impatient wait for *Joulupukki* was on. The excitement was palpable and almost went through the roof. The candles on the tree had already been lit and the real flames flickered brighter than any electric ones. Mika still wasn't totally comfortable with them, burning so close to the needles of the Christmas tree, but Anna-Liisa had assured him it was the way things were done, and that she was vigilant and very strict about fire safety rules. In fact, there was a bucket of water hidden behind the tree, just in case.

Soon bells began to jingle at the front door, accompanied by loud thumping, and Elina, Johannes and Aleksi raced to open it. Mika smiled as *Joulupukki* entered with all the traditional huffing and puffing and was led to sit in the armchair. Jussi Koivu delivered his lines with the ease of a seasoned veteran, telling the children how cold it was up in Lapland, while Mika took mental notes for his next year's performance. After the children had sung the welcoming song, the pandemonium of gift-distribution began.

When things had settled down to a roar, and *Joulupukki* had left, Mika felt in his pocket where he had tucked Anna-Liisa's Christmas gift. Tonight he would ask her to marry him, right there in front of the children. With that he would give up his bachelor status and at last surrender himself to the challenging—but also exciting and fulfilling—role as a husband and father.

About Karen Rossi

Karen Rossi (the pen name of Kaarina Brooks) has been a romantic since she was a child. She and her sister had their own "publishing company" and wrote about love-struck princes and princesses.

Today she writes grown-up romances where modern-day "princes and princesses" go through heart-wrenching relationship struggles before reaching their happily ever after.

She now also has a real publishing company, Wisteria Publications. Besides romances, she also publishes kids' books and non-fiction works, such as a cook book.

She lives in Southern Ontario with her husband and kitty-cat, Lilly.

www.wisteriapublications.com
brooks.kaarina@gmail.com